SOMETIMES IT SNOWS IN AMERICA

ESSENTIAL PROSE SERIES 96

MARISA LABOZZETTA

SOMETIMES IT SNOWS IN AMERICA

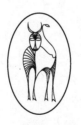

GUERNICA

TORONTO – BUFFALO – BERKELEY – LANCASTER (U.K.)

2012

Michael Mirolla, general editor
Lindsay Brown, editor
Guernica Editions Inc.
P.O. Box 117, Station P, Toronto (ON), Canada M5S 2S6
2250 Military Road, Tonawanda, N.Y. 14150-6000 U.S.A.

Distributors:
University of Toronto Press Distribution,
5201 Dufferin Street, Toronto (ON), Canada M3H 5T8
Gazelle Book Services, White Cross Mills, High Town,
Lancaster LA1 4XS U.K.
Small Press Distribution, 1341 Seventh St., Berkeley, CA 94710-1409 U.S.A.

First edition.
Printed in Canada.

Legal Deposit – First Quarter
Library of Congress Catalog Card Number: 2012938469

Library and Archives Canada Cataloguing in Publication

Labozzetta, Marisa
Sometimes it snows in America / Marisa Labozzetta.

(Essential prose series ; 96)
Issued also in electronic formats.
ISBN 978-1-55071-609-2

I. Title. II. Series: Essential prose series ; 96

PS3562.A2356S64 2012   813'.54   C2012-902885-1

For
Michael, Ariana, Carina, and Mark

Why must so many men be what they consistently are –
condoners of injustice or victims of it, doomed to soured
souls, never-ending rancor, and the needless bitterness
and sickening burdens of an unintelligible world?

Kenneth Roberts
Lydia Bailey

✯

"I'm scared of him," said Piggy. "And that's why I know
him. If you're scared of someone you hate him
but you can't stop thinking about him."

William Golding
Lord of the Flies

CONTENTS

I

Shelby House of Correction 1995

**********✯**********

The taxi and the ambulance showed up at the same time on the afternoon Fatma shot her husband. She had phoned for the taxi. He had summoned the ambulance that came accompanied by a squad car. If the taxi had arrived first, she might have got away.

Shelby County Jail and House of Correction was color coordinated, with uniforms that matched the cinder-block walls of the cellblocks: a sea of greens and corals and purples and blues to tell the women that they'd become a category – newcomer, pretrial, troublemaker, or psycho. If they enlisted in the culinary school, they got to wear white.

She arrived at the orientation cellblock on a Thursday, wearing tropical orange. The day hadn't mattered to her then, but she would come to hate Thursday. It was inspection day, the day that would remind her of Auntie's house, in which she had grown up and where the maids constantly scrubbed and polished.

While Fatma sponged down the metal toilet and sink in her cell during the weeks and months that followed, she would close her eyes and wander back to that colonial mansion Uncle Oliver had built. She could get away from herself that way. Then she'd open her eyes and catch her distorted image in the wavy slab of shiny metal that hung above the sink. (No glass was allowed at Shelby, nothing that might be used as a weapon or for self-destruction.) And she'd remember that she and her life had become warped beyond recognition. That they had become uglier than she had ever imagined they could be. That she had stumbled so far away from home, so far from Mombasa.

ISLAND GIRL 1966

********** ⭐ **********

She was born in Somalia, to a Somali father and a Saudi mother. Many Saudis lived in Somalia in those days; Arabs had been planting themselves along the Somali coast for centuries. Her mother's father owned three movie theaters, six gas stations, the entire bus system, the largest clothing stores, and a cannery that shipped lobster and other fish to Italy, along with bananas from his farm. There were plenty of Italians in Somalia too from their years of colonization: her father always said two out of three Somalis had Italian blood; the other third had Arabic. This, and the fact that the original Somali people migrated from Yemen, made Somali people different from other Africans – more like Egyptians, with lighter skin, longer noses, and straight hair. Other Africans didn't like them.

Fatma's parents had been neighbors in Mogadishu. When her mother was thirteen and her father seventeen, they ran away from school and got married. Fatma's grandfather never accepted his daughter's marriage to a Somali, whom he considered beneath his Arab lineage, despite the fact that Fatma's father had once been the son of a king. Her grandfather paid government officials to imprison his new son-in-law. It was an Italian-run prison, however, where spouses were allowed to bring in food and spend Friday nights, and Fatma's mother bore her father five children in five years. Acknowledging the futility of the situation, Fatma's grandfather eventually had her father released.

Her father entered the military, became a general, and traveled for long periods of time. He married other women in other cities and countries, but he never left her mother. He just loved women: young, old, rich, or sick. If he came upon a woman begging in the street, he would crouch down beside her and pet her, and if he fell in love with a woman in his hometown of Mogadishu, he would sleep with her but still come home to Fatma's mother's house to eat. According to Muslim law, the second wife must approve of the third wife, the third of the fourth, and so on, but the first wife must approve of all other wives. Fatma's mother never approved of any of them. In time her father divorced the other women, but he never divorced her mother. Perhaps it was her mother's Arab dignity that set her apart from the others. Perhaps she believed in the superiority of her race, despite the fact that she was married to a Somali, because she was beauty and brains and nerves of steel encased in crystal. Her elusiveness only made her children work harder to capture her love; it kept her husband tied to her. She, on the other hand, could have existed without any of them.

Fatma was her mother's fourteenth child. Her mother wanted to name her Fatimah, her father Fatma. They settled on Fatma; it was one of the few times her mother ever compromised. When she was three days old, her mother gave her away to her infertile sister and English brother-in-law, who lived in Mombasa, Kenya's prized island-city in the Indian Ocean. Some might have regarded this as a magnanimous gesture, but Fatma always felt that she was as expendable to her mother as an article of damaged clothing in her crowded armoire.

While Fatma's mother was a shrewd businesswoman, Auntie, her *shangazi*, was content to keep house in Mombasa for Uncle Oliver, who operated a cargo ship laden with coffee, tea, cotton, and animal hides from Kenya to Italy and on to his native Liverpool. Auntie was a kinder-hearted woman than her younger sister, and while she was not as pretty, with duller eyes and softer, unremarkable features, she loved Fatma more.

Fatma lived with her aunt and uncle in a big two-story brick house in Mombasa. It was several miles from bustling Biashara Street, with its modern kiosks and storefronts, but not too far from the narrow cobblestone alleys of Old Town, lined with stalls offering everything from colorful bolts of fabric to giant sacks of flour, and near the cannons and crumbling mud arches of what remained of Fort Jesus. She awoke each morning to the smell of brewing tea. Auntie knew how Fatma liked hers and put just the right amount of tea, milk, and sugar in the pot. Often there were eggs and fresh liver from a goat Auntie had killed, stuffing its stomach with broccoli, corn, and potatoes, sewing it up, and skewering the whole animal with a stick. She would cook it for hours in a red mud-clay oven as big as some people's houses that Uncle Oliver had made for her. From time to time she removed the lid and basted the meat with a garlic and oil marinade, turning the meat with the stick that protruded from holes on each side of the oven, roasting it until the flesh was so tender it fell off the bone. With the leftovers, she made cementlike potato patties studded with stew meat and vegetables. She poured black beans over them to make them more appealing to Fatma who hated vegetables, but this only made them less appetizing.

Fatma's pink-plaster-walled bedroom, with its gauze curtains that came alive in the evening breeze, faced the sea. On the beach tourists from Switzerland, Germany, and Holland shielded the fair skin of their scantily clad bodies with glistening concoctions and blended into the fine white sand. When Fatma went bathing, she wore a costume with three-quarter sleeves and a below-the-knee skirt that Auntie had made and that was typical beach attire for Kenyan women. Fatma not only believed that the tourists baked their bodies because they were envious of what little skin of hers they could see, but was foolish enough to think that, when they left for their cold gray lands, these foreigners would take with them as a souvenir their envy of the young girl who had been born just right, with honey tones and brown freckles that dotted her button nose and high cheekbones.

The tourism industry fed on the natural beauty of Mombasa, and Mombasa's economy feasted on tourism. Yet culture was never sacrificed for business, a notion that only added to Mombasa's mystique. Outsiders tried to capture it with a camera, but it was a world that opened and closed faster than a lens shutter. Fatma's family had always walked a thin line between life and death. "It is difficult for we Africans to extract the land from our blood and the blood from our land," her father said. "It is an inheritance from kingdoms past." Death followed life and life followed death, moment to moment. Alive or dead? Sometimes it was hard to tell. So it had been for her grandfather, the king of Somalia, who was poisoned by enemies. And so it would be for her father, Muhammad Hakeem, who would be assassinated by his brother.

✫

Promises had been made regarding Fatma's adoption. She would be raised Muslim, which meant that she would learn the Koran and speak only Swahili with Auntie and Uncle Oliver. When she turned four, every summer, she would be sent to travel alone by plane, with only a flight attendant looking after her, to spend two months with her brothers and sisters at her mother's thirty-six-room estate on the outskirts of Mogadishu, where she never felt welcome. There, Fatma would disappear to some cool corner of the sprawling ranch house with mazelike hallways for long periods of time and wait for her father to return. She was certain that the demand for her presence had come from him and not her mother, who paid little attention to her and then only to criticize her.

"She can barely speak Somali because she lives in a Christian man's home," Fatma's mother would say, ripping off Fatma's skirt and sleeveless blouse and replacing them with a long robe and a scarf over her head and neck. Then, squatting before Fatma so that her black eyes looked directly into her daughter's, Fatma's mother would accuse her of forgetting every word of Arabic too.

Fatma had not forgotten the language of her mother's people, the language Auntie sometimes used with her, the language of the Koran.

"Let her be." Fatma's older brother Hamal sometimes took her side. "She is only here for a short time." Then handsome Hamal, tall and dark like Fatma's father but with her mother's angled features, would take Fatma to the movies. He always hid one of her western-style outfits behind a tree beforehand. They would pick it up after leaving the house and stop at a relative's or friend's along the way so that Fatma could change into her own clothing.

One day Fatma asked Hamal why their mother didn't like her. He led Fatma across the street and into the shade of the arched porticos beside the sand-colored buildings, as if to have her in a more comfortable place when she heard his answer.

"Sometimes I do not think she cares much for anyone. Although our mother's house is very big, Fatma, the door is small. Do you understand?"

She didn't.

They returned home that evening to find their mother screaming and throwing pots at a Bantu man who was running down the gravel path from the house. Their mother had hired him to fix windows and now refused to pay him because he hadn't done the job to her liking. Bantu were the people hired to do odd jobs that Somali people wouldn't do even if they were starving, because Somalis thought they were above that type of labor. The Bantu, on the other hand, were hardworking people whom the Arabs had brought to Somalia from other parts of Africa to use as slaves. Somalis looked down on them and on their big lips and noses. Fatma was afraid of them. That night, however, it was her mother's behavior that frightened her, that put pains in her stomach and caused her to wet her pants. Hamal had been right: even a mouse couldn't fit through their mother's door, her heart was so small. Fatma would come to believe that her mother had married her father, a black man, only because he had descended from a family of kings and was powerful. Fatma, on the other hand, would always see her father as a kind man, robust and charming but too often absent, and whose attention was divided among too many children.

It was her uncle Ahmad who turned out to be the greediest of all. A four-star general, he led a military coup in the name of socialism and, promising to eliminate the society ruled by clans, seized control of Somalia overnight. Ahmad Siad Adan was Fatma's father's brother. When he banished Arabs and confiscated most Saudi property for himself, Fatma's grandfather was sent back to Saudi Arabia, but because her mother was married to Ahmad's brother, she was permitted to keep the cannery and banana farm, the clothing store, and the thirty-six-room house.

It was not enough for Ahmad to rid Somalia of Arabs and Italians; he thought religion also posed a threat to his presidency. At four in the morning during one of Fatma's visits to Mogadishu, soldiers banged on the doors of her mother's home and ordered the family to the center of town. All over Somalia the scene was the same: everyone, including small children like Fatma, was herded in nightclothes into the villages and made to witness the executions of sheiks and hajjis lined up with hands tied behind their backs. Fatma recognized many of them as neighbors and relatives. A captain gave the order, soldiers fired, and she watched the people she had grown up with fall into pools of blood. Though at the time she didn't understand the motive behind the madness, she was aware of the high social position of the victims. Whimpering, she waited for the soldiers to take her mother, who had made the hajj seven times and as a result was revered as a priestess.

"Keep still," Hamal whispered, tugging at her hand.

She tried harder than she had ever tried to do anything to keep still. She tried not to breathe. Her mother was spared again because her father, who trusted that his brother Ahmad would keep his promise and restore democracy to Somalia, was in those days allied with Ahmad. The demand for their presence at the executions had been a mere formality, Ahmad said. But in the end it would prove to have been as much of a warning to Fatma's family as to any other that the government of Ahmad Siad Adan would not tolerate resistance, even when led by priestesses and high priests, even when led by his own flesh and blood.

Fatma never spent another restful night in Mogadishu. She woke at odd hours and waited for the pounding on the door to echo through the long halls, for the firing of the guns, for her mother's death and even her own. Years later, after he had returned the Somali republic to a monarchy against the will of its people, Ahmad would flee Somalia, and the very Muslims he had sought to stamp out would take over his justice system. The legal process would be just as swift and definitive as ever: if you stole, your hand would be cut off; if you murdered, you would be killed; if you blasphemed or slandered, your tongue would be cut out.

When she was ten, things began to happen to Fatma's body. Blood trickled on its own from the secret fold between her legs where, when she was seven, a Somali midwife had used a sharp-edged razor to circumcise her. Hair appeared in private places. Painful mounds formed on her chest. Auntie pulled her straight black hair back and covered her body with long colorful silk outfits typical of Somali women – a burnt orange or mauve or multi-colored robe with long sleeves, and a white shawl that concealed her head and neck and bosom – because she had been born Somali and because now she was a woman and old enough to marry. This was, however, not enough for Fatma's mother, who also insisted on a veil to hide her face, exposing, as Saudi women did, only the almond-shaped eyes. Auntie, who never wore a veil, complied. Fatma became a prisoner of the sun she had loved and that now became trapped within the fibers of her robes, causing her pores to leak perspiration and her skin to prickle. Like a good Muslim woman she became accustomed to the discomfort, until it was as normal as the breeze off the ocean, as commonplace as morning tea – a reminder that she had not yet slid into death.

BETROTHED

********** ✪ **********

"**D**aniel Kornmeyer," the young man said, extending his hand. "*Hujambo?*" He was standing in the large foyer, surrounded by a hand-painted English country scene. Uncle Oliver had brought the wallpaper back to Mombasa from London, as he had the many pieces of antique furniture in the house. Two staircases rose on either side of him, leading to the second-floor balcony. Their ebony balusters and handrails had been carved by local Kenyans.

Uncle Oliver clasped the hand firmly, jerking it downward and back up again in one motion. This was what he considered the only way to shake a man's hand, as though testing to see whether his greeter was virile enough to keep the hand from being snapped off. "Oliver Widdowson. *Hujambo*," he said.

Daniel was as tall as the Englishman. This seemed to please Uncle Oliver, who was accustomed to towering over most Kenyans. When Daniel removed his dripping army-green plastic poncho, he revealed a body as skinny as paper, so thin he could be folded over and over again and put into someone's pocket for safekeeping, perhaps into his own narrow blue jeans. His hair was the color of weak tea and, tied back like a horse's tail, hung in one sopping coil down his back. He had what looked like the beginnings of a beard; Fatma would later realize that it was in fact a full beard, hard to make out because of its blond color. But that would not be apparent until she became very close to him, so close she could see the blue in his eyes and taste the curry on his lips. So close she could see two eyelashes pasted together with sleep.

"How was your trip?" Uncle Oliver asked in English, adding as Auntie cast a disapproving glance at him: "I'm sorry – as much as I'd like to, we don't speak English in this house, Daniel. Part of a promise to Fatma's birth mother long ago. We speak Swahili. Do you mind? The practice will do you good."

"The rain is not as bad here as in Katundu," Daniel said in Swahili.

"That's bloody good!" Uncle Oliver burst out in English and led Daniel into the dining room.

Daniel's eyes roamed as though he might find Fatma behind a cupboard or in a corner, like a scorpion that had entered through a crack. His English had sounded different than Uncle Oliver's.

"You'll get used to the weather," Uncle Oliver said, reverting to Swahili.

"I've been here almost two months already," Daniel boasted.

Uncle Oliver let out a hearty laugh.

"But only in one season. Would you like to bathe?"

Daniel must have felt uncomfortable at the prospect of climbing into a tub in a strange house, but Uncle Oliver's impeccable appearance made it difficult for him to refuse. Oliver's skin was scented with the green aftershave he kept on a marble shelf above the white pedestal sink in his bathroom. (Auntie had her own pink-tiled modern washroom.) His tawny hair, streaked with silver, was wet from his recent bath in the claw-foot Victorian tub and neatly parted. His crisp white shirtsleeves were rolled up to just below the elbow, signaling that he was ready – as a man should be at all times – to pitch in and work: change a flat tire in the mud, put up a fence, or load crates into his cargo ship.

But as usual there was nothing for him to do in the house that night. He liked this. His wife and her two maids, Kiah and Lisha, had taken care of everything: the table was set; the meat had been roasting for hours. The pitcher of lemonade rested on the ornate mahogany sideboard, lemon slices floating on the surface.

"Lisha," Uncle Oliver called out towards the kitchen, his deep voice resonating through the house and up to the second floor where Fatma was hiding. "Prepare a bath for our guest." He turned to Daniel. "I apologize for not having invited you sooner. I expected business to take me to Nairobi, where I thought we might meet, but the trip kept getting postponed."

"No problem."

During their conversation, Oliver Widdowson studied the young man's face. He had anticipated meeting Daniel Kornmeyer for a long time – from before he was born.

"Tell me, how is Walter? You certainly bear a strong resemblance to him."

"I'm not so sure you would say that if you saw him now," Daniel replied in his halting Swahili. His father hadn't weathered the years quite as well as Uncle Oliver.

Oliver had met Walter Kornmeyer, a GI, during the Second World War. Stationed outside London, Walter had gone into the city on a long weekend pass and was leaving a pub with some buddies when the air raid siren sounded. They took off for the nearest shelter but along the way, stumbled over an English soldier writhing in pain on the pavement. Too tight to think straight, Walter's companions refused to stop for the soldier.

Walter, however, did. He managed to get the man off the street and stayed by his side throughout the bombing. Afterward, he took the Englishman to a hospital, keeping vigil over him during his recovery from a burst appendix. The rescue had forged a bond between two men who had nothing much in common and who, in an effort to fortify their relationship, whimsically promised their firstborns to one another in much the way schoolboys seal friendships with blood. During the postwar years they exchanged occasional holiday cards, but the worlds they now navigated were as far apart as the distance between them, except for the fact that both had achieved fatherhood later in life than most of their peers.

Daniel was Walter's only child, and Fatma Oliver's only ward. Walter worried about his hippie son: he was too easygoing, too much of a do-gooder, and susceptible to the free sex and drugs of his rebellious times. Now he was about to serve two years in the Peace Corps, and Walter worried about the people he would encounter in his rural post; about the women he would sleep with, about the woman Daniel would be lured into marrying. Oliver, for his part, worried about his niece and her future in the unstable economy of Mombasa, and troubled Somalia, where Fatma's parents and siblings perched on the brink of political and natural disaster. America could be her salvation, Oliver told Auntie. At first Oliver had promised only to look after Walter's son during his stay in Kenya. Before long, however, the two men had had a lengthy phone conversation and had agreed that marriage might be beneficial to both their children as well as a fitting recognition of the pact they had made so many years before.

Uncle Oliver offered Daniel a scotch before his bath. The young man accepted, but the way he nursed the drink as he surreptitiously glanced around revealed that he was not a fan of hard liquor.

"You cannot see her, you know," Oliver said. "Custom."

"I know."

No, he could not see Fatma nor she him. But, crouched on all fours, an ear pressed to a floorboard in Lisha's room above, Fatma could hear him, and through a hole left by a missing sliver of wood, she could vaguely make out his image.

By the time the meal was over, the arrangement had been made. The deal Oliver Widdowson had agreed to on a lark years before became reality. Daniel and Fatma were engaged: he was nineteen, she eleven.

After a year of listening to Daniel's voice when he came to visit, Fatma could still only hear him as they took their vows on the white beach. Separated this time by the traditional division of the sexes in Muslim rituals, they were hidden from each other by several rows of men on one side and women on the other.

While the guests had partied for seven days prior to the ceremony – dancing to the musicians' drumming, and stuffing themselves with roasted goat, camel stew, wedding loaf-cake, and sweet potato pie – Daniel remained hidden somewhere with Fatma's brothers and she with the old women. Each night the midwife checked Fatma, the way she had checked her every Friday since the day of her first period, to confirm that her membrane was still intact and that she was worthy of a husband. If Daniel had been told that Fatma was no longer a virgin, he would have been given the option to cancel the wedding. It wasn't until after the ceremony, after the gold-embroidered veil that Fatma could see through but through which no one could see her was removed, that Daniel first laid eyes on her round face and high cheekbones, her Moorish eyes and small Somali features.

Daniel had been eager to marry. He was a "one-woman guy," he always said, preferring the security of one female upon whom he could shower attention. She was a native of a land that fascinated him, and the act would please parents he seemed unable to satisfy. No, marriage was not at all difficult for him.

Praise Allah, Fatma thought when she saw him face to face: at least he was handsome in his white collared dress shirt and khaki trousers. Marriage could never have been her decision to make. Neither the difference in age between Daniel and her, nor the fact that she was only twelve, was unusual in Mombasa. Still, Uncle Oliver had made an effort to persuade her: his business was faltering; Kenya was volatile; America offered a bright future. Nevertheless, she believed that she was being sent away, disposed of once more.

Everyone was at the wedding except Daniel's family and Fatma's natural parents. Her father was off fighting to reclaim the Ogaden and other Somali-speaking regions of Ethiopia, and her mother had gone to visit Fatma's grandfather in Saudi Arabia to boycott the ceremony. The fact that Daniel had converted to Islam had not impressed her: she knew he had merely gone through the motions (and without any formal study) for Fatma's sake. According to Fatma's mother, if you weren't born into Islam, you could never be Muslim.

Fatma's mother had come to Mombasa when she heard of the engagement. For the first and last time she entered her sister's home – a Christian man's home. Concealed by the long black *abaya* and *hijab*, the Arabian Muslim robe and veil that exposed only her jet eyes and spidery lashes and that she would not remove even for her sister, it was as though she hadn't entered her brother-in-law's home at all. She planted herself in the living room and spoke fast in Arabic, so fast the words seemed to fly like sparks from a tongue that couldn't keep up with the pace of her thoughts. Auntie's face was creased by pain as she sat opposite her sister. Fatma couldn't understand it then, as she peeked from behind a partially closed kitchen door, but Auntie's greatest challenge was her desire to please her husband and at the same time the mother of her adopted child. The plainer of the two women spoke calmly and softly, defending her marriage to a Christian, but the shrouded, sharp-featured beauty cut her sister's diplomacy to shreds. "What is it that you want?" Auntie finally pleaded. "I have raised her Muslim as you wished. I have not let her learn English." Fatma longed to tell Auntie that her mother had no say in the matter; she had given Fatma away. Yet a part of Fatma wanted her mother to win because she hadn't wanted to get married, to stop going to school, to belong to a man. Eventually her mother did accede to the marriage, but not before forcing Auntie to make one more promise, a concession that would remove her sister's claws from Auntie's skin but would sink them into Fatma's for good.

Fatma's oldest sister, Ayasha, came from Mogadishu, and Fatma considered her a stand-in for their mother. There were enough years between Ayasha and Fatma that Ayasha cared for Fatma when she visited the house in Mogadishu. Ayasha knew how to coax Fatma out of hiding and often came looking for her. She would groom and play with her little sister as if Fatma were her very own and shower Fatma with the affection their mother never gave. Of all Fatma's sisters, Ayasha most resembled their mother, and Fatma liked to pretend that she *was* her mother. Moreover, a recent event had brought Ayasha and Fatma even closer: Ayasha had married a Bantu, and their mother had disowned her.

Parenting came naturally to Ayasha, but children did not. All her pregnancies had ended in miscarriage. On the day of Fatma's wedding, she was once again carrying a child.

"Ayasha, I'm frightened," Fatma told her as they sat in the shade of a baobab tree.

Ayasha laughed. "All girls are frightened on their wedding night."

"What if I get shot in the head like the bride in Somalia?"

"Little sister, that was an unfortunate accident. She was the victim of overly excited well-wishers. No one here is shooting guns into the air." She smiled and placed Fatma's hand on a hard round belly that loomed like Kilimanjaro beneath her swollen breasts. "*This* is what makes it all worthwhile. *This* is the joy of what goes on between a man and a woman."

"I do not want to have any baby!"

"Maybe not now. But you will."

In Kenya, all the old women of the village watch the bride intently on her wedding night, since it is common for fearful girls to run away from arranged marriages, they are so young. The women escorted Fatma home from the celebration and waited in the hall, guarding the door, while she readied herself for Daniel. Afterward they would take her to the room where he was waiting and park themselves outside the door until the marriage was consummated and the midwife examined her one last time, for traces of blood – evidence of her lost innocence.

"I will not live with a white man," Fatma had boasted to friends, knowing that racial suspicion would make them more eager to help her escape. On her wedding night Fatma removed the white gown and crowned veil and put on men's clothing. Her friend Halima had given her the garments and she had hidden them days before under her mattress. While the midwife prepared her bath, she parted the gauze curtains and climbed out the bedroom window, down an iron trellis abloom with red roses whose thorns caught on her clothing and scratched her. Halima's father, a fisherman, waited for Fatma on the shore in his dhow and ferried her to Somalia in the night.

The waters between Mombasa and Somalia are rough, the current strong. It was nine days later when they reached the house in Mogadishu. Three of Fatma's older brothers, who had been in Mombasa for the wedding but who, after her disappearance, had flown back to Somalia, were expecting her. There was no welcome, no expression of surprise. They immediately began slapping and kicking her. Each time she fell, one of them picked her up and threw her back down on the floor. Even Hamal joined in the beating. They were careful not to touch her face; they didn't want to give Daniel an excuse to reject her. Like the time she had to stifle her sobs when the soldiers came to her mother's home in the middle of the night, she now concealed the pain she felt all over her body, the hurt in her heart. And she believed that, if her father had been in Mogadishu, her brothers would never have done what they did: while beatings were a part of the culture of Somali domestic life, her father had never laid a hand on her mother.

After they finished with Fatma, Hamal accompanied her back to Mombasa by plane. During the journey Fatma refused to speak with him; years would pass before she did so again. One would have thought Allah himself had knocked at Auntie's door for all the fuss made over Hamal for returning with Fatma. They celebrated with another feast. More determined than ever, that night Fatma escaped out the window again.

In Mombasa, if you asked someone to keep a secret, they would. All her friends were on her side. The first time she ran away, no one thought to look for her in a fishing dhow – fishermen were lower class, and she had been forbidden to associate with them, but for that very reason she was drawn to these people. This time Hamal went to every boat in the harbor, yachts and hiding dhows alike. By the time they came to the one in which Fatma had been hiding, the eighteen-wheeler food transporter she was on was headed for Uganda. There the driver met with another, who took her to Tanzania. "So, princess, you want a ride?" the drivers had said when she climbed into their trucks, because everyone knew and respected her. She was the granddaughter of a Somali king and the great-granddaughter of the king before him.

After Fatma had spent a week at a friend's house in Tanzania, the friend's mother had called Auntie, who came and escorted Fatma back to Mombasa.

"You're angry with me, Mama?" Fatma asked as they sat on the airplane. Auntie liked it when she called her "Mama."

"What do you expect, Fatma? To show such disrespect to your uncle, who has given you his home."

"Is he cross with me, Mama?"

"Quite."

"I don't care."

Fatma waited for some admonishment; instead Auntie turned toward the window, but not before Fatma saw her fighting a smile. So Auntie was not that upset with the runaway bride after all, Fatma understood. Perhaps she was even enjoying their little trip, though Fatma's behavior *had* been an insult to her husband, whose honor Auntie was bound to uphold.

This time there were no festivities upon Fatma's return to Mombasa. The old women were called back to wait by the door, and after their first night together, Daniel and Fatma left for Katundu.

KATUNDU

********** ⭐ **********

It rains nonstop for three months at a time in Kenya. Fatma and Daniel were married in late June – the end of the second wet season – when roads to small villages become too muddy or flooded to travel. They left Mombasa by train at eleven in the morning and reached Nairobi around seven in the evening. There they spent the night on a bench at the bus station because traffic to Katundu had been halted by the rains.

Daniel wasn't angry with her for running away. It seemed everyone but her brothers and uncle had found it amusing. Daniel had smiled a lot that day during the train ride and, while he was speaking Swahili quite well by now, she pretended his grammar wasn't good enough to understand. Still, despite his silence, she could tell he was anxious to show her, a native, a place in Africa where she'd never been.

While they waited for the buses to resume running, he laid out his sleeping bag on the bench, placed her duffle bag as a pillow, and urged her to lie down. He told her not to be afraid to sleep, that he would not leave her side. She wondered if he was guarding her to make sure she wouldn't run away again. She closed her eyes but didn't fall asleep, checking on him from time to time through her slitted eyes and, good to his word, always finding him on the floor, leaning against the backpack that cushioned the sharp edge of the bench seat.

By Kenyan standards, Katundu *was* a rich mountain village, where family farms grew coffee and tea, bananas and vegetables. It was the home of the Mau Mau warriors and of Jomo Kenyatta, Kenya's first president, to whom everyone seemed to be related. Katundu was Kikuyu land and, since she spoke not a word of it, her tongue became paralyzed. Although Swahili is supposed to be taught in all Kenyan schools, only those from Mombasa learn it in the home; everyone else speaks their tribal language. They say that, if you drink the salt water of Mombasa, you will speak perfect Swahili. As far as Fatma could tell, no one in Katundu had ever sipped Mombasa water.

Katundu was a rich village, but by Kenyan standards; the families might have owned their farms, but it was the companies they sold to that profited. The natives, long bound to the earth and the companies they served, seemed to have no desire for beauty and the comforts that progress could have brought them. Daniel admired this lack of materialism; Fatma found the Kikuyu mentality absurd. Why would anyone work hard for someone else if they didn't have to? she asked herself. Why would they work for almost nothing? This was certainly not the business philosophy of her mother and grandfather. The Kikuyu were stupid, she concluded. And while Daniel was a teacher – and white – and therefore respected in Katundu, she was still Somali, and believed that the Kikuyu didn't like her any more than other Africans did.

At the sight of Daniel's wooden frame two-room house which was attached to the one-room school where he taught English, she cried. "No running water? No electricity? No indoor plumbing? No maid?" She had never seen an outhouse, let alone used one at night, when she might run into snakes. And how it smelled!

Because of Daniel's status, Daniel paid women to bring water from the village, carrying it for hours in fifty-pound orange or yellow plastic jugs strapped to their backs with ropes that cut into their bony shoulders. Sometimes the women were very pregnant. Transferring it into buckets and standing on a ladder outside a three-sided wooden enclosure next to the smelly outhouse, the women poured the water over Fatma for her shower. "What are you looking at?" Fatma asked when they stared at her naked body. The women just smiled, having no idea what she'd said and making no attempt to understand her.

It was Daniel who taught Fatma how to wash clothes with this water and who tried to teach her how to cook. He liked to prepare a goulash that made her sick to look at.

"What is *that*?" she asked the first time he made it.

"You should try it before you pass judgment."

She had clearly offended him, so she tried it. She hated it. She had grown up with the rich, Italian-influenced food of Somalia, with Auntie's succulent roasts. But she ate it rather than learning how to cook: she was spoiled, having grown up with Lisha and Kiah as maids. The only thing she knew how to make was pumpkin dessert, because she had liked it and watched Lisha steam the pumpkin and scoop out the flesh hundreds of times. Lisha would let her stir the pumpkin and coconut milk and spices until it all became pudding. "Never stop stirring," Lisha would say. "Never let it burn." And while Fatma stirred, Lisha talked – about Lamu, the religious Muslim community north of Mombasa where she was from, and about jinns.

According to Lisha, the people of Lamu had always believed in the existence of jinns. Created by God out of fire, they were spirits who lived in trees, toilets, and other dark hiding places. Jinns could live in your mind, which could be helpful or damaging, depending on the jinn. They were ghosts. They could be guardian angels. They could be the devil. They could be healing or a death sentence, protectors or nuisances. To lose a good jinn was to lose a part of you. Auntie laughed at Lisha's belief in jinns and the stories she told Fatma. Auntie said the people of Lamu overused them because of their ignorance about disease and modern medicine. Jinns – good or bad – caused anything unexplainable. But Lisha held her ground. "You were born with a full head of hair and consequently an evil spirit, a bad jinn," she said repeatedly. "Your mother should have taken you to a healer right away to discover what the jinn desired, to make it go away. A goat would have been sacrificed and coriander burned. The sweet smell is pleasing to jinns. Now your evil jinn will plague you. But respect your good jinn. It will be your salvation one day."

In Katundu, Fatma and Daniel walked ten miles down a dusty dirt road into town to buy food and pick up mail. If they were lucky, they caught a *matatu*, a minivan that served as a bus, but these didn't run on any particular schedule, and at times it was faster to walk than wait for one. It wasn't the walking that bothered Fatma so much. Daniel always carried the groceries in his backpack, and besides it gave her something to do. It was the snakes that sometimes appeared out of nowhere and slithered onto the road that made her uneasy. Since coffee and tea plants attract them, snakes were plentiful in Katundu. Yet she couldn't help but feel that it was she who attracted the snakes, that having married a white Christian must have angered her good jinn and would always cause her to attract them.

Three weeks passed after their wedding before she let Daniel touch her again – really touch her. Their first night as man and wife in Mombasa had been something to get through. Daniel was clumsy about doing what a man does to a woman. She had lain rigid with her eyes closed throughout the ordeal, which was every bit as horrible as she had anticipated. The chattering and snoring of the old women who kept vigil outside the door had probably made Daniel nervous and led him to perform mechanically rather than make love. At the time she didn't understand the difference between these things. In Katundu, however, he began by stroking her hair with a smooth, gentle touch. When she turned away, he gently rubbed her back. Sometimes he passed his index finger over the tattoos on the insides of her forearms (which tickled her) and asked what each image stood for. They had been put there when she was a very small child. All her brothers and sisters had them. There was the flower, which was the family's symbol; then the hearts – one on each arm – that represented the love of both parents. And there was her name, crudely printed. Maybe having the names on his children's arms helped her father to tell one from the other, there were so many.

One night she lay there crying, because of Katundu, because of the Kikuyu, and because she was lonely, so she let him console her. While his hands moved in circles on her back, she turned to him. For the first time, he kissed her. It was a short kiss. Then came a longer one. Then a very long one. His hand moved down the back of her leg, then under her nightgown and up the front of her thigh to her breasts, large for such a young girl, where it roamed, like a hunter in new territory. Her nipples hardened and her breasts felt full. Her hips moved toward him, and, unlike their first night together, she actually saw him grow stiff and so big that she pulled back for a moment in shock. How could such a skinny man have such a giant *uume?* she wondered. As usual, Daniel understood. "*Si jambo la mara moja,*" he whispered – it takes time – and his hand played with her for a long time until she was wet and her private place beat like a heart. Then he turned her onto her back and got on top of her, careful not to rest his weight on her. Even then, she knew that Daniel's light body could never crush her. He reached under the bed and pulled out a small red packet that he ripped open with his teeth. He removed a round object and unrolled it down his *uume* like a stocking up a woman's leg. Her expression must have turned from bewilderment to hurt, because he sensed she thought he didn't want his *uume* to touch her. "*Hakuna mtoto. Mapema mno,*" he said. It was too early for children. It was all easier than the first night, easier than she could have imagined. He guided his *uume* into her slowly, awkwardly, but with little pain this time. Though he never admitted it, he wasn't very experienced himself. In the months that followed he tried to learn his way around her body, to discover how to make her desire him, how to satisfy her. They say that Somali women are circumcised to force a man to work hard to bring pleasure. But while Daniel may have worked hard, she had yet to really learn the meaning of pleasure.

She returned to Mombasa every chance she got. Most times Daniel stayed behind, even if he wasn't teaching, because she never hid her desire to go alone. She did not know how to spare the feelings of others, nor did she care to. No one had ever spared hers.

During the years she lived in Katundu, the summer reunions in Mombasa were the best times for her. All of her sisters and brothers—Auntie's nieces and nephews—came, including Rihanna, who had married an Italian and lived in Milan, and Kamilah, who lived with their grandfather in Saudi Arabia. They came from everywhere to Auntie's summer feast, where they laughed and ate and the small children ran around singing and playing games until they fell from exhaustion into their mothers' arms.

That first summer she returned, Fatma's sister Ayasha had given birth to a ten-pound boy named Kareem on whom she doted endlessly. "And this is your Auntie Fatma," she said, allowing Fatma to hold him. He was heavy and strong, and after a year or two was running wild like a captured deer set free. Ayasha spoiled him, everyone said. How could she not? He was her first and only child, born out of her forbidden union with a Bantu. Yet their mother's alienation had not left Ayasha starving, as it had Fatma. Ayasha beamed with joy in the presence of her gentle husband and strong little son, knowing full well that her mother's rejection had been the result of prejudice, that her husband had done nothing wrong.

Fatma cringed at the thought of having a big baby who seemed to grow like a jungle vine, and she tried to imagine how he could possibly have come out of the tiny hole that was big enough for an *uume* but never a baby.

"Do you miss me, Mama?" Fatma asked Auntie as she left Mombasa that first summer. To please Auntie, she had worn her Somali gown throughout her stay, not the jeans she had grown accustomed to wearing in Katundu. Uncle Oliver was loading Fatma's bags into the pickup; he turned and stared at Auntie, daring her to respond. Auntie's lips remained sealed. Then it was time to leave, to board the train back to Katundu and to face the little adjustments Daniel and Fatma would make whenever she returned, that would lull them back into the monotonous rhythm of Katundu and of being man and wife.

Every few months Daniel threw his own party. That's what he called it, but it was nothing like her family reunions. His school courses would end, and he would make a giant pot of goulash and buy lots of sweets. Three or four Americans – in appearance much like Daniel with their long hair and baggy western clothing – would show up at the door, other Peace Corps volunteers who taught in neighboring villages. One had a guitar, and they would all sing in English when she played and smoke marijuana, and eat. Sometimes they created small lines of white powder and sucked it up their nostrils with a tightly rolled American dollar bill – it had to be American money, they insisted. Fatma could not comprehend the nostalgia for their homeland and believed the magic powder would lose its potency if it passed through a five-shilling note. She would sit in a corner and watch them laughing, singing, and eating until their eyes became glassy and heavy and they fell asleep against the sleeping bags they didn't bother to unroll. One couple usually found their way into the schoolhouse and the rest could hear them rolling around on the floor, moaning and panting. Daniel never forced Fatma to take part in anything frowned on by Muslim culture, although her father had had a liquor cabinet that could have rivaled any Christian man's and that horrified Fatma's mother. Fatma often got light-headed just breathing the smoke that filled their tiny cabin in Katundu, and it frightened her. She did like the music, even though she couldn't understand a word. And she especially liked the fact that on these occasions Daniel had others to play with and left her alone.

She got used to Daniel. He was kind and she trusted him, but she never grew to love him. And she would never get used to life in Katundu, nor did she try. She was stubborn that way. She could have sat in on Daniel's classes, but she refused to learn English, feeling her mother's fingers digging deep into her shoulders, shaking them until her head nearly toppled, warning her to keep away. Perhaps that's why she continued to wear a veil, even though she wore western clothes in Katundu, where the days were long and boring, and where she spent most of her time planning her escape.

She missed her family. She missed friends like Halima and the fun they had had on the forbidden shore, where they used to jump from one dhow to another, playing hide and seek or screaming secrets that the deaf fishermen couldn't hear because their eardrums had burst from diving too deep for lobsters. Fatma missed Lisha and the stories Lisha would tell her in her bedroom or the kitchen or laundry room when she thought Auntie wasn't listening. Yet, when Daniel's commitment to the Peace Corps ended and he told her they would be going to the United States, she cried. She ran out of the house and was gone for hours. Daniel found her hiding under a baobab. "Never walk under that type of tree when you are unclean," Lisha had always said. "Evil jinns know when a woman is unclean and will enter her, possess her." She had her period that night, yet she lay beneath the baobab, sobbing. Nothing worse could happen to her than what was about to. An evil spirit had entered her body at birth, according to Lisha. *That* must have been the jinn that controlled her destiny. What else could it have been? she thought. It wasn't necessary to go to America, she told Daniel. It was Katundu she had to leave, not Africa. But Daniel had renewed his two-year-commitment once already. Eyes filled with compassion, he cupped her wet face in his hands.

"You will like it," he said. "I promise."

The notion that she might like America was inconceivable. She was fifteen and terrified that in America she would be lost.

II

CARLINGTON

**********⭐**********

The plane landed at Boston's Logan Airport on Christmas Eve. No one was waiting for Fatma and Daniel. They took a bus to the city of Rockfield, on the other side of Massachusetts, where Daniel's father met them and drove them to the small town of Carlington. It was like stepping into Auntie's icebox when it needed a good defrosting: Fatma's hands were numb, her toes throbbed with pain, the air smacked her face and left it stinging. Where had Daniel brought her? To the hell Uncle Oliver, on occasion, wished someone that had done him wrong would burn in. Only this hell didn't torture with heat, just the opposite. She had never seen anything like this before, except in a picture of the Arctic: white mountains three times her height were everywhere, a wall of snow so high in the middle of town, she couldn't see across the street. They walked on paths carved out of drifts several feet deep. Frozen snow glazed the rooftops, like the icing on sponge cakes she'd seen in fancy bakeries in Mombasa. Icicles like spears hung down to second-story windows. Vapor came out of their mouths when they spoke, and she feared her evil jinn was emerging, or her insides were rotting. Maybe she was dying. Daniel held her hand as she walked up the path to the front porch of his parents' house.

"You just missed the storm. Biggest one in twenty-five years."

Daniel translated what his father had said. "Snowed all day and night; then warmed up a bit and things started to melt, then the temperature dropped and we got another foot. I'm telling you, it was something."

His father was tall like Daniel. When he removed his puffy down jacket, Fatma would see that he was thin like Daniel too, except for a belly that made him look as though he might be carrying a beach ball inside his clothing.

Her feet had wanted to slide out from under her in the airport parking lot, which had seemed as slick as oil. But here in Carlington the air was dry, and white flakes flew around like bits of sawdust that disappeared when she caught them. The ground squeaked beneath her feet which were encased in a pair of patent-leather high heels in which she had been unsteady even in Kenya.

The house was large – three stories of avocado green shingles – but not nearly as large as Auntie's. On either side of the entrance were three levels of bay windows. At the third landing a woman waited by an open door with a pine wreath and a red bow on it. Daniel's mother was plain, not pretty and pale like the English or striking like the Saudis or the Italians. She seemed as bland as a boiled potato.

"Welcome," she said, her eyes avoiding Fatma's as she hugged her against a bosom as flat as Auntie's ironing board. Then she abruptly let go and took a step back so that she could study her new daughter-in-law's face. Her hands hovered above Fatma's shoulders as if she were deciding whether or not to touch her again.

"She's very pretty," Daniel translated.

Fatma tried to smile. She wanted to cry. Beverly Kornmeyer proceeded to fuss over her son, insisting that he had grown (which he hadn't) and that he must visit the barber the first chance he got because long hair on men, something she had never liked, was going out of style.

Daniel led Fatma to his old bedroom, which would be theirs now. The Kornmeyers had replaced Daniel's twin bed with a double mattress and box spring that left almost no space for a dresser and a nightstand. The white walls smelled of new paint. The two windows had narrow white blinds with a beige ruffled curtain across the top, just like the other windows in the house. Everything in America seemed to lack color. Fatma asked Daniel if all kitchens in the United States were upstairs. He laughed. "This is an apartment," he said. "We only live on the third floor." She assumed that Uncle Oliver had wanted her to marry Daniel because his parents were rich and thought it odd for a wealthy man to live in such tiny quarters.

"Then what is downstairs?"

"Tenants," he said. Then, to re-assure her: "Don't worry. This is temporary."

At dinner Daniel tried to translate everything he and his parents said, but Fatma was too tired and uninterested to keep up, and after a while told Daniel not to bother.

"You know that I'm Muslim now," Daniel told his mother when she set the pink pork, topped with pineapple rings and cherries and dotted with cloves, on the table.

"I know you converted to marry Fatma, but I didn't take it seriously."

Daniel took in a deep breath. Islam had seemed such an easy and logical fit when they were in Kenya, even though he had never been completely sold on the religion.

"What didn't you take seriously?" he asked. "The conversion or the marriage?"

Beverly apologized for having made ham. Daniel eventually ate it with relish; it had been his favorite. Fatma played with the food on her plate, sinking the peas and slippery pearl onions into the mashed potatoes just as Auntie had done when she made her patties. Surrounded by incomprehensible chatter, Fatma felt as small as those vegetables and, like them, longed to be buried. After the main course plates were cleared, Beverly placed a piece of pumpkin pie in front of her, and Daniel proceeded to tell Fatma that it was one of America's oldest traditional dishes, really the same as Mombasa pumpkin dessert.

"The only difference, Fatma, is that it's in a pastry shell, and the pumpkin comes from a can, and there's no coconut milk. Oh, and the spices are different."

"Then it's not Mombasa pumpkin dessert," she told him. Nothing in America, as far as she could tell, was like Mombasa.

Suddenly, Daniel's mother screamed and threw her paper napkin onto her plate. Fatma watched for Daniel and his father to do the same. Perhaps this was how one ended a meal in America. Fatma clutched the napkin on her lap, waiting for a sign to toss it onto her dish. Maybe the meal, praise Allah, was finally over.

"No!" Beverly cried out again, looking at Daniel for support. Daniel merely shrugged his shoulders, and Fatma saw a weakness in him she'd never noticed before. Daniel, who had cursed American imperialism and who had taught her how to make goulash and love, step by step, suddenly had no influence in this apparent crisis. Walter, with his balding gray head, blotchy skin, and pregnant-looking belly, was no different from Uncle Oliver, and enjoyed wielding power over Daniel and his wife. Only, unlike Auntie, Beverly dared to speak out.

"It's Christmas Eve, Walter!" Beverly said, her eyes welling up.

"Come on, Dad," Daniel protested, faintly. But Fatma could see that this house was no different from Auntie's, and that like Uncle Oliver, Daniel's father had the last word. Suddenly Walter was handing Daniel and Fatma their coats and ushering them out the door, leaving Beverly to sulk at the table.

They drove a short distance and pulled into a parking lot beside a smoky, nearly empty bar where, to Fatma's horror, topless girls were dancing on a stage. Asked for identification, Daniel showed her passport, which said she was twenty-one. He had had to lie about her age to take her out of the country. When one of the dancing girls approached their table, Walter stuffed a ten-dollar bill into the girl's g-string. Daniel shook his head; Fatma lowered hers. The room with its decadent behavior was spinning around her.

"I want to go home," she told Daniel.

"This is not customary, Fatma, believe me," Daniel said. "Just a little while longer, please. I haven't seen him in four years."

"America is evil!" Fatma cried to Auntie on the phone later that night. "The women are more naked than the foreign women on the beaches at home!" She told Auntie where they had gone, how she had looked in every direction, trying to avoid seeing the scantily dressed ladies and the groping men. Horrified, Auntie persuaded Uncle Oliver to wire money. Three days later, Fatma was back in Mombasa.

This time her brother Hamal did not have to travel to Mombasa. The fighting in Ogaden had sent millions of refugees into Somalia; the homeless were everywhere. Besides, opposition to Uncle Ahmad's rule was coalescing; Fatma's family wasn't safe. A military man like all her brothers, Hamal had taken care of himself by finding a diplomatic position across the border in Kenya. Unlike the sisters who had already moved to Europe with their husbands, or her spinster sister Kamilah in Saudi Arabia, the others – the unlucky ones like Ayasha – stayed on in Mogadishu, ready to defend their mother's estate.

"He is not rich!" Fatma cried to Uncle Oliver. "You said his family was rich!"

"He is rich compared to most Kenyans. And he is my friend. He saved my life."

"I know all about the war and the American who saved your life." She couldn't imagine Walter Kornmeyer saving his own life. "And if you send me back to America, there will be a third war."

"Fatma, you will adjust to the Kornmeyers. You will adjust to America. It's for your own good. There is no life for you here. There is too much instability. Business is bad."

Her other brothers were called to Mombasa. For two weeks they ate a lot and from time to time discussed her predicament until they reached a decision: she was Daniel's wife, and she belonged with him.

"One has to fit in wherever one is," Hamal quoted a Somali saying.

"You will learn to like living there," Uncle Oliver said.

"Just as you will learn to love your husband," was all Auntie said, drawing from experience and offering one of her own proverbs: "Patience is the key to tranquility."

Daniel met Fatma at the airport in Boston. It snowed all winter; she didn't leave the house until spring. She was not made for life in the bleak city of Carlington. She was an island girl.

Mombasa Eye

Walter Kornmeyer preached the golden rule. "It means be a good Christian," he said in a loud voice, as though volume would aid Fatma's English comprehension. "Do unto others as you would have them do unto you. Someday you'll understand this. Someday I hope you'll be one of us." Daniel didn't translate when she said that she already was one of them since she had one head, two arms, and two legs. Fatma had begun to think that Walter Kornmeyer's last good deed had been his heroic rescue of Uncle Oliver, because she observed that Walter said one thing but did another.

She couldn't understand his fascination with the strip club. Unlike Daniel, he didn't seem much interested in sex – not with his wife, at least, who watched talk shows until well after midnight, long after Walter had happily gone to bed without her. And while he preached his Golden Rule and gave in to tenants, neighbors, and others outside the family, from time to time Fatma could see frustration building within him. That's when he turned nasty to his wife and son – in a nice way. Looking back on it, Fatma would see that the times he claimed to be protecting his family from danger were the times he was trying hardest to gain respect, because his family were the only people he could control.

He gave Beverly less money for groceries, saying the economy was headed downward. He wouldn't let Daniel use the car. Although Daniel thought it was fine, Walter was sure there was something wrong with it. Walter managed the produce section of Fine Foods Supermarket. It soon became apparent to Fatma that all he knew was fruits and vegetables.

Beverly provoked her husband's tyrannical side. She often gave him a choice for dinner: steak or chicken, broiled or fried. If he requested steak, she made chicken. If he said broiled, she fried it. Fatma came to anticipate the dinner scenes that followed – the tightening of Walter's jaw as he gazed down at his plate, the deep breath, the murmuring. The next day, or even that night, a new restriction was announced, which made Beverly get all huffy or teary. Their marriage was a dance for which they set up their own obstacle course. Daniel seemed reluctant to translate at these times, perhaps hoping Fatma would remain oblivious to goings-on that he had grown accustomed to. But she must have understood enough for their behavior to rub off on her, because one day he would find herself caught up in a similar but far more dangerous marriage waltz of her own.

Walter made fun of Daniel's desire to help others – or at least Daniel's way of going about it – which seemed yet another contradiction of his Golden Rule. He discouraged Daniel from becoming a social worker and pushed him toward business, boasting that he would become an international entrepreneur. That's when Fatma learned that she wasn't the only prize Uncle Oliver had handed over to the Kornmeyers. He had offered to back the young couple in a venture, one he also stood to gain from. They would establish an artifacts shop. Uncle Oliver would provide the capital investment and inventory; Daniel and Fatma would run it.

Soon after Fatma and Daniel arrived in the United States, Uncle Oliver had sent Fatma a cashier's check for ten thousand dollars that was to provide the first year's rent for the artifacts shop, Kilimanjaro, to be located in the mall beneath the downtown Rockfield commercial towers. Jeannine Fournier, fresh out of law school and the daughter of Walter's boss, set about drawing up the contract for the business and arranging for the lease. The entire process would advance the careers of the younger generation and bolster the egos of the older. Uncle Oliver sent a list of instructions and provisions concerning the business. After a year, most of the profits would finance a second store in one of the wealthier Rockfield suburbs. If that one was successful, they would open another shop in Worcester, and yet another in Boston, until a chain of African-artifacts stores dotted Massachusetts and eventually the entire United States. Although Fatma would be the legal proprietor when she turned twenty-one, Uncle Oliver had made provisions for an increase in the cost of inventory that limited her profits. She couldn't help but feel that she had been sent to America to salvage his enterprise.

She began to understand bits of the conversations that went on around her but, in an attempt to remain outside of her in-laws' control, she refused to let on, finding it easy to dance Kornmeyer-style. While they waited for the first shipment of inventory, Daniel took a job delivering furniture in Rockfield and she spent her days with her mother-in-law.

"Do you want to mop the floor or dust?" Beverly would say, carefully pronouncing each syllable, her large mouth opening and closing so slowly Fatma had time to examine Beverly's silver fillings. Beverly held out a mop in one hand and a piece of Walter's old white boxer shorts in the other. She knew Fatma understood the exaggerated gestures she made when she spoke; she simply didn't understand that Fatma didn't do housework, that she was a princess. She encouraged Fatma to cook with her but, even when Fatma didn't resist, she did nothing to Beverly's satisfaction: Daniel's mother recut the kielbasa Fatma had sliced too thick or rescrambled the eggs she had not beaten enough. Fatma continued to work lackadaisically and used ignorance as an excuse to be rude to her mother-in-law because Beverly Kornmeyer's whiny nature irritated her no end.

"You don't like me, do you?" Beverly said one day as Fatma let the beef broth Beverly had just made vanish down the drain. A colander of neck bones and fat sat in the sink beside the bowl the soup was to have been filtered into. Fatma hadn't intended to do it; she had simply thought about doing it to annoy Beverly, and before she knew it she was doing it – and enjoying it.

While Daniel fell farther and farther away from Muslim culture, Fatma did her best to stay on the Islamic path around which her life had centered, though she did so more out of obligation to her parents and Auntie than from devotion. She knelt facing east five times a day on the woolen prayer rug with brightly colored swirls and geometric patterns that she kept rolled up beside the bed. Prayer before sunrise was the only time she felt comfortable, because at all other times Beverly was there in the apartment either watching or listening – eyebrows knitted up, lips puckered, trying to figure Fatma out. Beverly told Daniel she thought Fatma might have some personality disorder, since she spent so much time each day scrubbing her hands and forearms and feet and dribbling water on her crown like John the Baptist.

"It's Muslim ritual," Daniel told her. "They – we – have to clean ourselves if we've touched anything dirty or another person before we pray." He had spoken in the first person, but Beverly knew her son better than anyone else and, aware that religion had never been a priority in his life, she guessed he believed no differently where Islam was concerned.

"Even if the person is clean?" Beverly was the only person Fatma touched during the day, and only if they handed the other something or accidentally brushed in passing.

"No person is clean," Daniel said.

The morning after the soup incident, the prayer rug was nowhere to be found. By noon prayer time, Fatma still hadn't located the rug. At three o'clock she washed herself as usual and found Beverly in the mustard yellow housedress she wore every day, hanging the wash out on the clothesline that stretched from a post on the back porch to a telephone pole across the alley. She almost never used a dryer unless the temperature dropped below freezing. She liked the freshness of outdoors, she said, although she rarely ventured into it.

"*Msala?*" Fatma demanded to know where her rug was.

Beverly's puzzled expression meant she didn't understand.

Daniel came home and found Fatma in tears. Beverly said she had just wanted to clean the rug: it was so old and dirty, and she knew how important cleanliness was to Fatma. In a fit of insomnia she had put it into the washer during the night and then, because it was so heavy and would have taken so long to dry on the line, put it into the dryer and forgotten about it. "She's lying!" Fatma told Daniel (they still spoke only Swahili to each other) when he explained Beverly's motives. The episode had nearly destroyed the treasured carpet that had been with Fatma for as long as she could remember and that was now frayed, faded, and shrunken.

"You know she prays throughout the day," Daniel said to his mother.

"I only meant to help. I can't seem to do anything right around her. Please tell her I'm sorry."

"Tell her yourself," Daniel said.

"I'm sorry, Fatma. Really, dear."

Fatma thought Beverly might really be sorry, and that she probably had forgotten about the rug, but only because she had wanted to. Fatma's customs were as irritating to Beverly as Beverly's were to Fatma.

Daniel assured Fatma that, as soon as the store got under way and they had saved enough money, they would move into their own apartment. But Daniel seemed to be settling back a little too comfortably into the surroundings he had not so long ago cast aside for the unknown, and she feared it wouldn't be long before he forgot the urgency about a new apartment, or that when the time came he wouldn't have the nerve to leave if his parents didn't want the couple to go.

Fatma needed to get away from Beverly. As the sun grew stronger and birds began chirping, she took to walking into town. Downtown Carlington was small, several blocks at best – a dreary sort of place, especially in winter, with drab buildings and small unattractive shops so unlike the pastel hues of Old Town Mombasa. Each day she made a circle. She went down Centre Street, passing a few clapboard houses on her right, the shops on her left. City Hall was like her, out of place, an imposing brick structure with a large round stained-glass window and a rectangular clock tower topped with a weather vane. She crossed Butler Street with its Rivoli movie theater where Daniel always wanted to see complicated love stories with lots of dialogue she couldn't understand. She hated those movies that got Daniel excited and eager to make love. From there the street sloped downward to Front Street and the old redbrick mill buildings that were now an industrial park. Then came the river. It was the river that sustained Fatma in Carlington. In the heat of summer, which finally arrived like a miracle, she watched the dirty water and pretended it was the sea, and that she saw her family and all the fancy tourists of home in it. She pretended briefly that she *was* home, before she looped around and went up Ridge Street and back over to Union and the apartment. In the evenings when he wasn't working, Daniel joined her on a walk. He would put his arm around her, draw her close to him and kiss her on the cheek or forehead. But she always wriggled out of his grasp.

"It is really okay here. How many times do I have to tell you that?"

But it was so hard getting used to displaying affection in public, and the way women walked around with skin showing everywhere: bare arms and legs sticking out from shorts and skirts that just covered their behinds, necklines revealing half their breasts.

"I am who I am," she reminded him.

"I'm not asking you to change, Fatma. Just try to adjust."

"Daniel, I can't be new," she said.

The first shipment of artifacts arrived in midsummer, and Daniel quit his job at the furniture store. In the beginning Fatma went with Daniel each day to the shop, where she was to remain silent when customers entered, for fear they would think Daniel and she were plotting in Swahili to fleece them. As Daniel suggested, she wore colorfully festive outfits and headwraps not worn by Muslim women, and sat in a corner like a mannequin transported in a crate along with the other knickknacks. Before long he told her not to bother to come down at all, because the presence of a black woman in foreign dress must have been frightening the professional white clientele from the wealthy suburb. His decision suited Fatma just fine, since Beverly had begun to go to the shop every day to help out and she had even asked for a small salary. Time alone in the apartment would be like smearing cool salve on a burning wound.

What to do with Fatma, however, became the new Kornmeyer preoccupation. After dinner one evening Beverly sat munching on the raisins she had plucked from a pound cake, while Walter gobbled up the remaining loaf, which now resembled a block of Swiss cheese. (Sometimes Beverly picked blueberries out of a muffin, which Walter then finished off, or she spooned the filling out of a slice of pie, leaving him to devour the crust. It embarrassed Fatma when they did this, because it seemed such an intimate affair, a mutually satisfying act like making love. Maybe this was the closest they ever got to it.) It was time, they all agreed, for Fatma to learn English. Why she had resisted seemed of no interest to anyone, not even Daniel, who was growing impatient with her. She was going to apply for naturalization after she'd been in the States for three years, and she would have to be somewhat proficient in English. But her mother's hatred of Anglo-Christians had nearly severed her English vocal cords long ago and left them badly damaged.

Fatma agreed to go to school two nights a week. The classes were held at the high school. The teacher, Mrs. Dolan, was a stocky woman with red-framed glasses and short black-and-gray hair that stuck out like wet feathers from every part of her head. At the beginning of class, she made the students recite pronunciation drills out loud and in unison. She gave them a sound, and they made the changes she pointed to. *Luck, muck, tuck, buck, duck, suck, puck* they recited one evening. Fatma had never heard this kind of chanting coming from Daniel's schoolroom. When she had peeked into the room, Daniel was usually bent over a student's bench, whispering the correct pronunciation as the student read, trying not to embarrass the child. Fatma stayed silent as usual, until one day Mrs. Dolan pointed to *f* by mistake. "Fuck!" Fatma yelled, as loud as she could, along with the others. Most of them didn't understand what they were saying, but Fatma knew, because Daniel said that all the time when he was angry. Mrs. Dolan's face became as red as her glasses. It was the only time Fatma laughed in class.

The Cambodians, the Colombians, and especially the Russians made a lot of progress in Mrs. Dolan's class, while Fatma sat like a tiger trapped in a sandpit. This was not the kind of school she had attended in Mombasa, and these people were not her friends, who knew what country they belonged in. With each day away from home, Mombasa overran its boundaries until it spilled over the entire continent of Africa and was fast encompassing Fatma's world. She missed Auntie more than ever. She missed Mogadishu and her father and brothers and sisters. She even missed her mother.

Mrs. Dolan taught her students how to purchase gum and little packages of Kleenex, and how to order a Big Mac and Coke at McDonald's. Now on her walks Fatma went to a convenience store and bought a pack of Wrigley's Spearmint gum every day. She asked the Indian man at the register questions Mrs. Dolan had taught them: *How much is this gum? Do you have sugar free?* The Indian man would always mumble that he didn't understand. Daniel said he had a heavy accent of his own and shouldn't have criticized Fatma's English. "Fuck you!" she told him one day, fed up with his complaining. "Fuck you too," he said. It was the best English conversation she'd ever had.

When she spoke, some salespeople thought she was drunk and looked disgusted. Others looked at her with pity, and she knew they thought she was retarded. So she went back to saying nothing: she pointed to what she wanted, and gave the cashier a large enough bill that she wouldn't have to figure out the change. Then she discovered something easier. When no one was watching, she picked up the gum and hid it in her fist or up her sleeve. Sometimes she dropped it into her purse. It was gratifying, knowing she had pulled something over on the clerks. She chewed gum in English class, which infuriated Mrs. Dolan.

Daniel told Fatma that she was just being stubborn, that she had a flair for languages. But while she had grown up speaking Arabic, Somali, and Swahili, English was the language of the devil, Lisha had said.

It wasn't until she met Miss Greene, however, a woman about Beverly's age who lived in an apartment next door and worked in the X-ray department of a hospital in Rockfield, that speaking English began to matter. Beverly could never mention her without saying, "Miss Greene, the nice heavyset black Baptist lady next door." Fatma never knew whether the description was a warning for Fatma to lose weight, because she too was short with a generous bosom and a thick waist, or to remember that she was also black, or to convert. One day, when Fatma was returning from her walk and Miss Greene from work, Miss Greene invited her up to her apartment. They sat at a kitchen table covered with a big orange and cobalt floral-print cloth that reminded Fatma of Kenya. Enormous green vines erupted from large planters, and walls were painted yellow, orange, and red. Miss Greene was big, with a fanny that spilled way over the seat of her chair and breasts that could have nursed all the starving babies of Somalia. Fatma wanted to climb onto her lap, pull one out of her sweater, and start sucking. She wanted to get lost on Miss Greene's lap. She wanted to smother her face in those two giant pillows until she suffocated from joy.

Sometimes Miss Greene worked through the night, sometimes on weekends. "I'll leave a light on in the kitchen and, when you see it, morning or night, you'll know I'm up having my coffee, and you come by," she told Fatma, who began to work harder at school so she'd be able to understand her new friend.

Sitting at Miss Greene's table, Fatma took in the sweet scented oils the older woman used in her hair, which she pulled back into a small knot, and listened to the stories Miss Greene told about herself. Miss Greene would say things several different ways, until Fatma grasped the meaning, whereupon Miss Greene celebrated by opening her big mouth so wide with pleasure that her gold tooth caught the light and sparkled like a star in the night. Then Miss Greene would clap her hands to encourage Fatma, as though she were a baby learning to say *Mama*.

She'd come north from Virginia a long time ago, but her parents had died at an early age from some disease or other and left Miss Greene pretty much on her own. She talked about places like foster homes that Fatma couldn't really imagine but that, in her mind, connected them like an umbilical cord of abandonment. She had never married, either. Fatma didn't know any women except her ugly sister Kamilah who had never married. But Miss Greene wasn't like Kamilah; Miss Greene was beautiful.

"Don't want no man in my life, child. Don't want to raise no man. Don't want to answer to no man. Ain't got time for no man."

She didn't have to convince Fatma about living without a man; marriage had never been her choice. She wanted to be free like Miss Greene, and she wondered what it could possibly be like to live alone. But she was incapable of doing this in America, and she would never be allowed to do it in Mombasa.

"Why I just sit all day? I see everybody go work," she told Miss Greene after they had begun to meet regularly.

"You have a business."

"I cannot be there."

"Then we'll go down to the Skills Center and sign you up to learn how to do something," she said. "I see you need your own career."

"Like what?"

"Like, I don't know, child. Something with your hands. Something where you don't need to talk none."

When Miss Greene wasn't looking, Fatma helped herself to things she didn't even need – a bar of soap from a stack under the bathroom sink, loose change on the kitchen counter, one of the many tubes of lipstick in the medicine cabinet. Fatma liked having things that were Miss Greene's, anything that had touched her warm smooth skin.

After a few months of classes, Fatma did learn something useful – circuit boarding, probably because it was mathematical and, as Miss Greene had said, she didn't have to talk none. Miss Greene helped her fill out an application from an electronics company in the industrial park.

"No one is going to hire you," Daniel said. "Not until you can speak English better. And you could, if you put your mind to it. You already speak three languages."

Daniel was always so doubtful. So cautious.

Fatma was careful to dress nicely on the day of the interview: a navy skirt that came down to her calves and a sweet-potato-colored blouse. She oiled her hair so that it shone and pinned the sides of it back with two rhinestone barrettes that Daniel's mother had given her for her eighteenth birthday. Her earrings were the gold oval loops Daniel had bought in Nairobi on their first anniversary. She wore high quilted nylon boots even though there was no snow. She wore boots every day in winter to keep her toes from freezing. She put on Miss Greene's lipstick. She was getting used to wearing makeup like American ladies, like the ladies of Kenya who worked in expensive shops, like the whores of Somalia.

"Mrs. Kornmeyer?" the woman in personnel at Gemtek called out.

When Fatma approached her, the woman's jaw dropped, and Fatma knew it wasn't her outfit that impressed the woman. She was getting used to many things in America.

"We must have made a mistake," the woman said. "We must have called the wrong person."

"You make mistake – about color of skin." Fatma pointed to her own face.

She was understanding English but she was hating America.

Gemtek paid Fatma thirteen dollars an hour to sit on an assembly line and put circuit boards together. They had made another mistake, too: they had no rule about workers wearing safety goggles. Five months later, Elsa Martinez, a young Puerto Rican who sat next to her, had a fan going on a hot summer day. The fan blew the molten solder she was working with into Fatma's right eye. Someone should have taken Fatma straight to the emergency room where Miss Greene worked, but instead they had her finish her shift. By the time she got home she couldn't see out of that eye. Beverly took her to a doctor who performed laser surgery; however, the solder had spent too much time in her eye and had gone in too deep. The scarring would come back again and again, like a recurring nightmare.

She gradually regained her sight after putting drops in her eye, and she was given glasses for close work and reading, but her eye was red and teary all the time. She called it her Mombasa eye – the eye that wept for home.

Miss Greene thought Fatma's accident was all her fault, because she had helped her get the job at Gemtek. She felt so bad she did something nobody had ever done for Fatma: she apologized. Though Fatma loved having Miss Greene's things, she never stole from her again.

THE PENNY HOUSE

********** ⭐ **********

The week Miss Greene was working until four, she and Fatma had their coffee late in the day. Fatma talked to her about Daniel, about how she might like him better if they had more space instead of being on top of each another.

"I saw an advertisement for a penny house," she told Fatma and began rummaging through a thick stack of newspapers on one of her kitchen chairs. She was still feeling bad about Fatma's eye and seemed to want to go out of her way to help her more than ever.

"A what?"

"It's a government house. You put down a penny and get a really low interest rate. But you got to meet their qualifications. Talk to your Daniel, but don't take too long. They go faster than ice cubes on a summer day."

"This can be problem with Daniel," Fatma said.

"See what I mean about men, child?"

⭐

"No way! We don't have a prayer," Daniel said that night as he and Fatma lay in bed. The open newspaper in front of his face prevented her from seeing his expression. "Here's an article on Somalia," the voice behind the newspaper said, changing the subject. He tried to keep her up to date on what was happening in Africa, sharing news whenever he came across something in the paper or heard a story on the radio. While they were still in Katundu, Somalia had declared a state of emergency after its defeat in the Ogaden war. It had broken its alliance with the Soviets, who had supported Ethiopia. This and the Soviets' invasion of Afghanistan had led to a strengthening of Somalia's ties with the United States. Daniel insisted on reading the article to her.

"The U.S. is supplying monetary aid in return for the use of air and naval facilities at Berbera, but remains hesitant to provide military help while Somali forces maintain operations in Ethiopia. Added to this is the growing concern that Somalia will renew friendship with Libya. Opposition movements continue to spring up in Somalia along the border, threatening the government of General Ahmad Siad Adan – "

"You're talking too fast for me to understand," she interrupted in Swahili.

"Try to talk in English, Fatma. You need the practice. You'll be applying for citizenship soon."

"Daniel, I hear nothing from my brothers and sisters. Nothing from Ayasha. Nothing. So we talk, Daniel – in English – about house." She couldn't worry about her family right now. They didn't want her home, and she hadn't visited for some time. She couldn't help but feel selfish and worried about her unhappy existence. "All we need is five hundred for application and fifteen hundred in bank," she said in English. "That we have got."

"Forget it, Fatma. Do not waste your time." He pronounced each word distinctly to make sure she got the message.

She had expected as much. Kilimanjaro had yet to produce a cent of profit. Oh, people wandered in and out of the store on their lunch hour and admired the five-foot-tall hand-carved giraffes, the intricate designs woven into baskets. They pawed over the jewelry, the brightly colored outfits, and the lustrous ebony masks. "It's lovely, but where would I put it?" they'd say, or "It doesn't fit with my color scheme," or "I couldn't walk the streets in that." Those searching for Halloween costumes or something to display in schools during Multicultural Week found the wares far too expensive. Aside from purchasing the occasional necklace or miniature zebra or leopard, customers left empty-handed. Sometimes they roared with laughter at the absurdity of an article. You can't force your culture on others: some things – some people, she was learning – were meant to blend in with the landscape of their own countries, or else they stand out like a sore thumb – objects of ridicule, always out of place.

She stopped trying to convince him about the penny house and began to play with his *uume* instead. He stopped laughing at her.

While her mother had done her best to rid herself of Fatma, she could never dilute the blood that also flowed through her daughter and that carried her trait of determination, of survival. Fatma was descended from a long line of tycoons, and she understood that production was nothing without a market. There didn't seem to be a market in Rockfield for the African artifacts, and she tried to tell Daniel this, but he wouldn't listen. Daniel was a sweet man, but he could never see beyond his short nose. The business was going to fail, and part of Fatma was going to be happy to watch it go down. She was here, in a place she hated, where no one was going to rescue her. And why would she expect them to?

She sent in the application and, in the spring of 1984, Daniel read her the letter saying that they qualified for a government loan at a three percent interest rate. They moved out of the Kornmeyer triple-decker and into a two-bedroom house on Poplar Street in

Rockfield, just over the city line, in a neighborhood called Forest Acres. Fatma's only regret in going was that she had to leave her lovely Miss Greene, who had suggested the penny house in the first place.

"Where is forest?" Fatma asked Daniel.

"There was a forest once. That's what happens in America. Things get swallowed up little by little. People get swallowed up."

Some of the forest remained, but now it was only a small park that Daniel said wasn't safe at night, and hardly in the daytime, since it was filled with drug addicts and pushers. "You might say the forest became a jungle," he said.

She thought they used that term a lot in America. Everything bad was a jungle. What did they know about jungles? Her father was a hunter: he covered the walls of her mother's home in Mogadishu with stuffed heads of tigers and lions and other animals that roamed the high plains of Kenya. The first thing he had taught Fatma to kill was a deer. She remembered that it was her tenth birthday, and he had come, as he always did for her birthday, to Mogadishu. From there they had gone on safari to Kilimanjaro: they often went there or to Serengeti, but first they passed through the jungle, where you could kill all the deer you wanted. In Kenya, people killed with a purpose: for food, for clothing, for decoration; but deer, nobody cared why or how you killed them, her father told her.

The .22 double barrel was heavy, and it hurt as it kicked back into her shoulder the way a frightened child jumps into its mother's arms. It had taken only three attempts. Her father said she was a natural. She had a good eye, the other men in the group, including father's oldest brother, Abdullah, agreed. They ran to cut out the deer's liver and collect its blood in a cup. Handing them to Fatma, they made her bite into the raw meat, then sip the blood.

It's something every hunter does after his first kill, they explained; if he doesn't, he will bring bad luck on the rest of his hunting days. They laughed as she gagged on the soft, warm meat. They cheered when she threw up the blood as the heat rose from her bowels to her skin and her stomach convulsed. Her head pounded. She had liked the killing part, though, halting a quick animal in its tracks. But it had been a doe, and she had felt bad about leaving its baby without a mother. The men only clapped their hands with glee and toasted her success – *their* success.

Later that night, as she lay awake and the others slept, her Uncle Abdullah, who had always appeared ancient to her, crouched beside her mat. As the eldest member of the family, he was the most respected. He was also the kindest and fairest of the brothers – fairer than the ruthless General Ahmad, gentler even than her father, Muhammad. Perhaps his benevolence had come with age, for he was much older than his brothers, or because his military days were far behind him.

"You are all right?" he whispered, his face so close to hers that his moustache tickled her.

She nodded, though her stomach was still queasy.

"You are brave, little Fatma," he said. "You are the good General Muhammad's daughter. And remember that your name comes from Fatimah, the Prophet Muhammad's favorite daughter." He patted her cheeks until the knots in her stomach dissolved and she fell asleep. Simple words. But words too heavy with meaning for her little ears to take in at the time.

Fatma's father never took her on a lion hunt. "It's too risky to mind a child and hunt for a lion at the same time," he claimed. He would go with only three other men. While it is cowardly to shoot a lion for sport, to battle it with your hands, as her father did, was acceptable. A knife may be used to counter the lion's claws and thus level the odds a bit. Her father sought only king lions. Not all lions are kings, not even all males, but the king lion truly rules the jungle. Fatma had seen animals quake and panic when the king roared. "You know it when you see a king: he looks you straight in the eye, and his look says, 'Don't come near me or you'll die.' He can hear the drop of a needle, smell you from miles away," her father said.

Not many men can outsmart a king lion, which likes to trap the hunter, going past him for thirty or forty miles, then returning and surprising him when he is tired and least expects it. People spent months searching for lions. Fatma's father did kill a female lion one time in self-defense and then took her cubs to Fatma's mother's ranch to raise as pets. Fatma used to ride them when she was two or three years old, the way toddlers ride big dogs. But her father had to shoot one of them after it ripped off the arm of a neighbor's boy. "Once a lion has tasted human blood, he becomes addicted," her father explained. "And he cannot stop from killing humans again."

Besides a store that sold used auto parts on one corner and a fish-and-chips take-out on the other, empty lots filled with broken beer bottles and greasy bags surrounded Poplar Street. The park had no trees, just a rusty swing set and a broken slide. Some Poplar Street owners were making an attempt to fix up and maintain their homes, most of which were similar: an open front porch (two narrow windows on the second floor above it); either clapboard or shingled; painted a pale color like sky blue or pistachio green. Daniel and Fatma's house – like they themselves – was two-toned and different from the rest: white clapboards on the bottom half and brown shingles on the top. Fatma liked it. She had Daniel paint all the rooms a bright yellow, because she wanted her house to seem sunny during the dreary winters. She went to a discount store and bought brocade drapes for all the windows – gold and red and royal blue – that went down to the floor and could be tied back with braided ropes. Beverly was horrified by their ornateness; Daniel thought them a bit gaudy, but they made Fatma feel like a princess.

It was time to stop using condoms and try to have a child, Daniel said. He was eager to fulfill a final promise that Auntie had made to Fatma's mother. Since Daniel had let Fatma decorate the penny house the way she wanted, she accommodated him. She let his penis dig deep into her while she held her vagina open as far as she could.

"What in the world are you doing?" Daniel asked when he saw her lying on her back the next morning, her legs in the air.

"Keeping seeds from slipping out."

She drank milk and ate broccoli and soda crackers, even though she hated them, because Daniel's mother said this would take away the morning sickness. But the bleeding came month after month, until one month it stopped, and her breasts became larger and sore, and she could no longer zipper her pants. Her belly swelled faster than a sail at sea, and it became difficult to sleep at night or even to get out of bed. This was what her sister Ayasha had been desperate to have happen to her? This was supposed to have made marriage worthwhile? But no promise had been made concerning Ayasha's pregnancy. Carrying a child had not been a gross inconvenience for her, as it was for Fatma; she had been able to keep her son. Fatma, on the other hand, would be forced to give up hers. Because the only way Auntie could get Fatma's mother to agree to Fatma's non-Islamic marriage that day they sat in Auntie's parlor had been to promise that Fatma's firstborn male would be turned over to the family to be raised Muslim. The only way Fatma's mother would agree to her marriage had been to punish her for it.

Nature, however, had a trick up her sleeve. Her doctor was concerned about the amount of weight Fatma was rapidly putting on, so he ordered a test that confirmed what he suspected: she was carrying twins, a boy and a girl. Her family would never separate the two infants, nor would they take both of them, since they wanted only a boy; the promise thus became null and void. Daniel admitted he never really believed they'd hold them to the promise anyway. Fatma was free then to embrace the babies growing inside her. The bigger she got, the better she felt – except for the fact that Beverly insisted on accompanying her on doctor's visits and showing up at Poplar Street unannounced, with pink and blue fuzzy sleepers, undershirts the size of her hand, and coupons for diapers. The furniture store where Daniel used to work gave them a big discount on two cribs and a twin carriage.

In the last trimester of her pregnancy, Fatma became terribly homesick. Beverly said she should be nesting instead of dreaming of faraway places. Perhaps Fatma did need to make a nest, but the tree in which she wanted to build it was Mombasa. She quit working at Gemtek, since she had planned to leave when the babies were born anyway. Also, she no longer needed a job to feel productive. She was doing nothing these days, yet she was amazed that she was not only still creating, but twofold! She ignored her doctor's advice and left for Africa for Auntie's summer feast, hoping to see Ayasha and say, *Look what I've done! Just like you!*

She knew the chances of Ayasha being able to leave Somalia were now remote.

Over the years Fatma and Daniel had become sloppy about taking their malaria prevention pills when returning to Mombasa. Uncle Oliver financed their trips, which he considered to be more about reviewing his American business endeavor than visiting with his daughter. On the other hand, Auntie fussed over Fatma more than she had when Fatma returned from Katundu. But in her time away from Kenya, Fatma had become more American than she realized. More susceptible, she came down with malaria on her return to Rockfield, and the babies arrived early. Her daughter was stillborn; her son died three hours after birth.

Daniel was quick to suggest that they have another child as a way of coping with the loss. Fatma, adamant that there would be no more babies, returned to Gemtek, stepping out of what now seemed to have been an eight-month nightmare. She was allergic to the birth control pills her doctor prescribed. Her body rejected an IUD. Daniel promised her that he would go back to using protection. But Daniel wanted another baby.

In December, Fatma's father phoned. She hadn't seen him since before her marriage to Daniel, over seven years ago. Now he was at the Somali embassy in Washington, and he wanted to see her.

More Promises

As Fatma rode the train to Washington, she kept the image of her tall and handsome father, General Muhammad Hakeem, before her. No sooner had she stepped from the train at Union Station than an elderly black chauffeur removed his cap and bowed his head in respect, saying, "Come with me, Miss Fatma. I'm here to take you to the embassy." His voice was melodic, with the texture of velvet. He picked up her suitcase and led her down the platform, through the busy terminal, and out the glass doors to a limousine parked by a fountain flanked with flags from different nations. She was still wondering how he had been able to identify her so easily when he opened the door with such haste that she knew she should get in quickly.

"Fatma," her father said, smiling. He bore only a faint resemblance to the man she had adored all her life. She dove, nevertheless, into the backseat as though it was the Indian Ocean, and the essence of Africa swallowed her whole.

He wore his dark dress uniform, with tassels at the shoulders and medals on the chest. He lifted her small chin with his large fingers, callused by years in the military. He studied her, then pulled her face, warm from excitement, to his own perfumed skin.

"How beautiful you are, daughter," he said in Somali.

"America goes well with you."

She forced a smile. His words couldn't be farther from the truth. All the safaris and plane rides with him now seemed concentrated into a moment, a short journey, a drive up Massachusetts Avenue.

Massachusetts. It was as though she had traveled all day to wind up where she had started that morning, as though her father and the land he represented had been consumed by the country she hated. She half expected to find her very white mother-in-law waiting for her at the door of the Somali embassy. She would be hanging a Christmas wreath and fretting about the words for her greeting to her Muslim daughter-in-law, just as she had the first day they met. Only on this day Fatma would have to introduce Beverly to her father, and Beverly would become even more flustered, more confused, and look even more foolish confronting this imposing black man. They turned onto Connecticut Avenue – still too close. To Fatma's relief, they next pulled onto a street called Wyoming and into the driveway of a house whose entrance was marked by the blue Somali flag, with its large white star in the center, hanging above it. Her cousin Ali, the ambassador, stood waiting at the doorway.

They ate in the embassy dining room, at a table draped in white cloth and set with fine china and silver. Now she saw her father clearly for the first time: he was old, not so much with age as from weariness. His hair had turned gray, his onyx skin was cracked like the worn leather of his finest saddle, and his stature appeared diminished. He was not quite as powerful as she remembered.

"So, you are an American now, my daughter," he said.

"Never. I will never be an American."

"Are you not a citizen yet?"

"I am. But I will never be an American."

He and her cousin Ali smiled. "You will become an American," he acknowledged, "but you will always be Somali, even before you are a Kenyan." The pinkish tips of his fingers tapped his heart which had transported, from continent to continent, all the troubles of his homeland.

"Why have you come?" she asked.

"To see my friend President Reagan."

She knew that, but she would have liked him to say that he had come to see her, that Washington just happened to be a more interesting place in which to meet than Rockfield, Massachusetts. She also knew that he would speak to her of their family through politics, because politics *was* their family. Whether he was explaining how to approach an animal before the kill or how to feed a country of starving nomads, her father had always spoken eloquently, uttering every word as though it were falling upon the ears of thousands. Today was no different.

Ali nodded, affirming every utterance he would later translate when her father delivered the same speech to the president of the United States. She felt proud that her father was sharing his work with her. She knew that it was his medium for communication, and that he rarely separated himself from it. What she didn't know, however, was the imminent danger he was in.

He plucked several purple grapes from a cluster in a dish in front of him and placed one after another in his mouth. He chewed them slowly, then swallowed, taking in a deep breath that would allow him to go on. "We fear the drought will extend into Somalia soon. The country is at the brink of civil war – disaster. That is why I have been unable to come see you during your visits to Mombasa. That is why I have come to Washington. To ask for the military aid America has refused to give us in the past. Only I have come to ask it for myself."

"I don't understand."

"I have broken with Ahmad. I have been hiding out in Uganda, forming my own resistance to his rule. Ahmad has brought only ruination to our land, and I intend to overthrow him. Ali is on my side."

Ali's expression remained fixed, neither confirming nor denying his allegiance this time.

"Why always bloodshed?" she asked, not expecting a reply.

"Because war has no eyes," he said sadly. Then, turning upbeat, perhaps in an effort to make her feel better, he added, "Do you know that your mother is pregnant?" Ali looked up in surprise.

It had been twenty years since her mother was pregnant with Fatma. Her mother was fifty-one, and Fatma resented her for having got herself into this situation, when Fatma's birth had seemed such a burden.

"She hasn't spoken or come to see me in nearly eight years," Fatma told him.

"Your mother is still your mother, though her legs be small." He shook his head and laughed with wonder and pride at her mother's capabilities – and his own accomplishment generating a child at their age. "She's on her way to Riyadh shortly, to stay with your grandfather while she delivers."

"Will she keep this child?" Fatma asked.

He leaned closer as though to focus on her better. "Fatma, you were given to your mother's sister because your Auntie was infertile. That is the only reason."

His words were little consolation.

"Your husband is well?" He changed the subject.

"Daniel is fine."

"He is kind to you?"

"Yes."

"His people?"

"I hate them."

"Fatma! And this business I have heard about with your Uncle Oliver, the store?"

"It's going fine. Soon we will open up a second store," she lied, as he nodded his approval.

"Fatma," he said sternly, "promise me something, daughter. If anything ever happens to me, you must never return to Somalia. Your life will be in great danger."

"But my sisters and brothers – " she protested.

"Never, I tell you."

"I promise."

He took her hands and held them with their palms up, looking down with satisfaction at the tattoos that lined the insides of her forearms, as though no matter where she went, she would always belong to him.

"Never forget our family, and that your mother and I love you."

He would always be blind where her mother was concerned.

"And babies?" he asked.

She looked up at him in surprise. She was sure word about the twins had reached him.

"Yes. Tragic." He patted her hand in acknowledgment. "I mean *more* babies."

"Not yet," she said. *Never*, she thought.

When the meal was over, the chauffeur took her to the nearby Sheraton Park Hotel. After her father's meeting with the president the following day, they would have supper again at the embassy before he departed. An accident must have occurred – a broken glass, a spilled bag of chips – because a bellboy was vacuuming the hotel lobby when she entered. In Mombasa, Auntie never let the maids sweep at night; it stirred up the evil spirits who would get into mischief that would plague you in the morning. She washed her face and brushed her teeth and slid her body between the stiff white sheets, unaware that she and her father had dined together for the last time.

The telephone woke her. At home she never answered the phone; she found it difficult to understand English without seeing gestures and facial expressions. It took her a few moments to get her bearings. After speaking Somali all evening, she hesitated to pick up the receiver, fearing her tongue would be paralyzed. A familiar nausea rose up into her chest. She swallowed in an attempt to trap whatever wanted to make its way out.

"Hello." She braced herself for the words that would come from nowhere into her African ears, concentrating very hard to understand them. It was not difficult; they were in Somali. It was Ali, telling her that her father's plans had suddenly changed during the night. The civil unrest in Somalia had taken a turn for the worse; the country was in utter turmoil. His brother Ahmad had summoned her father and cousin to Mogadishu. He wanted to reconcile with her father; he needed his help to set things right, for the sake of the country and for his own sake. Ali and her father were to leave immediately for Somalia. A car would arrive in a while to take her around Washington or to the train station, whichever suited her. Had she eaten yet? Ali wanted to know. He would have room service deliver a nice American breakfast: sausage and eggs, toast, coffee. The thought disgusted her.

She felt dizzy, and her nausea intensified. The train ride, the heavy meal, the excitement of the day before had got to her. She was still in her nightgown when breakfast arrived. She sat at the table and took a few bites of dry toast, sipping the tea she had asked the bellboy to bring in place of the coffee. When the nausea passed, she dressed and met the chauffeur in the lobby.

"Wouldn't you like to see our Capitol, or maybe the Air and Space Museum?" he asked. "How 'bout the National Zoo? It's right up the street."

"No zoo," she told him. "Where I come from, animals go free. I like train please."

"Whatever you say, Princess."

No one in America called her princess. He worked for the embassy; he had met her father. Ali had informed him of her family's lineage; that was all there was to it. Still, for the first time in America, she was afraid for her life. Her father had frightened her about their family's predicament. Why was he so trusting of this stranger? Enemies were masters of deception. At Union Station she grabbed her bag from him and, being much younger and quicker on her feet, she disappeared into the crowd.

Her mother and father died on the same day. It was only fitting: they had never been able to stay apart from each other for very long. The morning her father and cousin arrived in Mogadishu, Uncle Ahmad called all the powerful military and political leaders to a state-of-emergency meeting. He was taking no chance that his Revolutionary Socialist Party would be defeated in the forthcoming election, leaving Fatma's father to take over the government because of his strong ties with the United States. Just as the lion lures the hunter and then circles back until he is trapped, her father and cousin were taken prisoners at the phony meeting, taken out into the street, and executed in public. Her mother went into premature labor on her flight to Saudi Arabia; she suffered a heart attack, and she and the baby died in the air.

Fatma was numb. Oddly enough, her thoughts turned to Ayasha, who would be again welcome at the ranch in Mogadishu. Foolish Fatma, still unable to comprehend the magnitude of Somalia's plight, failed to understand that the grandeur of her mother's mansion would soon be a thing of the past, and that the building would soon resemble the remnants of the decaying Fort Jesus.

Fatma went to Saudi Arabia to be with her family during their period of mourning. Unbeknown to Daniel and to her, she had conceived again, against her wishes; Daniel had tricked her. If she had been listening carefully, she might have heard the baby crying, and she might have changed her course. But then, a baby cannot be heard weeping in its mother's womb. Surely it must have wept, knowing that her family had a way of making mothers out of aunties and strangers out of mothers, and that even death couldn't cancel the promise Auntie had made to Fatma's mother in that living room years ago. Promises, based on duty and respect, were her family's way of life.

Anger and resentment about the conception of the child she found she was carrying, coupled with the fear of losing another baby to some horrible complication during delivery made her desperate to get the birth of the monster over with. She believed she could detach herself from this one – just let it develop in her belly, concealed beneath the abundant fabric of a black abaya and matching *hijab* – and then see to it that there would be no more pregnancies. She would stay in Saudi Arabia after the mourning period was over and the rest of her family had gone back to their homes, and she would not tell Daniel about the pregnancy until she arrived back in Rockfield with his infant. She would not let him or Beverly help her grow this child like the last time, make her look forward to its birth, make her love it even before it was born. Her intent to punish them would backfire, however; in the end, she would be the one to suffer most.

So many years had passed since she'd last seen Grandfather and been in this home that was as big as some hotels in the congested capital city of Riyadh. A child never thinks that one she considered so old could grow even older, but of course Grandfather had. He moved about slowly in his long flowing white robe with the help of a shiny black cane, his hand tightly wrapped around the carved gold handle. With each step, he dug the cane determinedly into the intricate designs of colorful silk carpets. His frame had curled forward, which caused the cloth of his white headdress to fall around his face like a theater curtain that couldn't decide whether to open or close. But his mind was sharp, and what his eyes could no longer detect was seen by his loyal servants, who not only waited on him assiduously but also tended to Fatma day and night.

An accident that had happened to their parents, Kamilah was as ugly as Fatma remembered her. It wasn't that she had inherited all the bad features of their mother and father, because they had no bad features, and while some of the siblings had emerged as combinations of the two, Kamilah looked as if she couldn't possibly have come from either. Her features were distorted, as was her personality. Fatma knew people from Mogadishu and Mombasa who were quite homely but whose looks went unnoticed because, Auntie used to say, unlike the rest of us, their homeliness freed their spirit from their body and allowed their temperaments to blossom. It was not so with Kamilah and her sour disposition.

Fatma used to think that Kamilah felt bad about her looks, but this trip to Saudi Arabia convinced her that, despite what others may have thought of her, Kamilah felt quite superior to most people. Certainly she felt superior in every way to Fatma, living here in a luxurious palace, having Grandfather cater to her every whim.

Fatma tolerated Kamilah because in Saudi Arabia she too lived in luxury again, reminded of what it was like to come from a respected family of means. She let herself accede to her grandfather's invitation to stay because he made it easy for her to manage the inconvenience that carrying a new life imposed on her body. And she began, as before, to grow attached to the creature that kicked and lurched inside her and whose foot or bottom she could see moving beneath her skin. Once again she enjoyed a sense of productivity and purpose. "Come home. Your visa will expire," Daniel told her each time he called. But Grandfather had connections; no one bothered her, not even Daniel, who after a while resigned himself to her time away.

When Riyadh's spring temperatures reached unbearable heights, Fatma went with Grandfather and Kamilah to Grandfather's summer home in the mountain resort city of Taif. She never had to go to doctors' appointments; Grandfather had doctors come to her. He gave her a tape player so she could listen to the music that was forbidden in public. She ate well, slept long hours, and swam in Grandfather's pool. She accepted the way Grandfather and his servants doted on her, unaware that they were waiting to see the sex of the child that would emerge from her womb, plotting all the while, just like her Uncle Ahmad had plotted against the Somali people, to rob her.

She named her son Hussein, because it meant "little beauty." The very day he was born, Grandfather informed her that Hussein would remain in his home and be raised by his faithful Kamilah, who was now past her childbearing years. Fatma threw herself on her grandfather's mercy and pleaded with him to let her keep Hussein. He was not her firstborn, she argued; the promise had died with her twins. But the days of getting her way with her grandfather were over. Hussein would be raised in Saudi Arabia.

"Then I too will stay here," she told Grandfather, who warned her that her Christian husband was not welcome in his Muslim home. "I will stay here without him," she cried.

"Fatma, you do not seem to understand. This was your mother's wish. This was the agreement. We will not dishonor your mother."

His frail voice nearly broke with emotion as he spoke, and she could see that her mother, so like him, had been his favorite among all his children, his grandchildren, his great-grandchildren, and that he had been no less obsessed with her than Fatma's father had been. It was her mother's spirit that Grandfather longed to hold on to, and the child she had lost on her way to visit him. Fatma had merely served as her mother's surrogate, and now Hussein would be that child for her grandfather, that spirit. Foolish Fatma! She had sought to deceive, only to be deceived herself. She tried her old trick of fleeing, to no avail. There was always a servant with a watchful eye in the garden where she fed and rocked Hussein or in the nursery where she kept vigil over his sleep. At night servants guarded the doors. Just as Grandfather had imprisoned her father, she was now his victim.

She had come to Saudi Arabia with a spiteful broken heart; she left with a shattered one. Grandfather allowed her one month with her son, but one hour would have been kinder. She was escorted to the airport in Riyadh and put on a plane with a one-way ticket that Grandfather gave her. She also carried his .22-caliber pistol, which she had managed to steal, and determination to return one day and claim her son.

Hostess with the Mostess

********** ⭐ **********

After Hussein's birth, Fatma and Daniel's marriage was never the same. Daniel said he was sorry and that he hadn't impregnated her without her consent. "Sometimes these things just happen," he said, but she didn't believe him. Now they were finally free to have children of their own, he pointed out, trying to console her. "Nasikitika!" he whispered each night when she turned away from him. "I'm sorry."

She refused to go out of the house, staying in her bathrobe all day and mostly sleeping. The lack of exercise added extra pounds to the weight she had gained from her lavish lifestyle in Saudi Arabia. She stopped praying. Some nights she jumped out of bed, screaming that the house was on fire.

"Get baby! Get baby!"

"Hussein is not here. He's safe," Daniel would say, wrapping his arms around her, but she wriggled out of his embrace and threw punches at him, until she found herself back on the bed, sobbing for hours.

To Fatma's surprise Walter Kornmeyer called Uncle Oliver and asked him to help retrieve his grandson – *their* grandson. But Oliver retorted that Walter had liked the ways of Fatma's people only when it had suited him, and that he and Fatma should have known that like himself, they were people of their word. Walter Kornmeyer called her family barbarians.

Although Daniel begged her to, Fatma would not go for counseling. The notion of talking to a complete American stranger about what had happened was impossible. Daniel took it upon himself to procure antidepressants, but she refused them, swearing that he was trying to poison her. He began to secretly stir the drugs into the fruit punch she liked, and he prayed she would become thirsty. That is how, after several months, she began to come out of her misery, until one morning she emerged from the bedroom, dressed and wearing makeup, and announced that she was ready to go back to work. She needed to get away from Daniel. While he may not have intentionally gotten her pregnant, nevertheless he had. She had lost another baby, and he had done nothing about it; even his father had made some effort to have Hussein returned. She understood the Kornmeyers' contempt for her for hiding the pregnancy from Daniel; well, she had only contempt for their son. Betrayal is the thief of trust.

Gemtek was not hiring so Daniel set up an interview for Fatma with a different electronics firm that made circuit boards for airplanes. "Getting back to work will do you good," he agreed. The personnel manager asked her what languages she spoke, other than halting English.

"Swahili."

He raised an eyebrow.

"And Arabic and Somali."

He bent over his desk and murmured so as not to let his colleagues overhear. "You know, International Airways is always looking for women like you. Attendants who can speak several languages, especially African ones and Arabic, are hard to come by. They don't pay as much as some airlines, but flying for free isn't so bad."

Talking fast into the receiver, as though he'd discovered a diamond mine, he called International Airways. He even filled out an application for her. The next day a car came to 135 Poplar Street and took her to JFK, where she began her training. The money was more than adequate. Even Daniel, who was struggling to make ends meet with the artifacts business, became optimistic.

Twelve women made up the group: three Japanese, three Germans, two Americans, two Brits, one Kuwaiti, and Fatma. International Airways put them up at the airport hotel during their three-week training period. They took them shopping in Manhattan, measured them for uniforms – navy blue dresses that fit snugly around their behinds and tailored matching jackets – and entertained them with four-course meals that began with cocktails, continued with wine, and ended with nightcaps. Groomed as special hostesses who would be catering to an elite clientele, they were taught the difference between Cabernet and Shiraz, between cognac and brandy; how to mix drinks like screwdrivers and bloody marys; how to serve liquor straight up or on the rocks. They needed to know what kinds of drinks men of certain ethnicities might want, in case the men were too inebriated when they boarded the plane to place their orders. Until now, she had always refused alcohol, since it was against her religion. Her father's secret liquor cabinet had been a source of great contention between him and her mother.

Alcohol was no stranger to some of the other trainees, however, who drank until their speech slurred and their bodies slumped over those of the male employees who escorted them. For a few, like Fatma, their long-stemmed glasses were nearly as full at the end of their meals as they were at the beginning. Eventually the prodding of their male hosts and the desire to fit in meant the sips became more frequent, and the liquor started going down more easily. Fatma found that champagne and vodka took away her self-consciousness and loosened her tongue considerably, advancing her English by light years.

She never resumed praying. The other hostesses and she were always together, and their religions didn't seem to demand such devotions. She wanted to fit in; she was tired of sticking out like a giraffe in America.

On the last night of her training she called Auntie to let her know she was getting on with her life and that despite the pain inflicted by Auntie's promise to Fatma's mother, Fatma still loved her.

"I have a job with an airline," Fatma told her. "I'll be making big money, traveling to Milan and England. I'll come to see you soon."

"Be careful, *binti*," Auntie said. "You know these businessmen."

Fatma indeed knew businesspeople; she had grown up with Uncle Oliver and Grandfather and her mother, hadn't she? And she intended to find a businessman just like them – a Saudi, with connections.

They flew to London, then Frankfurt, and sometimes Rome: four of them in one corner of first class, four in another corner, and four in the middle. Every fifteen minutes they checked on passengers. "How are you doing? Would you like another drink?

Do you need an extra pillow? Would you like to lie down?" "Only if you lie with me," was a common reply. Most of the women soon learned to laugh the invitations off. A few women, like herself, had come from restrictive cultures and they turned into utterly different people during their shifts away from home. They were the ones who responded to the men's requests with "When we land," and who always kept their promise.

Fatma became the first to unlock the hotel room's liquor cabinet at each new destination, realizing that she shared her father's appetite for its contents. Alcohol lightened the heartache she had carried away from Saudi Arabia and even helped her mend fences with her in-laws. Walter Kornmeyer found one aspect of her new job – the tag sales – very much in his own interest.

Before landing, the hostesses needed to clear out all the duty-free liquor on the plane so the cabin could be restocked before the next flight. A bottle of vodka went for two dollars, a case for twenty. Fatma worked six or seven days a month, and Walter had her flying schedule memorized. Less than an hour after she arrived back home, he would pay her and Daniel a visit.

"Tax man is here," Daniel would announce, hearing his father's knock at the door.

"Any Dewar's today, Fatma dear? Fournier loves Dewar's." Walter looked around in anticipation of the carton.

"Dewar's and Seagram's," she'd say.

"Come for dinner sometime. Your mother would like to see you, Daniel."

"Just me?"

"Both of you, of course. You know I meant that, Daniel."

"No, I didn't actually. But you can still buy the booze."

Walter had found a new way to win people's hearts. He handed salesmen and deliverymen these bottles in return for shipments of perfectly ripe bananas and crisp greens, and for keeping Fine Foods supplied with harder-to-come-by commodities like star fruit and persimmons, coconuts and horned melons, that his competitors could not find. Fine Foods prospered, and Fournier, who was also presented with a case from time to time, rewarded Walter handsomely, with a pay raise and more importantly, with respect. Walter gave bottles to department managers and cashiers on their birthdays and a case on special occasions such as engagements and births. Thus International Airways benefited both Walter Kornmeyer and Fatma in the same way – it made them friends. When she found a Saudi diplomat who was fond of drinking and who asked her to keep him company, she answered, "When we land."

She met him that evening in the London hotel whose name he had scribbled on a cocktail napkin, sitting with his jacket off, tie undone, bearded and fat, swishing ice chips around in a glass of scotch. Excusing herself, she went into the bathroom, where she kicked off her navy blue stacked-heel shoes, unknotted the red and blue neck scarf the hostesses wore, and stripped down to her black lacy underwear. It wasn't as hard as she'd imagined it would be, as long as she thought about Hussein. She took a miniature bottle of scotch out of her purse and doused her entire body with it, as she had once seen a woman do in a movie Daniel had taken her to. Sitting on his lap, she told him about Hussein, while he fondled her breasts. She undid his zipper. She had barely touched him, when he squirted like a fountain, then asked – more out of embarrassment than consideration – what he could do for her.

The Saudi was a man with connections. Alas, so was her grandfather. When she landed at Kennedy at the end of her week's shift, she was called into Human Resources and informed that she had made her last trip to Europe. From now on she would be flying only to Miami and Jamaica twice a month.

✳

Elsa Martinez had known about Fatma's attempt to return to Gemtek. Fatma supposed that Elsa had always felt guilty about shooting solder into her eye, and that's why she began to call Fatma from time to time. Daniel referred to Elsa as the "shitload of trouble," but Fatma cared less than ever about what Daniel thought.

Elsa told Fatma she had a friend in desperate need of help. Would Fatma please take a package to the friend's auntie in Kingston? One evening while Daniel was at the artifacts store Elsa came to Fatma's door and delivered a small gift-wrapped package and a sign that read *Malik* to display in the airport in Kingston. Elsa knew that hostesses were not searched at customs.

"You doin' a good deed, *chica. Dios te bendiga.*"

When Fatma landed in Kingston, a young Jamaican man approached her, saying he was Elsa's friend's cousin. He thanked her for her trouble and asked how long she was staying. The following morning, as she prepared to board her return flight, he brought her a different gift-wrapped package in a shopping bag, a gift from his mother to Elsa's friend. "To Angel. Love Auntie," the tag read. Elsa met Fatma at Kennedy and hurriedly ushered her into the ladies' room. She disappeared into a stall. Fatma could hear her ripping the package open; wads of crumpled newspaper fell to the floor.

"You done a good thing, *chica*," she announced when she emerged. "*Te juro.* I won't ask again." Handing Fatma a small red change purse, she told her: "Let's say it's what I couldn't give you when I ruined your eye. A gift from my friend for your trouble. To the hostess with the mostess." She cackled, revealing a large gap between her yellowed upper front teeth.

Fatma didn't open the purse until she was home, locked in her bathroom. Her good deed had earned her a thousand dollars, which she kept secret from Daniel. The satisfaction of having got away with something far outweighed the illegality of the transaction.

Soon afterward Fatma was saved from deciding whether or not to do Elsa's friend any more favors when International Airways filed for bankruptcy and folded. She tried other airlines, but new standards for stewardesses had been imposed: in order to reach the overhead compartments they now had to be five feet five without heels. Fatma was five-two.

She dreaded going back to life as she had known it with Daniel and the Kornmeyers, a life without status and the opportunity to be away for days at a time. Poor Daniel. He had taken a child from Africa and planted her alongside him, hoping that as she matured their two cultures might intertwine and they could grow strong together and produce a family. How he had longed for her to feel comfortable in this country of his.

She *had* grown up. And now the once ghastly America that he had yearned for her to desire – the America that offered freedom for women – finally appealed to her. She wanted, like Miss Greene, to take control of her life, to break free the way Elsa and the other hostesses had and experiment with the temptations all around her. She would find her own way back to Hussein; listening to others had only brought her heartache. She would punish her mother for her death, which had removed any possibility of their making up for the years wasted between them and which had saddled her with the ultimate promise. She, Daniel, Grandfather, Uncle Oliver, even Auntie had taken turns chiseling at her heart until it had crumbled and like dust blown away, leaving her empty and guiltless and free to hurt everyone who had taken part in destroying it.

III

IBLIS

Auntie's maid Lisha used to tell Fatma that angels were made of light and that God could see what was inside them. But man was made of clay that hid his lust and violence, and his muddled brain led to dishonesty and stupidity.

All the days and nights Fatma amused herself in Lisha's room, Lisha talked about Iblis, the fallen angel of God, and how he had refused to bow to Adam, the first man, because he thought that Adam was inferior. She said that Iblis's rebelliousness and disobedience caused him to be cast out of heaven. "You see, Fatma, my little sweetheart, God gave Iblis three qualities missing in other angels: pride, desire, and doubt, and those are what led to his downfall. Pride caused him to desire more than others did. Believing that his own ideas were as valid as God's led Iblis to doubt God's intentions. Iblis roams the earth today in search of people who question God's commandments. He murmurs seductive words in their ears and makes them go astray. Iblis is the devil."

Americans believed that jinns were beautiful harem girls or superstrong men who lived in lamps and who, when the lamps were rubbed, emerged to magically grant wishes. The truth was that jinns were spirits: good ones behaved like guardian angels; bad ones – the fallen ones – followed Iblis. Though Auntie always scolded Lisha when she heard her filling Fatma with preposterous notions about jinns, it was becoming increasingly apparent to Fatma that jinns did indeed inhabit her. Whether this had occurred at birth or as she lay unclean beneath the baobab tree, somewhere on life's path she had come to a fork and chosen the wrong way. Iblis was closing in on her. She was bad right out of the womb, which was why her mother had given her away. Bad for having married a Christian. And now she was bad for wanting to deceive that Christian and for refusing his love. Bad for having doubted her destiny. She was no less greedy for power, really, than her Uncle Ahmad Siad Adan. "Bad always finds bad," her evil jinn whispered in her ear as she tossed and turned each night. "Bad Fatma. Bad, bad girl."

Elsa Martinez lived with her three children and her mother in a rundown rent-subsidized apartment. She was dark complexioned like Fatma, but stockier – denser – with long curly black hair and clothes so tight Fatma could see through the seams. Fatma missed her time with Miss Greene, whom she had never gone back to see. Perhaps Fatma knew that her friend would have tried to dissuade her from the thoughts she entertained. Perhaps her thoughts would have disappointed Miss Greene or perhaps Fatma had no interest in the advice Miss Greene might have offered, since she had made up her mind to taste life on her own. But she hobbled on one foot in America, while the other remained implanted in rich African soil soaked with tradition and human blood. Across the continents her legs stretched. Her African foot never caught up with the American one: it merely kept her displaced and off balance. "Africa is here," one foot beckoned her. "You are an American now. Be glad. Africa is not safe," the other whispered.

She told Elsa about her mother and father, her country, even about Hussein. Elsa would nod and let out moans of sympathy, understanding every word of Fatma's halting English. Elsa even cried; she was a good actress. And while Fatma would quickly have been able to size up an individual in Kenya or Somalia, she faced new rules in America: a different set of codes, signals, and humor that Daniel tried to warn her about. Her judgment played tricks on her. Who was good and who was bad, who was genuine and who was false, who was funny and who was not, were perceived according to her needs at a given time.

Elsa brought over rice and pork that Fatma now ate, though with reservations. How could Elsa afford to take food from her children? Fatma asked, when Elsa revealed that she had been laid off at Gemtek. Elsa vowed that she never stole from her children, that she would never let them go hungry, that she would do whatever it took to see that they didn't. She began to cook at Fatma's house, which bothered Daniel no end. Not that he complained; Daniel was a patient man – too patient. But Fatma could see the disappointment in his face when he returned from work to find Elsa occupying his kitchen. Sometimes he made excuses for not eating with them and left. Sometimes he sat down to dinner, but with a jaw almost too tight to chew food. *Good. Maybe you'll starve to death,* Fatma thought. *Maybe that will be the way to get free of you.*

Together Elsa and Fatma shopped for groceries that Fatma always paid for, including the bag Elsa took home to her children. It was worth it to be able to move around comfortably with another woman, with no man's demanding penis dangling between them. Yes, Elsa and Fatma became good friends, equals in age and as immigrants. She was Fatma's first girlfriend in America.

They went to Steigers department store and shared a dressing room. Their elbows banged into one another's soft tummies and behinds and breasts as they tore outfits on and off. Elsa's breasts were big and round, with large dark nipples. One day she caught Fatma staring at them. At first she was mad. "What you gawkin' at, *chica?*" she said. "You funny or somethin'?" Then she laughed and said she was only kidding. She took Fatma's hand and put it over one of her breasts. "Nice, eh?" she said. "Even after three *niños*. These titties are real. Not that jelly some ladies inject into themselves." They *were* nice, hard and smooth. Fatma saw the black fur between Elsa's legs when she tugged her jeans off and her panties came partway with them. Elsa saw Fatma's too. One day Elsa stuffed a blouse into her panties. She said the plastic security tab was missing, and that it only fair: it was meant for her. She took nail polish from the drugstore. She took doughnuts from the bins in the supermarket and dropped them into her large purse, just the way Fatma had stolen in Carlington. Elsa said that was what you did in America. You had to live by your wits when the chips were down. "What chips?" Fatma asked. "Your luck," she answered.

Elsa taught Fatma the satisfying tastes of nicotine and coffee, nicotine and sugar, and especially nicotine and alcohol. She kept a tin of small hard raspberry candies she sucked on while she smoked. That's what really hooked Fatma on cigarettes: the raspberry candies, and feeling independent and sophisticated. Every day they swore they would look for new jobs, but then they went out to lunch or shopped instead. It was like being back at International Airways, except that Elsa was much friendlier than the other hostesses had been. Fatma wanted to be like Elsa, to maneuver with the assertiveness and confidence she exhibited, to have men look at her and to look right back. She wanted to wear clothes like Elsa – clothes she never imagined she could wear – a size smaller than her own so that her breasts peeked out of low-cut knit tops. What she didn't want was to be alone.

Elsa listened to Fatma when she described her family and her unhappiness with Daniel. While she listened, she took in the leather sofa, the new TV, and the rugs and curtains Daniel and Fatma had worked for. Fatma interpreted Elsa's ravenous scrutiny as a compliment; she was proud of what she owned.

"If there's something you like, maybe I can make it," Elsa offered Daniel over dinner one evening.

"What's your children's favorite dish?" Daniel responded.

Elsa put down her fork and stared straight into Daniel's eyes. In a soft sweet voice she responded, "Plátanos – *los maduros*."

"Maybe you should be home making it for them."

"I'll teach Fatma how to prepare it."

"Maybe Fatma can go to your house and make it for your children," Daniel said.

Daniel and Fatma had a fight that night. She had never seen him so angry. "Why you don't like her?" she demanded to know.

"Because I don't trust her. She's using you."

"For what?"

"For your nice house. For your food. And who knows for what the hell else."

"Like your father use me for liquor?"

"At least he paid you for it."

"She's my friend."

"She ruined your eye. She's no friend. Why isn't she home with her kids?"

"Her mother watch them."

"*She* should be watching them."

"So now you perfect father. Too late."

"This has nothing to do with our son. Is this what it's all about? Are you trying to get back at me for Hussein? I've told you a million times I did not intend to get you pregnant. You're the one who went back to Saudi Arabia. You played right into your crazy family's hands."

"Now they crazy. You like them when you come to Kenya, though. You like them when you marry someone too young to know better. You never understand Muslim family. You think you do, but you don't. You never understand me. You never understand my loneliness here. When I tell you about Hussein, you never even try to get him back."

"Why did you wait until you'd already come back home to tell me?" he asked. They'd been over this dozens of times; he looked as though he was about to cry. Daniel had always been weak.

"You could do something after. You never fight, Daniel. You never try."

"We can have more children, Fatma. The promise is over."

"No! No more loss."

"We can try to go and talk to your grandfather."

She didn't believe a word he said. She no longer trusted him.

"I'm tired of listening to everyone. No more. And now you don't even like I have friend. Too bad."

"That's not true!" His look said he longed to touch her in some way, to feel the warmth of her arm, the softness of her face, but she stood still and impenetrable as steel. "There's something about Elsa that's all wrong. *You* can't see it, Fatma, but I can. She's not like you. You're a princess."

She looked around at the walls of the small house and laughed. "Some princess," she said. "Maybe you don't know this princess."

"Come on, Fatma. She's this close to a hooker." He drew his thumb and forefinger together. "Maybe she *is* a hooker. You've been here long enough you see them in the center of Rockfield. You know who I mean." He made a fist and knocked it on the table as though he didn't know what else to do with it.

"She's my friend! She make me happy." She lit a cigarette. Daniel grabbed it out of her mouth. For the first time he frightened her.

"Look what the smoke's doing to your eye."

Her and Elsa's smoking made the Mombasa eye smart and tear up all the time. And because she didn't care if Daniel was right about the smoking and about everything else, she knew they had come to the end of their journey together.

"I hate you," she said.

That night she dreamt there was a porch roof beneath the window in the bedroom, just as there had been outside her window in Mombasa. She jumped onto the roof and slid down the pillars into a dhow, for Poplar Street had turned into a canal of sorts where her old friend Halima and Halima's father waited for Fatma with a basketful of Auntie's roast pig. Even the vegetables appealed to Fatma.

"How did you get here?" she asked Halima.

"It was easy."

"Where are we going?"

"To Saudi Arabia. We have come to take you to Hussein."

"But how did you know about him?"

"This is a dream, Fatma."

Fatma wept with joy. She was about to tell Halima how her

brother Hamal had beaten her when she ran away from Daniel the first time, but the boat began to rock so forcefully that she spilled out of it into the hard sea and hit her head.

"Open your eyes and save yourself, Fatma!" Halima cried from the boat.

But her eyes would not open.

"Open your eyes!"

The voice grew louder, and Fatma realized she had fallen out of bed. She was glad her eyes were too swollen from crying to see Daniel kneeling above her, pleading with her to open them. There was numbness where her aching heart used to be; she was deaf to the wailing of the child inside her empty womb.

Daniel was afraid to let her go, afraid that she would make mistakes, afraid she could not survive alone. He had seen her into womanhood, but even mother birds push their babies out of the nest.

"It's never only been about Hussein," he said.

"No."

"Still, I was always hoping."

"I try, Daniel. I try for long time."

"I'm not abandoning you," he assured her. "We've come to a decision."

"I know."

"I hope to God you do."

"He look like you, Daniel. Hussein look like you."

Daniel left without any fuss: he was a peaceful man, always a gentleman – the only man Fatma would eventually realize ever really loved her. They closed the artifacts shop. He went back to school to study social work. She would one day come to think of herself as his first case gone wrong.

LADY LIBERTY

********** ★ **********

Daniel gave her the house on Poplar Street, along with some cash. He said the house had been her idea anyway, but she thought it made it easier for him to leave her. Occasionally Elsa spent the night, and it reminded Fatma of being with her sisters when she visited the ranch in Mogadishu. That house had so many rooms she had always slept alone, but the one on Poplar Street had only two bedrooms: hers and Daniel's, and the small nursery. Fatma liked sharing her bed with Elsa, laughing about men they had run into that day while they drank vodka and smoked cigarettes with nobody's disapproving eye on them.

One night while Elsa was sleeping, Fatma cupped the soft breast that had fallen out of her camisole like a melon ripe for the picking. Elsa's skin was silky smooth, and Fatma kissed her all over her plump face. Elsa continued to sleep undisturbed – that is until she opened her eyes and Fatma realized she had been awake for quite some time. Fearful of Elsa's reaction, Fatma backed off. But Elsa smiled and guided Fatma's hand under the sheet and inside her panties. She moved it around her moist secret spot until she pressed Fatma's hand so hard it hurt and Fatma felt the spot pulsate as Elsa moaned with delight. Now both of them were breathing heavily, but only Elsa had been satisfied. Unconcerned about Fatma's gratification, Elsa turned her back and said, "Ay, look what you made me do, *puta*."

Surprised by what she'd just done and confused by Elsa's reaction, Fatma lay watching Elsa sleep for hours, until she too drifted off. When she woke in the morning, Elsa was gone. Weeks passed without a word from her. Fatma hated living alone on Poplar Street, in such a remote part of the city, in a house filled with nothing but sadness. Daniel would have helped her plan her next step, and she missed having him to manage the little messy details of living in America and to blame for everything that went wrong.

When Fatma told Auntie about the divorce, Auntie was beside herself. What was a young woman to do in such a big country without a man to protect her? Uncle Oliver said he was disgusted with the whole bloody bunch of the Kornmeyers, including Fatma, for having made such a disaster of Kilimanjaro.

"Come home, *binti*," Auntie begged.

"Pay your own way," Uncle Oliver added.

Fatma did not go home. Nor did she continue living in the house on Poplar Street. She phoned Jeannine Fournier, who had set up their business contract and had taken care of their divorce. Jeannine convinced her not to sell the house until she had a good job and some plans for the future. "After you pay off the mortgage, you'll have nothing left. You could become homeless, you know. That's how it happens in America," she warned Fatma, who understood that she would one day need a home to which she could bring Hussein. "Besides, it's not worth much right now in this market," the lawyer added. Fournier agreed to list the house as a furnished rental and be the escrow agent of an account into which went the rent and out of which came the mortgage payment and her fee. Fatma put down a deposit on a one-bedroom apartment above an Italian deli on Main Street in the south end of downtown Rockfield. It was tiny but clean, with crisp floral bed linens and sheer white curtains over mini-blinds. There was a worn but clean cut-velvet sofa, a matching gold recliner, a coffee table on beige wall-to-wall carpeting, and a kitchenette with a built-in china closet. The bedroom could barely hold a bed with a blond wooden headboard and matching dresser. The bathroom was tiled – gray on the walls, white mosaic on the floor. A pink shower curtain showed two large swans facing each other as though engrossed in conversation.

Mrs. Lucchese, a widow, owned the flat and ran the deli along with her son, Sal, and younger daughter, Pia. Mrs. Lucchese, who had immigrated to America with her parents when she was a little girl after the Second World War, was probably a lot younger than she looked, with salt-and-pepper hair cut in a style that resembled an artichoke. She never wore makeup, and her black-rimmed glasses matched her hair and hid her eyebrows. The Luccheses told Fatma that there used to be a big Italian population in the south end of town. To Fatma, it sounded like Italian Somaliland, in the southern regions of that country. But just as the community of Italian Somaliland had been altered when her uncle Ahmad had deported the Italians, so too had the south end of Rockfield begun to change by the time she moved there. Puerto Ricans from the north end of town were moving in and inserting, themselves among the Italians: Iglesia Cristiana Pentecostal sat sandwiched between Angelo's Barber Shop and Danza's Bakery; Diaz's Pawn Shop – WE BUY AND SELL IT ALL – appeared between Casa

Lisa and Little Venezia Café. The Hispanic storefronts looked like afterthoughts, with their carelessly hand-painted signs taped onto the windows; the Italian ones were filled with family photos of christenings and weddings and graduations for all to see. *We are established and fortified, and we were here first*, the Italian stores proclaimed. A few travel and insurance agencies, with their fancy wooden signs engraved in gold, expressed the hope that Rockfield might be headed for yet another resurgence even as scruffy men in castoff parkas, shaking and smoking cigarettes, peered out from dark alleys.

Nothing happened in Rockfield after five, when the lawyers and insurance agents went back to their sleepy suburbs. Except for the occasional night when teenagers piled into the Civic Center for a rock concert, then ran back home as fast as possible when it was over, the town was dead. But for others, Fatma would soon learn, nighttime was when Rockfield came alive: with junkies and prostitutes, drive-by shootings and gambling rings. Iblis slithered through the alleyways and vacant tenements.

The Luccheses had a cousin who owned a pizzeria up the street and was caring for his sick wife. Getting her up in the mornings and ready for bed at night consumed a lot of time; he needed someone to come in first thing to mop the floor, clean the glass cases, turn on the ovens, and take the dough and cheeses and other ingredients from the refrigerator so that everything was at room temperature when he came in to begin cooking. Was Fatma interested, they wondered?

It wasn't as glamorous as working for the airlines, but it was less boring and confining than putting circuit boards together, and she had to start somewhere if she was going to establish herself in America and make a home for Hussein.

She awoke to the early morning perfume of garlic and basil and thyme, of sausage and eggplant frying, of simmering red tomato sauce that rose up from Mrs. Lucchese's *salumeria* and entered her bedroom without knocking, just as Auntie's cooking had in Mombasa. Sitting at a little round kitchen table beneath the window that faced the alley, she drank her coffee. She called this her country home, because a tree branch brushed against the windowsill and she breakfasted with the birds. The front windows, in contrast, looked out onto Main Street, but she liked that view too: the bustling traffic in the early morning; the sound of vendors rolling out their awnings and sweeping their sidewalks the way Mrs. Lucchese's shy son, Sal, did – the way Fatma did too, as soon as she picked up the key from the Luccheses and walked up to the pizzeria. It was a welcome contrast to the isolation of Poplar Street.

"Pay attention!" Mrs. Lucchese warned her, because the streets were still dangerous at that hour. Fatma believed she was more worried about someone stealing the key than harming Fatma.

Most days Fatma wore a suit or a dress with high heels and a fake white fur coat, as though she were going to work in a bank rather than a pizzeria. She descended to the second floor where the Luccheses lived and then down one more flight to Main Street. Some mornings Pia would be leaving for the university at the same time, in her jeans and black peacoat and sneakers, her long brown hair shiny and smelling of coconut, and she'd walk with Fatma to her bus stop. Over time a short walk adds up to many minutes, and Pia was easy to talk to. She never pried.

"I can't imagine living so far from my family," she said one day. "I envy your courage."

"It wasn't my choice. Courage come with choice. Like you for choosing school."

"I'm not going to scoop mozzarella balls for the rest of my life." Then, realizing her words were like a fistful of pebbles tossed into the air without a thought for a landing place, she added, "Not that it's a bad thing to do. My family's done well, and I'm proud of them."

"Don't worry. I don't clean pizzeria rest of my life either," Fatma said.

"What would you like to do?"

"Be successful business lady, like my mother. Like *your* mother. You?"

"I'm going to be a doctor," she yelled as she sprinted across the street to catch the bus.

It took only two hours to clean the pizzeria, and afterward Fatma often sat in Little Venezia sipping cappuccino and daydreaming of ways to trick her grandfather and sister to win back Hussein. At that hour the customers in the café were mostly men – old and young ones both, who talked excitedly, their tones ranging from whispers to loud outbursts and even arguments. But there was never any fighting. Some played cards; others discussed serious issues, their heads bowed close to one another; then they got up abruptly and left as if on a secret mission. Others ran in and out, holding newspapers folded in quarters and open to the horse-racing schedule, and through the front window of the café she could see them at the pay phone on the corner, excitedly placing bets.

Fatma liked living upstairs from the Luccheses and sitting in Little Venezia. She liked being surrounded by people who were similar to the ones she had known in Italian Somaliland. It took away the loneliness that came with liberty. Sometimes she sat there for hours, because all she seemed to have those days was time. She had let herself forget about the rent from the Poplar Street house that her lawyer was putting into an account for her; perhaps one day it would be enough to send Fatma back to Saudi Arabia or to hire someone to steal Hussein. But she would need more money to take care of her son; besides, she needed something else to do. She had never liked being idle. She walked into stores with Help Wanted signs in the window, but she became so nervous and tongue-tied that her English was more mangled than ever.

"Do you have experience in flower arranging?" "Where have you waitressed before?" "Are you old enough to serve liquor?" The last question was the only one she could answer yes to, but no one was interested enough to check her identification. "Why can't they learn to talk English good?" the baker at Sweet Grace's Cake Shop said to his wife, as though Fatma were invisible. It was exactly the way the Kornmeyers used to talk about her. "You black lady want work in Chinese restaurant?" the owner of Hung Lee shouted for all the diners to hear before bursting out laughing.

When the manager at Juicy Burger asked if she could assemble forty-five burgers in ten minutes during their peak hours, with no chitchatting, she landed another job in America.

On her first day she had just sprinkled onions over ketchup and begun laying down the pickle slices when she heard a familiar cackle at the register behind her. She looked up to see Elsa Martinez paying for her lunch.

"Fatma!" She waved.

Fatma went back to building her hamburger. When her shift ended at two, Elsa was waiting for her.

"Where *you* been, *chica*?" she said, throwing her arms around Fatma.

"Where you been?" Fatma pulled away.

"I'm sorry. I had to go away for a while. What? You think it's because of what we did that night? Don't be silly. I forgive you."

Fatma grew hot with embarrassment and anger as her co-workers watched them. Then Elsa put her face close to Fatma and whispered, "I got into a little trouble, that's all." Returning to full volume, she went on, "You look good, *chica*! You're not back with Daniel, are you? How long you been working here? Maybe you can get me a job."

In Kenya they say you can live without a brother but not without a friend.

Even though she'd been hurt by Elsa, she thought how nice it would be to have a friend again, one she could actually do things with and not just walk to work with, one whose unpredictability was like a big surprise package.

"Come on, *chica*. Let's go to the movies. My treat. There's a good action picture around the corner. A lot of fighting and hardly no talking. Real easy to understand. Just like you like."

And Elsa was right. It was just like Fatma liked.

COLUMBUS DAY

********** ⭐ **********

There began to be days when Fatma did not walk to the bus stop with Pia, days when she barely made it to work because she had been up late the night before drinking with Elsa at the Royal Lion on Gaylord Street. The Royal Lion had a few tables, one disgusting bathroom, and a window lit up with BUDWEISER – KING OF BEER in neon. *Even beer wants to rule the world,* Fatma thought when Elsa had first taken her there. The small white cinder-block building was surrounded by a chain-link fence. *No running in or out of bar.* Service for *paying customers only* painted on the door announced the caliber of its clientele, the familiar faces of people who were becoming her friends.

When Fatma had first met Mrs. Lucchese, she thought her nose was too bumpy and way too long for her to be considered attractive, but after a while she didn't notice her nose anymore. Her voice was what struck Fatma with a reprimanding tone that made a simple *Have a nice day* an order, as though she was mad at the world. There were days when Fatma emerged from her flat and heard Mrs. Lucchese disapprovingly call her *la dormiglione* – which she gathered meant something about her sleeping late – to Sal, who would be wiping down a counter or the glass beverage case. Days when Fatma felt vulnerable among the crowds of dark suits and long coats that poured out of the office towers. Days when she felt naked alongside figures who held portfolios securely under their arms, tight against their bodies like Turkish towels, as they scurried across Main Street to the courthouse or to lunch at Casa Lisa. Days when she wanted to run back into the safety of the dark and seedy Royal Lion.

Sometimes Mrs. Lucchese caught her returning home at six in the morning, as the energetic woman and son were getting ready to open for the day. Fatma would try to sneak into the doorway so she could shower and change before she picked up the key to the pizzeria. She sneaked because she knew what the older woman must have been thinking about her – what Auntie would have thought of her. But Mrs. Lucchese always saw Fatma and motioned for her to come into the store, handing her an eggplant *panini* left over from yesterday or the fatty end of a slab of prosciutto. As Fatma took it Mrs. Lucchese would cast an accusing eye at her and slowly shake her head. It's not nice, her look said, for a young woman to be out at all hours of the night. Where's your family? Where's your mother?

On one of those lazy mornings the trees on Main Street blazed like a brush fire – red, orange, and gold. Something was different about this particular day, however. Something was happening in Rockfield, something that people were beginning to position themselves for. Seated at the curb in beach chairs, with jugs of drinks at their sides and squirming children waving miniature Italian flags, they scanned the empty street as though a movie were about to begin. They kept coming, carrying bags of popcorn and cups of coffee, forming a giant snake that wound itself around State Street and up the hill. The police were there too, setting up barricades and rerouting traffic. Fatma could hear distant drums rolling like a thunderstorm. People craned their necks to see up the hill and around the corner. Down the street came a large group of men holding a purple Knights of Columbus banner; the mayor, waving, walked behind them. A group of marching teenagers played shiny brass instruments. Then a float carrying a strange-looking ship made its way down the hill. A short man in a velvet jacket, tights, and a big plumed hat waved from a platform on deck.

"*Mira*, Cristóbal Colón." A young man pointed; a toddler sat on his shoulders, its legs curling around the man's neck like a boa. "*Y la Santa María*."

"It's not the real one," his wife said, holding another child's hand.

"No shit," the man said annoyed.

Of course. The Columbus Day parade. Daniel had taken Fatma to see it her first year in America. The dislocation happened some weekends: there were days when she felt she was living her life inside out, when she lost track of time and purpose; days when only the ringing of the church bell signaling the Masses at Our Lady of Mount Carmel reminded her of the hour.

She stepped into Little Venezia for a double espresso to help her wake up, and glanced down at a newspaper left on the table. *Somalia Faces Serious Food Shortages as Civil War Rages*. She saw the word *Somalia*. She had heard it at the Royal Lion during the late news broadcast. The other patrons' eyes would find hers. They'd jerk their liquor-logged heads in the direction of the TV on the wall behind the bar when a green spot on a map of Africa appeared for thirty seconds, as if to say, *Here you go, Fatma. You're on. This is about you.*

Somalia. The word wandered around her brain like a nomad roaming the dry plains. Her throat became parched; she took a sip of the coffee – no relief. She tried to focus on the narrow column and she read slowly, syllable by syllable:

> *A major humanitarian crisis has arisen in rural Somalia, especially around Bardera and Baidoa in the south, largely due to the destruction of relief food stocks in April of this year by the remaining forces of former President Ahmad Siad Adan. The number dead from starvation is already estimated at 300,000. The escalation of fighting between ruling clans continues to keep the country in a state of anarchy. The UN's slow response to the crisis and failure to stop the fighting has been widely criticized ...*

She couldn't read any more because her Mombasa eye was tearing all over again and the print blurring. In fact, both of her eyes were tearing. She couldn't remember the last time she had spoken to Auntie. How sad and disappointed in Fatma Auntie must have been not to hear from her. She tried to recall her brothers and sisters: there were twelve – no, thirteen. She counted them on her fingers as she named each one. She tried to imagine the lives of those left in Somalia.

Three women around Auntie's age were sitting at a table behind her. She watched their images in the smoky mirrors on the wall supported by marble arches while she listened to their conversation. They had probably just been to Stella's Beauty Salon up the street for their weekly wash and set, because their blond, red, and black hair looked like lacquered helmets. Dyed helmets, of course: had to be, at their age. Each picked at pastry, poking their forks into the *sfogliatelle* or *cannolo* or *rum babba* in front of them as though searching for a hidden prize.

"I like Gloria. She's nice. You think she ever calls me?" the redhead said. "She goes to Friendly's. You think she ever asks me to come along?"

"I used to see her in church at confession on Saturdays," the blonde said. "That's when confession meant something. Now they've made it so easy no one wants to go."

"Nancy Reagan was on *Charlie Rose* the other night," the brunette said.

Fatma had trouble following their conversation. She blamed her less-than-perfect English, never considering that the enormous amount of alcohol she consumed each night was slowing down her brain.

"They say Reagan has Alzheimer's," the redhead said.

"That's tragic," the blonde said. "To lose your mind. A lot of things happen to us when we get old, but to lose your mind ..."

Maybe I have Alzheimers, Fatma thought.

"At least she'll have help to take care of him," the brunette said. "What would we do?"

Who would have help? Gloria?

"Imagine, a president! With such a sharp mind! It's a pity." The redhead shook her head.

"I write everything down now," the brunette said. "Everything. And I take vitamin E."

Fatma wondered if vitamin E would sober her up faster than a cup of coffee.

"What time is it? We're missing the parade," the blonde said, and they began to gather sweaters and large leather pocketbooks.

A smiling man strolled in. He was fair, in his mid-to late forties, with wavy brown hair flecked with silver combed carefully in place. Fatma could smell his musk cologne from where she sat. Not as tall as Daniel, he was much more muscular, his upper arms bulging out of his short-sleeved polo. The shirt was lavender. She remembered this because it was an unusual color for a man to wear, and because he was the first man she'd been attracted to since – maybe forever. He was a clean-looking guy, the kind who wouldn't tolerate wrinkled garments or loose buttons, whose clothes fit him like those of a mannequin in a good men's shop, who sucked on breath mints all day. She didn't notice much else, since she was holding a napkin to her right eye to catch the tears. He kissed one of the old men on the cheek, sat down, and ordered an espresso. When he smiled at her, she became self-conscious. She got up to leave, remembering she and Elsa had talked about meeting up for the parade.

"*Buongiorno*," the old men said as Fatma passed by.

She nodded, trying not to meet the gray eyes of the younger man.

"Miss!" one of the women called out. She was pointing to the leopard-print shoulder bag Fatma had left hanging on the back of her chair, and Fatma's armpits tingled with embarrassment. The younger man's smile broke into a grin; he had enjoyed unnerving her.

"I don't like the way you sound," Auntie said when Fatma phoned. "You sound tired. You are working too hard. Are you sick?"

Then she told Fatma that Uncle Ahmad's government had collapsed. That the Somali embassy in Washington had closed. That Ahmad, having been refused asylum in Kenya, fled to Nigeria. And that Somalia – and her family – was starving.

"Come home, *binti*," she pleaded.

"Soon, Mama."

✴

Elsa and Fatma were eating fried dough later that afternoon, just enjoying the crowd, when a Jamaican man in khaki slacks and a crisp white-collared shirt approached them. Blacks in Rockfield believed that Jamaicans were after their jobs, so they treated them badly. But Fatma got along with Jamaicans, because she was also a foreigner who didn't feel accepted by the other blacks in Rockfield.

"How are you, Elsa?" he asked in a heavy Jamaican accent.

"Who's that?" Fatma asked after he'd passed.

"A friend."

"Why you don't introduce me?"

"I forgot."

"Who is he, Elsa?"

"You remember when you did me that favor when you were working with the airlines? Well, that's who paid you."

"You never tell me what's in package."

"Ay coño, sometimes you really are a stupid African. I don't know why I even bother with you." She took a drag on her cigarette, threw it down on the sidewalk, and left it burning.

On a good day Elsa was full of compassion. On a bad day she could slice you like a switchblade. Relationships, Fatma was learning, were like that, with many turning points – little sparks of truth – that bring two people closer together or drive a stake between them. Either way, from that moment on, everything is different.

"He's a dealer," she said. "I used to work for him. But then I got into trouble. Where do you think I was when I was away?"

"I think – "

"You thought I got mad at you for feeling me up." She laughed. "I kind of enjoyed it. But we're done with that, right?" she quickly added, her expression sober.

Fatma wouldn't have minded being intimate with Elsa again, but it had been more important to keep her friendship. What interested her now was the fact that this good-looking, polite Jamaican was working a job that made a lot of money. She often believed that what Elsa liked about her was the fact that she knew her way around better than Fatma did, that she could speak English better, and that she could be the leader. But even though Fatma couldn't express herself as well as she would have liked, there were things she understood that Elsa could never begin to comprehend. Daniel had appreciated this quality in her and sought to cultivate it, but she was looking for someone who wanted to be with her, not someone who wanted to make her better.

It seemed to Fatma that this might be a way to make more money – to bring her son back sooner, to help her family in Somalia, she rationalized, knowing full well that Iblis was surfacing again, bringing out the greed in her and filling her with false pride, the belief that she was ever so clever, cleverer than Elsa, clever enough to get away with something in America.

"Can you introduce me?" she asked Elsa.

The moment Fatma met India, she knew she wanted her as a friend. She was different from Elsa – different from the rest of the women she worked with at Juicy Burger, different from the crowd at the Royal Lion. She was tall and straight, thin and elegant, and she was black like Fatma.

Isaac and India's apartment was on Trumble Street, a few blocks off Gaylord and not too far from the Royal Lion. Elsa took Fatma there, thinking she might be able to work her way back into Isaac's good graces, yet she did so reluctantly. Fatma could tell when Elsa introduced her to India, that she was jealous of India, afraid that Fatma might prefer the beautiful Jamaican to her. Although Isaac told Elsa he didn't want to work with anyone anymore, he must have sized Fatma up that first night as someone special, because the next morning he came to the pizzeria. Yes, he could use her help, and yes, there was much money to be made running errands for him that he no longer used Elsa for, because Elsa had stolen from him; users could not be trusted. And if he was pleased with Fatma's courier services, there was even more money to be made in cooking.

"I can't cook," she told him.

He smiled. "Oh, I think you can learn."

Isaac had a flat on the other side of town. It was a laboratory of sorts, an empty apartment in a decent building that he also rented by the hour to other dealers who wanted to keep their business a secret. It was a place where Fatma could learn to make money, a place where he wanted to spend less time, because Isaac was very cautious and didn't like having attention drawn to himself.

And that was how she began to work one more job in America. While Mrs. Lucchese was cooking up a storm at the deli, Fatma, whose only miracle in the kitchen had been putting together a deluxe burger, would develop a most lucrative skill of her own over on Broad Street. After working her shift at Juicy Burger, she headed for what she called the double-barrel building: two semicircles of brick and windows running up four stories on either side of the entrance. It was across from the Baptist church and one block from the mosque, just a few streets down from the courthouse and the towers filled with attorneys' offices. It was in a nice section of town, a place unlikely to draw suspicion.

When she passed the mosque those mornings, she closed her eyes in the hope that the imam, who sometimes appeared in the doorway and studied her as she walked past, would not be there. She was aware that he knew, without seeing the black *buibui* or hearing the sound of her voice, that she was no ordinary woman on her way to work. He knew what her mother would never let her forget: he knew she was a Muslim woman. Once in the double-barrel apartment, however, and out of his sight, she closed the door on all that had been bad as well as good and decent about her childhood.

"You ever did anything bad?" she asked Pia one morning as they walked.

"I let Johnny Premiano feel me up in an alley after school when I was in fifth grade. Wasn't much to feel." They both laughed.

"I mean really bad."

"I used to steal from Stop & Shop in high school. It started with snatching a cookie from an open package. Then I started being the one to open the package and take a cookie. I progressed to taking entire packages that I slipped into my backpack. It became an obsession. Crazy. I just liked getting away with something. One day I put in an Eskimo pie, and the store detective saw me, and I knew it. He followed me around while I did more shopping, but I just wouldn't put back this damn melting ice cream bar. It was like a game I was playing. I even went through the checkout and paid for everything else but the Eskimo pie! He nabbed me the minute I walked out of the store."

"He arrest you?"

"He took me down to this disgusting cellar filled with crates of what smelled like rotting fruits and vegetables, and he put the fear of God in me, as my mother would say. He told me I could go to jail for what I'd done. That I would disgrace my family. After the lecture he said that I was 'too pretty to go to jail' and that he'd give me a second chance. I didn't know what I was more afraid of: him, jail, or my mother finding out. Anyway, it cured me."

Fatma knew the thrill of getting away with something. She had felt it when she ran away on her wedding night, when she stole from the convenience store and Miss Greene. And she felt it now. Every other Tuesday, Isaac arranged a connection in New York City: maybe in Harlem, maybe lower Manhattan, maybe even midtown; it was all the same to Fatma. Her job was to meet Isaac's friend, who was usually a nurse's aide, in the lobby of some hospital, where they made the transaction right out in public. She gave him an envelope with money; he gave her a bag of powder. Then back she went to the flat in Rockfield, where she began to cook the way Isaac had taught her.

She put some of the powder and water into an empty baby-food jar, added a pinch of baking powder to harden it, and simmered it over a low flame on the stove. Once it solidified, she cut some of it up into very small wedges the size of a fingernail, putting two or three of these into plastic bags. She packaged some of the loose powder for clients who sucked it up their nostrils in restrooms during their workdays as easily as they popped sticks of chewing gum into their mouths. And she added a pinch of tranquilizer or anything else addictive that Isaac gave her and cooked it into the crack she gave cabdrivers for her rides to New York.

Isaac said his customers were upscale, with discriminating taste. They were safe clients with too much to lose from exposure, professionals like doctors and lawyers and even judges, who knew enough to eat before they got high so they would come down fast. They were rich junkies who could afford to eat. He said it was just a matter of time before drugs like this would become legal anyway, but in the meantime they needed to take advantage of the demand. It was like getting into the stock market at the right time, he said. They were foreigners but they were as smart as anyone else; why shouldn't they make their fortunes while they could? She didn't know anything about the stock market, but she knew some things about business. Uncle Oliver had been wrong about the market for African artifacts in Rockfield; Fatma had come to that conclusion early on. But from what Isaac said, there was clearly a demand for the goods *he* was selling. At times even Daniel and his friends had taken powder into their nostrils in Katundu. And if she was as cautious as Isaac, there would be nothing to worry about.

"Think of it as an adventure, Fatma. You are like Christopher Columbus. You are discovering a new America," Isaac said. "And watch the drinking, my friend. Stay alert."

"Pay attention!" Mrs. Lucchese had said. Keep alert, Fatma. Keep alert.

"And watch out for Elsa," Isaac added.

Elsa had been right: besides the promise of being able to make money, what had attracted her to the business was India, and Fatma tried hard to make India like her. Fatma visited her from time to time and took her gifts, the way Auntie had taught Fatma to give to hostesses. Sometimes she went with flowers for the kitchen table or chocolates. In a way, Fatma courted India. And there were times when Fatma thought she had won her over when she was as warm as melted butter on a slice of toast as she knelt on her bony knees to scrub a molding or scrape up something that had spilled onto the red-brick-patterned linoleum floor. Unlike Isaac's laboratory, this apartment was in a deteriorating section of the city. And while India kept it clean, it was sparsely furnished and its walls, the color of dead skin, needed painting. This surprised Fatma, until she realized that Isaac and India not only frugal saved every penny they possibly could, but that nice furnishings would only have raised suspicions about illicit income. Isaac also worked off the books, just as Fatma had, as a cook in a Greek take-out restaurant, and even that was a step up from the situations of other tenants in the building, who were on welfare and most of whom were addicts.

What the apartment lacked in style it made up for with the rhythm of their orderly life, like the smell of spices India used that seduced Fatma as they talked over coffee. India couldn't wait until she and Isaac had made enough money to quit the drug business, get out of Rockfield, and begin a family like normal Americans. They had tried when they first arrived in the States, but it had been too difficult for them to find any substantial work from prominent black employers, even though Isaac had worked in a bank in Jamaica. "We're different," she told Fatma, including Fatma in that *we*. "And we're ambitious. The others resent us for it." It soon became apparent that it would have taken them a lifetime to achieve the comforts they sought. One thing had led to another, and Isaac had become a dealer. "A person has to do what a person has to do. If they don't get it from you, they are going to get it from somebody else," she said. "It's just a business, Fatma. A means to an end."

Fatma's longing for India must have been all too obvious and was probably distasteful to India, because there were times when India withdrew from Fatma and seemed as preoccupied as everyone else and as cold and remote as Fatma's mother.

Perhaps those days in Rockfield marked the emergence of the other Fatma. The notion was not so extraordinary. Her life was unfolding like a song in double time: two mothers, two countries of origin, two children in one birth, two jinns – and, eventually, two husbands.

THE FEAST

********** ✪ **********

She should have listened to Isaac; she should have watched Elsa more closely. She should have remembered that whoever walks with unworthy people becomes unworthy. Elsa should have remembered that also. Bad always finds bad, Lisha used to tell Fatma. Bad Fatma. Bad Elsa.

It didn't take long for the entrepreneurial blood that flowed through Fatma's veins to help her make money out of money. She used her new income to purchase more cocaine than Isaac had ordered on her trips to New York, and she established her own clientele in the bathroom of the Royal Lion and the alleyway behind it. Some of Isaac's classy customers became her customers, because she undercut Isaac's price. Two or three wedges of pure cocaine brought her between twenty and fifty dollars, depending on the going market price for a hit. A large cut – one chunk that kept someone high for hours – sold for eight hundred.

Elsa and Fatma were drifting apart. Fatma was caught up with her jobs: one that kept her honest, one that made her rich. And Elsa was caught up in hers. When they did meet, it was at the Royal Lion, where they sat at the bar, drawing on cigarettes with one hand, cradling drinks with the other, while their feet played on the rungs of their wooden stools.

"Why we come here?" Fatma asked her one night after she had drunk a good number of vodkas the way she liked her liquor – straight up.

Elsa swung her long shiny mop of black curls now streaked with blond toward Fatma and looked at her as if to say *You know damn well why you come here.*

"I tell you why we come, Elsa. To hide." The Royal Lion had not only become a place for Fatma to do business but a place where she was known and even respected. The clientele masqueraded as a circle of friends who left whatever lives they led away from the place outside of the bar. The Royal Lion became their own secret world of camaraderie and depravity.

"What's the matter? Isaac finally get you in trouble, *chica?*" Elsa said with a certain amount of satisfaction. She hadn't been jealous only of India; Isaac had never given her more work.

"We come to hide from *us*, Elsa." Fatma tapped her breast. "From ourselves. When your neighbor's wrong, you point a finger. But when you wrong, you hide."

"What the fuck are you talking about?"

Fatma didn't answer. In Kenya they say *Who does not even understand a look, does not understand long explanations.* And so Fatma ended the conversation because Elsa was always ready for a good fight.

"Maybe you helping yourself to a little of Isaac's inventory. Better yet, maybe you helping yourself to his wife, funny girl." Then she gave that loud cackling laugh of hers that made even the semiconscious look their way. "So tell me, what are *you* doing with all your money?"

"You know I save it for my family."

"Oh, right. You're going back to Africa or wherever you came from. Like I buy that."

"What *you* doing these days, Elsa?"

Since Fatma had known her, she claimed she'd worked as a hairdresser, in a mini-mart, as an aide in a nursing home, and more recently as a model for a wholesale lingerie company. But she never had any money.

"I'm a secretary for a plumbing supply store," she said. "For a big boss with a big *pinga*." She held her hands a foot apart.

"Maybe we drink too much, Elsa."

"Maybe you're no fun no more, *chica*. And maybe you can pay for my drinks. I got to meet my boss right now. He's taking me to dinner."

"It's midnight."

"Maybe he said breakfast." She laughed again and slung her large gold lamé purse over her shoulder.

"Why don't you put some air-conditioning in this shithole," she told the bartender. With her tiny skirt riding up toward her waist, she gave him a flash of her furry patch as she maneuvered off the stool, and he smiled. "Fuck you," she said, tottering away on her stiletto heels.

Fatma assumed Elsa meant the bartender, but she couldn't be sure.

She had gotten so plastered that a few hours later, the ringing of the phone almost didn't wake Fatma up. It was a sweet, sober Elsa, asking if Fatma would please come down to district court at 8 a.m. "Bring lots of cash," she said. "I'll pay you back." Fatma tried to ask what had happened, but someone grabbed the phone out of Elsa's hands, saying that her time was up.

Fatma wasn't sure what prompted her to help Elsa and expose herself to Rockfield's legal system. Maybe Walter Kornmeyer's Golden Rule had actually had an impact on her or maybe the side of her that liked to live on the edge prevailed, because she went to the pizzeria earlier than usual to get her work done, then took a taxi down to a place she had worked meticulously to avoid – the courthouse. She was directed to a courtroom where she found Elsa sitting in the front row with a bunch of hookers. From where Fatma sat, she could see one side of Elsa's face: her smudged eye makeup made her look like a raccoon, her lipstick and rouge were worn off, her hair was all tangled. She appeared exhausted, all the bravado sucked out of her, and Fatma wondered what her night in an American jail had been like.

"Case of Commonwealth versus Elsa Martinez," a clerk sitting at a desk in front of the judge called after a while. A man in a tan suit got up and stated that he'd interviewed Elsa and that she was entitled to appointed counsel. Then the judge said something about a public defender, bail, and another hearing, and a court officer led Elsa out.

Fatma didn't know what to do, so she sat in the back watching the other women in skimpy shorts and skin-tight skirts and low-cut tops like Elsa to be called. Some got to walk out. Some, like Elsa, got led away again. A man slid into the seat alongside Fatma.

"Are you Fatma Kornmeyer?" he asked.

"Yes."

"Nick Benson." He extended his hand. "The court's appointed me to represent Elsa Martinez. She told me you might be here with her bail."

"I have money."

"Did you understand what just happened?"

"Not really."

"Your friend was picked up for common nightwalking." He looked surprised that Fatma wasn't familiar with the term. "Tricking. Prostitution," he explained. "She also violated her probation, so her probation officer has requested a preliminary hearing. Can you stick around for another hour?"

Fatma nodded. Benson flashed a half smile and left. She wasn't really surprised, but she was irritated that Daniel had had Elsa pegged from the moment he met her. She could leave now and be done with her once and for all, but she wanted to stay, and not solely for Elsa. There was something familiar about her attorney, and something very attractive. And how dangerous was it, really? She had plenty of lawyers who were clients. A lawyer wasn't a cop. She found a pay phone and called Juicy Burger to say she'd be late.

At about eleven, Elsa was brought back in. Her tired eyes swept the courtroom and, meeting Fatma's, she smiled with relief. The man in the tan suit who identified himself as her probation officer handed her a sheet of paper. When her name was called this time, Benson stood in front of her and Elsa sat down. A lawyer in a gray suit asked for bail of two thousand dollars. Fatma had brought only one thousand. She wondered if she should take the money up to them anyway, but then the lawyer in the gray suit said something about bail for an old case being revoked.

"This case is continued to July twentieth for pretrial conference and hearing on violation of probation," the judge said.

Fatma kept waiting for someone to ask her to step up with the money, but they led Elsa away. She never turned around to look for her friend again.

Fatma sat there for a while thinking they might bring Elsa back into the courtroom. When it finally emptied out, she left. It occurred to her to tell Elsa's mother what had happened, but she had never met Elsa's mother, or her children. She wasn't even sure where to find them, because according to Elsa they moved around a lot. They didn't have a phone; Elsa had always used a pay phone.

Then she scolded herself, the way Mrs. Lucchese might have done, for giving a rat's ass about Elsa.

She was standing in front of the elevator when the man who had introduced himself as Elsa's lawyer approached her again.

"You still here?" he asked.

A little laughter in his voice gave it a sexy, youthful quality that attracted her. She tried not to stare into his eyes, but she was trying to determine if they were gray or green. She said she felt foolish for having hung around so long.

"I'm sorry, but with two prior offenses, probation violations, and dirty urine, bail was more than a long shot," he said. "But thanks for waiting just the same." He took a few steps away; then turned back around to face her. "Can I ask you something? What's a nice girl like you doing hanging around someone like her?"

Now she wanted to run as fast and as far away from the building as possible, before they locked her up too. But the attorney's smile indicated he was concerned about someone who had been pulled into something she knew nothing about. Little did he know.

"I'll do what I can for your friend. But don't make lunch reservations too soon."

She skipped lunch that day; the smell of the burgers she put together made her nauseous. The courthouse had frightened her more than she realized. Recalling Elsa with her hands cuffed behind her back and being led away like a captured animal made Fatma's throat dry and her head pound. After all, Elsa had been her guide to freedom in America.

To make sure no one was watching her, Fatma now asked the taxi driver who picked her up for her New York trips to follow her for five blocks before she got in. Isaac was sending her more often now, sometimes three times a week. She routinely checked the locks on Isaac's flat several times before she began to cook. She closed the blinds. She turned on the radio to drown out any sound she might make. Isaac had told her not to deposit large amounts of cash, because this was a giveaway. She hadn't deposited any. She bought nails and a hammer, and nailed shut the drawers of the built-in china cabinet in her flat where she kept her money.

Trouble was brewing like a monsoon over the calm seas as it always does. It had all been too simple. People got arrested every day: she had seen it with her own eyes. It had been as common as someone carrying a cup of coffee out of Dunkin Donuts.

She met Isaac at Steigers' Department Store later that day, and they exchanged shopping bags – one that had her cooking beneath clothing wrapped in tissue paper, and the other with her salary in cash similarly hidden. From the moment their eyes met, Isaac sensed trouble. "Come visit us tonight, Fatma," he said. "India misses you."

In the warmth of their kitchen, over steaming coffee and fresh-baked rum-and-walnut buns, Fatma told Isaac and India what had happened to Elsa and admitted that she was worried about getting caught, and that she had probably made a mistake by showing her face in the courthouse. Her friends' expressions never changed.

"But you are not Elsa," Isaac said. "That is why I asked you to work for me. That is why she doesn't anymore."

"Just remember that it's not forever," India said.

"You're not Elsa. You are Fatma." Isaac said it like a mantra, as though waiting for Fatma to deny it. "You are not Elsa. You are Fatma, aren't you?"

"Yes," she said.

"Liar!" Isaac screamed, his face contorted. "I don't mind that you started your own business. I understand that. I even understand that you've stolen some of my clients. But I don't understand your using my flat, and without the decency to tell me. And jeopardizing my clients and all that my wife and I have risked by going to a courthouse to protect scum like Elsa. We are finished. Give me the key and go." With steady hands that surprised even Fatma, she boldly removed the key from her key ring and threw it on the table. Yes, she still had the cursed pride of Iblis. "And don't try to use my suppliers in New York." His voice resumed its calm. "They know you are untrustworthy. You are dead to them."

But Isaac was wrong. In the cocaine jungle, money speaks louder than loyalty. While her trips to New York became much less frequent, a few suppliers were quite willing to continue selling her the cocaine she was now audacious enough to cook in her own apartment. She found it exciting this new challenge of keeping her business a secret from Mrs. Lucchese. What did distress Fatma was losing India, who had shaken her head in disapproval at Fatma's behavior. Fatma loved Pia, but she adored India – her beauty, her determination, their shared culture. She was Auntie and Ayasha and Fatma's mother all rolled into one. Fatma would find a way to make big money, to hire the best in order to confront Grandfather. But she would never find another India.

Then Nick Benson called to tell Fatma he thought she might like to know that Elsa would be spending six to eight months in jail. It had been nice of him, Fatma supposed, and something that considerate lawyers did. She had thought of him a lot after their meeting at the courthouse. He was the kind of man whose face and smell you carry to bed with you at night, whose image tugs at your vagina and makes your heart race. The corners of your mouth curl upward as you remember the sound of his voice.

The second time he called, he asked her out. He called at least once a week for the next month. He called on the morning of the feast. Wouldn't she just have a cup of coffee with him? Despite the attraction, she refused. Isaac had been right about Elsa leading Fatma into trouble; she had stupidly tried to help Elsa, and now Elsa's lawyer was after Fatma.

"The feast – it's not what it used to be," Mrs. Lucchese, in her long white apron that barely covered her large breasts, said, heaving a sigh and filling rolls with tomatoes, fresh mozzarella, and basil on a hot August day. Despite the vendors in their trailers selling pepper and sausage grinders, pizza, and fried dough stuffed with anchovies or dusted with powdered sugar, the crowds gathered for the Feast of Our Lady of Mount Carmel would be in for her panini. "Used to be such a special day. What a party! Everything's changed." Mrs. Lucchese looked at the crowds of Puerto Ricans wandering the streets. "What do they celebrate? You tell me."

"What does it matter who's celebrating, Ma?" Pia said. "As long as they celebrate. Today we're all Italians."

"Are you Irish on Saint Patrick's Day?"

"Come on, Ma."

"Beh!" Signora Lucchese uttered, thrusting her palms up in the air as if to say, "So there you have it."

"Shh!" Pia whispered, indicating that her mother had offended Fatma.

"Why? She's Irish?"

Pia rolled her eyes, mortified by her mother's tactlessness.

Mrs. Lucchese handed Fatma one of her panini. "Mine is better than what they got out there. And don't forget. They gonna carry the Madonna at two. That's when you make a wish. The Madonna can make your dreams come true!"

Fatma thanked her for the roll and went out into the muggy crowded street. She liked the feast: the colored lights strung from lampposts that were draped with red, white, and green flags; the rock and roll music from the stage set up at the end of the street; the little man with an accordion trying to compete with them as he strolled through the crowds singing "*Mala Femmina*." Except for a few of the older Italian women who, enraptured, nodded their heads to the beat, nobody paid any attention to him.

The giant Madonna was being paraded down the street now on a float, bouquets of flowers all around her. Daniel's mother had a statue like that on a pedestal in the foyer, and she used to explain all about the Virgin to Fatma in the hope that, one Sunday, she might want to accompany her to church. "Just to see what it's like," she would say. Beverly's Madonna wore blue and white; this giant one had on an elegant brown-and-gold velvet dress with a heavy gold crown and a string of pearls. But just like Beverly's Madonna, this one had long blond hair, which made Fatma laugh: didn't they know what women looked like in Fatma's mother's part of the world? Fatma's ex-mother-in-law's Madonna had stood alone with her arms stretched out, beckoning to the world, while this bigger-than-life-size image held her son, the Baby Jesus, dressed in a matching outfit down to the pearls and blond hair. This Madonna wore a long white satin cape trimmed with gold and a rosary of white roses around her neck. As six men in dark suits slowly carried the float that supported her, parishioners, mostly women, flocked to her and pinned dollar bills onto her gown in a show of devotion or perhaps in hopes of having their prayers answered, of a miracle happening.

Maybe Elsa's lawyer had pinned one on her himself that day, because Fatma had just turned off Main Street and was strolling on Gaylord toward the Royal Lion when he pulled up to the curb in a convertible filled with so many flowers it looked like one of the floats.

"I've been looking for you," he said.

People stared at him as though he was crazy, sitting in a car filled with floral arrangements. Fatma was embarrassed. A cruiser pulled up alongside the convertible.

"What's up?" the policeman asked the lawyer.

"Nothing, officer. My fiancée and I were just having a little spat."

"Your *what*?" Fatma said.

"Either get in," the policeman ordered Fatma, "or you get outa here," he said to the beautiful man in the car. "Just stop blockin' traffic. Can't you see there's a feast goin' on?"

"Give the guy a break!" a man in the crowd shouted.

"My boyfriend don't give *me* no flowers, bitch," a girl yelled.

"Let me at least drive you home," Nick Benson said.

Then Fatma did what she did best: she ran – away from this lawyer who had not only drawn the attention of a crowd but of a police officer to boot. They were all laughing – the crowd behind her, the children she passed on the street – as she ran up Gaylord toward the safety and obscurity of the Royal Lion. She ran until one of her high heels got caught in a crack in the pavement and her ankles, which were always weak, gave in.

She was on all fours when Benson pulled up alongside her again and got out of his car to help her up.

"Now will you let me drive you home?" he asked.

"No."

"Please," he begged, looking like a puppy dog.

"No! Thank you," she added, softening.

"Your knees are bleeding."

"It's nothing," she said.

"I'll call you – again," he said.

He went back to his car, while she, scraped knees and palms stinging, continued to walk toward the Royal Lion, unable to stop thinking about this sexy man who, unlike Daniel, knew how to fight for what he wanted. But what exactly did he want? To learn more about her business? To get her locked up? Or was it possible that he was truly enamored with her? It would be easy to fit a man like this into her life, and where Hussein was concerned, so very useful. It occurred to her that, despite the humiliation and pain, maybe it was a special day after all, just like Mrs. Lucchese had said, a day meant to end happily – a new beginning. Maybe someone – maybe the Mother Madonna or maybe her good jinn – was looking over her shoulder after all.

At the Top of the Hub

********** ⭐ **********

At seven p.m., Fatma was sure she had been stood up. At five past, Nick appeared at her door carrying a dozen long-stemmed red roses. He wore a black silk sports jacket, a sky blue shirt, and a yellow-and-blue-striped tie. He seemed nervous. How could someone as handsome and successful as he ever be nervous? she wondered. *All men wobble on stilts from time to time*, Auntie would have answered.

"Can I come in?"

She was embarrassed by her sparsely furnished room. She'd become so obsessed with accumulating money that, unlike the house on Poplar Street, she hadn't spent any of it on fixing up the apartment. Taking in the few dated remnants of Mrs. Lucchese's early life with her husband, Nick complimented the place all the same.

"It's cozy," he said. "Do you have a vase for these?"

She didn't.

"A jar will do." He smiled, and she was glad he did because he had looked so serious standing in the doorway.

She went into the kitchen and took a quart of sour milk from the refrigerator, emptied the milk into the sink, and refilled the container with water.

"Kind of art deco," Nick said. "I like it."

"Good thing you don't give me all those flowers in your car from feast," she said.

"I have a confession to make. A guy I know is a funeral director. Sometimes there are too many flowers for the gravesite. The mourners don't want them, and he doesn't know what to do with them. I did him a favor."

"What you did with them?"

"I put them on the Madonna's float and said a prayer." He brought the palms of his hands together. "But I bought these. That's why I'm a little late." He placed the flowers on the table by the window overlooking the tree.

"My country place," she said.

They both laughed at the notion.

"I'd like to have a place in the country someday," he said, "away from the rat race."

"This one is easy to get to. It remind me a little of home."

"Where's that?"

"Mombasa. And Somalia. And my mother is – was – Arabian. Is long story."

"Well, come on, Scheherazade," he said, taking her arm. "We have all night. And hopefully another thousand."

They drove to Boston, and then Nick took her higher – to the top of the Prudential Center. She was at the top of the world, all right, drinking martinis, eating Oysters Rockefeller, and staring down on the city lit up like a Christmas tree. Nick had asked for a booth so they could sit side by side, and when his leg brushed hers, she cemented her leg to the warmth and pressure of his.

Attempting to win over Nick wasn't hard. She had never been excited like this about anyone else – not Daniel, certainly not Elsa, and not the few men she'd kissed in a dark corner at the Royal Lion, where she had let their liquor-and-tobacco-laced tongues linger for a while. But she never went home with them and she never invited them to her place. And if she found out later that they were married, she admonished them out loud, for everyone to hear, with the saying: *A rooster doesn't sing on two roofs*.

"Your eyes are so exotic," Nick said.

No one had ever called her exotic before. She wasn't exotic in Africa. There was a club in downtown Rockfield with exotic dancers, but she didn't think he meant that she was one of them. Her stepsister Jamila, the tall and willowy daughter of her father's youngest wife, was exotic, with a neck so long it could accommodate twenty gold bands when most people could wear only seven or eight. She had been discovered in Somalia by a news photographer at the age of thirteen and sneaked out to England. Now she was a famous actress – "the exotic Jamila," people in Europe and America called her. But Fatma was short and busty, with a round face and freckles across what she considered a too-small and uninteresting nose.

Fatma tried to deepen her voice and make it sultry. She visualized the verb conjugations that Mrs. Dolan had used, searching for the correct tense endings that were still hard for her to keep straight. He was a lawyer, educated. But nothing she said seemed to bother Nick, who made her feel like an ebony sculpture that should be polished until it shone.

"You know, that day in the courthouse wasn't the first time I'd ever seen you. I recognized you from Little Venezia last Columbus Day. You were sitting next to a bunch of old ladies, but I don't think you were with them. You looked a little tired."

She was ashamed to think that he had seen her so hung over. Of course she hadn't appeared much better the morning she'd met him at the courthouse, when she sensed something familiar about him but couldn't put her finger on it.

"I was with my father-in-law, Vito Rossi," he said, "when I saw you at Little Venezia." Her smile vanished, and he quickly added that it was his *ex*-father-in-law. "I'm divorced now," he said.

"Me too. You still friends?" She had meant he and his wife, but he continued to talk about his father-in-law.

"I like Vito. But my ex-wife's a bitch, to put it bluntly – a pathological liar. She told brutal stories about me, so Vito cut me off. In fact the last time I saw him was that morning I saw you at Little Venezia. I guess there's always a silver lining, as they say. And your in-laws?"

"I could never be friends with them," she said.

"Anyway, I was kind of sorry I hadn't spoken to you in Little Venezia. Then, at the courthouse, it hit me after a while that you were that girl. Can't get much luckier than a second chance."

"You have children?"

"Three. Of course they're pretty much grown up now. And you?"

What would he think of a woman whose own family had taken her child away from her?

"A boy. He's far away right now."

He didn't pursue it. When he asked her what she did, she timidly told him about the pizzeria and Juicy Burger. To compensate for her lack of status, she let him in on a little secret she didn't like to talk about in Rockfield. "In Somalia, I'm princess. Royalty."

"So you really are my Scheherazade!" He beamed.

Nick excused himself several times that evening, and she suspected that he was attempting to escape a disappointing evening, a date that had been an error in judgment. Each time he returned, however, he was happier and more eager than before.

"The bladder gets lazy at my age," he offered.

✳

On their next date, Nick took her to his office suite. It was the first time she'd been inside the towers. It was plush – just like Nick. Browns and rusts and forest greens with leather couches and dark wood furniture that, he made sure to inform her, was tropical mahogany. He proudly walked her through the suite, pointing out his secretary's desk, his office, and the library with floor-to-ceiling bookshelves lined with fat legal volumes. Then came the coffee room and Tom O'Brien's office.

"Your partner?" she asked.

"Oh no. I've never had a partner. Being married to one person at a time was all I could handle. On the other hand, I guess I didn't handle that too well, either. I admit it: I like to be the boss. Much less complicated. That way, anything goes wrong, I have no one to blame but myself. Tom's just out of law school – Western New England. I get most of my associates from there. They stay a few years, pick up a little experience, and then go off on their own or join some bigger practice. It works. I prefer a change in secretaries from time to time too, before they start thinking they're the office manager. I've seen what happens when lawyers get too dependent on secretaries."

"How Elsa can afford you?"

"She didn't have to pay me. I'm part of the bar advocate program. The court picked me from a list of its lawyers. We represent clients who don't have enough money to hire an attorney. In our legal system everyone's entitled to a trial by jury with representation. That's the great thing about it. However, I have to say I'm glad enough people can afford to pay us esquires."

Nick used a lot of words she'd never heard. He was the kind of man she had expected to find when she came to America. Someone of her family's status. A man with connections. This was what her uncle had promised.

He took her hand and led her back into his office. Encircling her with his arms he told her he'd always wanted to make love on the couch.

"Here?" she asked.

"Why not?"

"What about Tom?"

"It's Sunday."

He pressed her body to his and kissed her forehead. "You going to get shy on me here, Princess?" he asked.

She nodded.

"Do I have to undress you?"

She nodded again. And so he did.

"I don't like your boyfriend," Mrs. Lucchese said one morning.

"Jesus, Ma," Pia moaned as she placed freshly baked loaves of bread onto slatted wooden shelves along the wall behind the counter.

"And you, don't take God's name in vain. Just because you're gonna be a doctor, don't ever forget that God will always be smarter than you."

"What you don't like, Mrs. Lucchese?" Fatma asked.

Mrs. Lucchese, out of habit, wiped her clean hands on her big white apron in preparation for revealing something really important.

"The eyes." She pointed to her own eyes. "I don't trust his eyes."

Fatma shrugged her shoulders, as if she couldn't care less what the old woman thought, and turned to leave for the pizzeria.

"They say he left a wife and three children," Mrs. Lucchese called after her.

"People say many things," Fatma answered, walking out the door.

"Move in with me, Fatma," he said one night in late fall as they lay on a Cape Cod beach. They were bundled up in hooded jogging outfits, huddling beneath a blanket, looking up at the stars like two actors in a romance movie. "You know I've fallen in love with you."

He couldn't afford to take much time away from work, so he enjoyed what he called "quick getaways" – long weekends in Bermuda or Puerto Rico or, as now, Cape Cod. They were staying in a bed-and-breakfast facing the sea in Truro and had spent the afternoon walking the empty streets of Provincetown. Nick liked the beach in the off-season; he didn't like crowds. He also preferred videos at home to going to the movies; Fatma didn't mind this, except that he chose films with complicated plots and fast-paced dialogue that she didn't dare interrupt to ask about because Nick was annoyed if he missed a key word. And while he often said hello to people he knew when they passed on the street, he never talked about his friends, with the exception of George, an undertaker with whom he played golf and whom Fatma never met. Some guys were just like that, Pia said.

The beach was all theirs the night he asked her to move in with him. She turned toward him, wanting to see his face – his eyes – clearly when he said he loved her, but all she could make out was his profile in the dim moonlight. All she could really hear was the crashing of the waves.

"What do you say?" he persisted.

"When we get married," she answered. *A woman has to hold something back from a man she plans to ask a favor from – even if he drives her wild*, she thought. It had kept her father coming back to her mother all those years.

✷

At Christmastime Nick took his staff to a fancy restaurant with a band, and all the drinks they could handle. Emma, the new secretary, was younger than Fatma had expected, and had a boyfriend who spoke only when someone asked him a question. He hadn't worn a suit like Nick and Tom, yet it seemed that even his dress shirt and khakis had been too much for him to handle.

"Have you ever seen Nick in a courtroom?" Tom asked Fatma.

"Once." Instantly she regretted the answer, hoping she wouldn't have to relate the story about Elsa and her common nightwalking.

"She's never seen me litigate, if that's what you mean," Nick said.

"You should come to one of his defenses. The guy's amazing."

"Okay, okay, that's enough," Nick said, but Fatma knew he enjoyed seeing her being impressed.

"When I watched Tom the first time, I couldn't believe it was him up there interrogating those witnesses," Tom's pregnant wife, Madison, said. "And when he gave his closing – it was a murder charge – I was in tears. So was most of the jury. He won, of course."

"Nick taught me everything I know."

"Come on," Nick said. "You have a law degree."

"You know this is where the real training happens," Tom added.

"This your first baby?" Fatma asked Madison.

"Second. We have a girl. We got married right after college. It's a boy; we already know. I was hoping for another girl. I have two sisters and we're really close. Boys are so energetic; I'm not sure how I'm going to manage working with two. I'm a kindergarten teacher. I don't think I can stand to leave both of them all day so I can be with twenty-two other children. I mean, I hated missing Isabella's first step. She took it in day care. It really upset me."

Try missing everything, Fatma wanted to say, downing her third vodka on the rocks although they were still on the appetizers.

"I told you, you don't have to work," Tom said, patting her hand. "Business is good." He cast a look of gratitude toward Nick.

"How are those golf lessons going?" Nick asked Tom.

"I'm working with a pro at a virtual course this winter. I should be ready to take you on this spring."

"We'll see."

"I hope you're not turning him into one of these absentee golf husbands," Madison said. "Can't you play tennis? Golf takes too long."

"Take it easy," Tom gently cautioned, not wanting to ruffle Nick. He sounded the way Nick had when Nick had tried to tone down Tom's compliments.

But Nick wasn't bothered by what Madison had said. He deemed it the perfect time to take the envelopes from the inside pocket of his jacket and present Tom and Emma with their bonuses.

"We're having a housewarming on the twentieth," Madison said. "We hope all of you will come." Then, turning to Fatma, she asked: "What do you do?"

"She's in retail," Nick said, and called for the check.

"You don't see your children?" she asked later that night when they reached his condo. "It doesn't bother you?"

"Of course it bothers me. I miss them. But I hope they'll come around one day. It hasn't been that long. They just need time. These things happen in divorce, especially if you're married to a wacko. One party poisons the kids about the other. The kids feel sorry for that whining parent because they're the weaker one, and the next thing you know, they turn against the strong parent. It's probably better you never got to know your son before you lost him."

She had told him about Hussein, and he had been sympathetic. Now he was telling her she was smart to leave well enough alone. How was she ever going to persuade him to go up against her family? She was upset, so he presented a peace offering – in his own interest.

"We could have a baby, just like Tom and Madison."

The thought actually appealed to her. This she could do with Nick.

"But only if it looks like you," he added.

He had been sitting next to her on the couch, and he bent over and kissed her. His lips were cushiony and moist, and she could have sucked at them all night, but he asked her to do what he liked her to do – to take off her clothes. She could never look at him when she did this, and so she focused on something else – the lamp on the end table or the switch plate on the wall.

"Slow down, Princess."

He got up to put some dreamy music on, but he never took those gray eyes off her. She unhooked her bra and let it fall to the floor.

"Hold them," he said.

By the time her pants and underpants were off, so were his, and his penis, big and swollen, was aimed straight at her. She went over to the couch and knelt in front of him. She put his penis between her breasts and rubbed it until it erupted. Then Nick made her lie down on the floor and licked her until her body shook and she couldn't stand it anymore.

"Will your family disapprove of me because I'm so much older than you?" he said afterward. "I could be your father."

"You have lot to learn about my culture."

"And I want to, Fatma. I want to go to Mombasa. And we'll find Hussein."

His last statement surprised her. It was all turning out as she had hoped – even better. It was all going according to plan.

"Tell me something. Did your husband ever make you feel the way I do?"

She didn't answer. She didn't want to talk about Daniel. It didn't feel good; it didn't feel right. She laid her head on Nick's broad chest, curling the long bronze and silver strands around her finger.

"Sorry," he said. "I don't know why I asked you that."

But it wouldn't be the last time he did, as though he couldn't help himself, and it made her uneasy. She didn't like to see a weak side of him.

IN MUSLIM LAW

**********✮**********

"I stopped by Juicy Burger today for lunch, but you weren't there." Nick's statement demanded an explanation.

"You ask for me?" Fatma hadn't even taken off her coat. They were at Edelweiss, where she was meeting Nick for dinner a few days into the New Year.

"No. I figured you must have gone home early or not come in at all for some reason. Not feeling well?"

"I have bad stomach ache, and they let me go home."

"I called but you didn't answer. I swung by your apartment. It was all the dragon lady could do to tell me she hadn't seen you all day."

"Mrs. Lucchese's not bad, Nick. It's just her way."

"You mean it's just that she doesn't like me."

"Maybe. She's proud lady. She doesn't like when you tell her what to cook."

"Where *were* you?"

"Upstairs. Sleeping. The Luccheses don't see me every time I go in and out building. Guess I don't hear phone."

"You must be feeling better, otherwise that spätzle and bratwurst you just ordered is going to sit like lead in your belly."

"I'm much better. And hungry. I don't eat all day."

"Good. I'm glad to hear it." He took a sip of his scotch and put it down without taking his eyes off her. Then he broke into a little smile, as if he hadn't believed a word she'd said, as if he knew she'd been down to New York, as if he'd caught her in her own game. "By the way, the correct word is *didn't*, you didn't hear the phone and you didn't eat all day."

He hadn't wanted to go to Tom and Madison O'Brien's party. "I talk to people all day," he said. "When I'm off, I need a little quiet – a little down time." Still, he went, to please Fatma.

The O'Briens lived in a suburb of Rockfield, in what Nick called a bedroom community, on a street of new houses that were all the same. There wasn't much furniture in the house, only the necessities.

"It's getting there," Madison said. "I figured this was a good time to have a party, before we put down any carpeting. Would you like to see the rest of the house?"

"Sure," Fatma said.

"You go ahead," Nick said. "I'm going to fix myself a drink." Fatma followed Nick upstairs. When she showed her the master bedroom, Fatma couldn't help picturing Tom and Madison making those babies in that big bed. Before Madison slowly opened the door to her daughter's room, she put her finger to her lips.

"I don't have to," Fatma said.

"No. No. It's fine. Just be quiet," Madison whispered. "Once she's down, she's usually out for the night, thank God."

In the illumination of a nightlight, Fatma saw her in the white crib, her padded bottom almost in the air, her face red and plump, thumb in her mouth.

"I know she shouldn't be sucking it, but it's so cute," Madison said.

Fatma thought it would hurt to see her, but it didn't. For the first time she felt excited about having another child of her own, and hopeful about Nick helping her find the one she'd left behind. She had gambled on being on her own, and it was paying off big-time.

Downstairs, Nick was standing in the same spot, about a foot from the entrance to the kitchen, not far from the island that served as a bar. He handed Fatma a vodka tonic.

"Ready to go?" he asked after she had downed her drink.

"We just get here."

They stood there for the remainder of their short time at the party, Nick changing his position only to go to the bathroom to attend to that weak bladder, then resuming his post, as if he were a bearing wall that might bring down the entire house if it were taken away. He was pleasant enough when other guests introduced themselves but he never initiated a conversation.

"Had enough?" he asked after a while. "Parties just aren't my thing."

A man brushed by Fatma to get to the bar. When he excused himself, she looked up at him and their eyes locked in recognition. He turned away quicker than she did, poured two glasses of white wine, and found a different way back to his wife, or whoever the woman waiting for him was. Fatma had seen him often at the Royal Lion. He wasn't one of her clients, but men of his caliber didn't frequent the Royal Lion just to drink. When she was with Nick, she ran to the bathroom at his place, or to the ladies' room when they were out, to check her pager. Later, a doctor, a cop, even some judge's messenger would be in the alley behind the Royal Lion no matter what hour of the day or night she stipulated. It had been easy for her to slip in and out of two worlds as it suited her, but now the worlds were moving independently, threatening her plan and frightening her as they transgressed their boundaries.

Nick arranged more getaways, to Vegas, Palm Springs, Cancún, and other exotic places. Most weekends they went to Boston. He tended to business while she spent time at the hotel's shopping mall or in the jewelry district in Downtown Crossing. They'd meet back at the hotel room, where Nick would pick out a new outfit for her to wear, and soon she was that lady with gold bracelets and diamond pendants, dining among the elite of Beacon Hill at the Top of the Hub, looking down on her kingdom. Occasionally Nick chose a small place in Cambridge – perhaps Indian or Mexican – and they sat close to each another in a dark corner booth while waiters in white pleated shirts and black pants grilled chicken vindaloo, or flamed bananas at their table.

Nick slipped off his shiny black loafer and beneath the floor-length tablecloth ran his toe up and down her leg. He put his arm around her, and drawing her closer, kissed her until the taste of scotch and the smell of cologne weakened her and she could hardly hold back an orgasm. Finally, he whispered something outrageous, something no one in the restaurant could have dreamed he was saying, like: "Next time, don't wear panties." With his face so close to hers, she could see little red veins throbbing at his temples, like rubber bands about to snap, and she worried not that Nick would never find Hussein, but that Nick would leave her because she didn't know how to love him.

✳

"I have a little surprise," Nick said, taking a glass of vodka out of her hand and setting it and his scotch on the coffee table. They were watching a movie at his condo in Connecticut, just over the Rockfield city line. It was a moment when she felt happier than she'd ever been, one of those rare times when all the puzzle pieces finally fit together, and one fears that the sudden ringing of the telephone, a sneeze, or even a slight breeze might scatter them all and make them forever irretrievable. She hadn't wanted Nick to move a muscle, but he got up to go to the bathroom, she assumed, as he often did. This time he went into the kitchen and returned with a miniature liquor bottle – the kind she used to serve on airplanes – and a plastic bag with a familiar-looking pebble in it, a small piece of aluminum foil about an square, and a fork. Poking holes in the foil with the fork, he shaped it into a tiny cup. He took a drag on his cigarette, filled the cup with burning ashes, and put one of the pebbles on top of the ashes. He fitted the cup to the open neck of the bottle and sucked at a hole on the side of the bottle. Then he handed it to her.

"I don't," she said. She may have been a drunk, but when it came to tasting her wares, she had listened to Isaac and India. "It's just a business. A means to an end," India had said.

"Come on, Princess. I think we can be honest with each other after all this time."

"I'm honest."

A little bewildered, he pursed his lips and raised his eyebrows.

"Look, I know you have a side thing going. We all have our little secrets." He held the pipe up as an example of his own.

"How you find out?"

"Your friend Elsa. Defendants often try to implicate – name – others to get off easier."

"You know all this time?"

"I didn't say anything because I didn't want to scare you away. I wanted to wait until you knew me better, until you trusted me. You do trust me, don't you babe?"

She did trust him, and that's why running into the guy at Madison and Tom's party had shaken her up. Rockfield was a small city, and the world of addicts even smaller. She had had bad dreams afterward about Nick finding out and leaving her, and dreamt she was down on her knees pleading with him not to go, grabbing at his legs, his shoes, anything she could get hold of. She would wake up the way she used to on Poplar Street when she dreamt about Hussein, sobbing into a wet pillow. She couldn't lose Nick.

"I quit business, Nick."

A look of surprise washed over him.

"But I never use, Nick." She had drunk too much as usual, and was getting confused. She needed to keep her wits about her. Pay attention, Mrs. Lucchese had said. She needed to stick to the plan, but the plan was overtaking her.

"We drink, don't we?" he said, his smile returning. "Well, there was a time in this country you could go to jail for drinking. Did you know that? And it's just a matter of time before marijuana and cocaine are made legal. And we don't waste money and time defending street junkies. Drug cartels will disappear, and everyone will just smoke socially, like I do. Just like we drink. And you can resume your business, because it'll be legal. Of course, you won't earn nearly as much money. By the way, what are you doing with all your money?"

"I save it for my family."

"Of course. That's a good thing."

"Sometimes I think we drink too much, Nick."

"No, Princess, we don't." He spoke with authority in a calm and reassuring way, drawing her in word by word, breath by breath, keeping her in suspense as she watched his lips form every syllable, making his opinion known just the way the men in her family did. That had been the problem with Daniel; he hadn't known how to make people listen to him, how to convince them – especially Fatma.

"I'm under a lot of pressure with my job, and I need to unwind. But we can cut down if you're not comfortable. We can cut down anytime we want, I promise, because we're not like the others who let it consume them. We're people who know how to stay in control. Every now and then I take a little sniff of powder when I go to the john. That's it. That's all. Keeps me regular. On special occasions, like now, I smoke. It's like drinking champagne. We're just going to take a little hit, and then I'm going to make passionate love to you. You're going to feel like it's the Fourth of July." He started to sing: "Skyrockets in flight, afternoon delight." Then, holding out the pipe: "Do you know that song? Come on, Scheherazade. Take a hit."

And she did, because Nick was more than a means to an end. There are some people – some things – that, if you really love them, can wield that much power over you.

On a frigid morning in early March, Nick and she drove to the countryside, to a town named Hamilton, forty minutes north of Rockfield. They entered a forest and then a clearing with a lake that was frozen in spots. The road continued alongside the water. After a curve to the left, an enormous wood-frame house appeared.

"Let's get out," Nick said, pulling up to it.

The smell of new cedar shingles reminded Fatma of the air in Mombasa. There was not another house in sight.

"Be careful," Nick said as he led her along the iced-over driveway to the front door.

"Who we visiting?"

"No one," he said, putting a key in the door.

The ceilings were high – cathedral, he called them. The carpeting and walls were cream colored, the kitchen filled with cherry cabinets and stainless-steel appliances, and the stone fireplace reached up to the ceiling. In the great room, atrium doors formed a glass wall that overlooked the lake.

"Imagine. Once there were houses – a whole town there." He pointed to the lake.

"What happen?"

"They flooded it. The government took it over, turned it into a reservoir."

"What about people?"

"Bad luck, I guess. What do you think?"

"Mean. Like something they do in Somalia."

"I mean the *house*." He laughed.

"Beautiful!"

He was grinning now, the way he did when he knew he had done something really fine. She could see his chest expanding with pride, and she thought he might pound on it with both fists like a gorilla would.

"Good thing you like it, because it's yours."

"What?"

"I bought it. That's where we'll plant the garden." He pointed in the direction of the atrium doors, although she couldn't tell exactly where he meant; everything was covered in snow. "So we can look out at it every spring and summer morning and watch the flowers grow. When do you want to move in?"

It had been the wrong question to ask her – it was out of sequence – and, as much as she wanted to say yes, she refused again. She had to regain control of her plan.

"I need to marry if you want that we live together," she said.

His expression went from confused to hurt.

"Didn't you think I would marry you?"

"In Muslim law," she blurted out, feeling her dead mother's chains around her neck.

"How about tonight, Scheherazade?"

There was, of course, a bouquet of roses on the table in the restaurant that evening. Nick had arranged to have them there. The waiter poured two glasses of champagne, and Nick took a black velvet box out of his pocket. Inside, sitting in white satin, was a yellow gold ring with a modest pear-shaped diamond. It wasn't quite as large as Fatma would have liked.

"I'm going to treat you like a real princess," he said.

"I *am* real princess," she reminded him, but Africa was fading from her mind; she had helped obliterate its memory. She told Nick she had met Daniel in school in Mombasa, that she had been one of his students, and that they had fallen in love: maybe to impress Nick, maybe because at that moment she couldn't remember the real circumstances. For an instant, however, she felt an urge to tell him everything again, only this time the truth, never skipping a detail about the ranch in Mogadishu, about the dogs she used to ride, and the hunting trips to Kilimanjaro. Yet she refrained because she knew her past would loom too large over Nick's world, a world in which he liked to be in the forefront. Then the instant passed, as did the urge.

They didn't go to the Arabian mosque in Rockfield to get married that evening. Nick said he knew a woman whose brother Ishmael was a sheik, and that it would be more intimate, more personal that way. The place didn't seem to be a mosque at all, just an ordinary home. Fatma's brain had become far too muddled, more muddled than the average flawed human brain, as Lisha would have said, to question the circumstances that night. A woman, perhaps the sheik's wife, gave her a red silk sari whose worn hem was soiled and frayed to put on over her low-cut pink taffeta dress. She stood beside Nick in his shiny dark suit. They repeated some vows in English, signed a paper, and it was over. She was deliriously happy.

Nick waited in the car while she told Mrs. Lucchese that she had married and would no longer be living in the apartment. The older woman shook her head in disapproval; nothing ever pleased her.

"Now what'd you go and do that for?" Sal, who rarely said anything, asked Fatma. He had never questioned her comings and goings, but it was clear that when it came to marriage, the line between blacks and whites should be drawn.

"*Pazzi*. Tutt'e due." They were both crazy, Mrs. Lucchese muttered. "What's the use to talk? You did it already."

After Fatma broke the news, Pia disappeared. Fatma was walking back to Nick's car when she came running after her, wearing her old maroon sweatshirt with UMASS written in big white letters across her breasts. She hadn't bothered to put on a coat.

"It's a tablecloth my grandmother made." She handed Fatma a flat package neatly held together with a lavender ribbon.

Fatma could see through the tissue paper that the cloth was white, with different-colored birds and flowers embroidered on it. Pia's grandmother had to have given it to her that way, Fatma thought, because there hadn't been any time for Pia to wrap it.

"It belong to you," Fatma told her.

"Not really. Not until I marry, and I have no intentions of doing that for a long time."

"I can't."

"Please. I want to give you something. I hope it brings you luck. Believe me, I have plenty of others. All my grandmother ever did was embroider."

"Thank you." Fatma threw her arms around Pia, thinking that Italians were as superstitious as Muslims: always talking about luck, as though they never had a part in the way their lives turned out.

Nick beeped for Fatma to get into the car. "Be happy!" A grinning Pia called out, waving. Then, hugging her shivering body, she ran back into the store.

Fatma hadn't taken anything from the apartment, because Nick told her he wanted her to have everything new. But Mrs. Lucchese came roaring out of the store and told Fatma she wanted all of Fatma's stuff out – everything clean.

"If you don't take it, I'm gonna burn it," Mrs. Lucchese said.

Fatma ran upstairs and emptied the contents of several drawers into a suitcase. The money she used to hide in the china closet was nearly gone now: a little of it had been wired to Auntie, the rest recycled in a way – back to where it had come – to some other street junkie to support Nick's and her habit, to chasing that first high. The rest of her belongings Mrs. Lucchese could burn.

Tomorrow she and Nick were going furniture shopping; they were starting out brand new.

"*Ninakupenka*," Fatma whispered in bed to Nick the first night in their new home. She hadn't spoken Swahili in years.

"What did you say?" he asked.

"I love you."

THE HOUSE
OF THE FIVE-HEADED MONSTER

********** ☆ **********

Fatma quit working at the pizzeria and Juicy Burger. It would have been impossible to get to Rockville, living way out in Hamilton. Daniel had tried to teach her to drive not long after she arrived in America, but early on she had crashed into a police car and refused to get behind the wheel again. Now she regretted that decision. She asked Nick to give her lessons. "Sure," he said. But he never made the time, seemingly preferring to keep her dependent on him and to know where she was at all times. "Besides, how would it look?" he said, explaining that the wife of a prominent attorney couldn't be seen shredding mozzarella, refilling red pepper and parmesan cheese shakers, sweeping the floor, and assembling burgers. He assured her money was no object and promised to start sending some regularly to her family, as soon as he sold his condo in Connecticut and paid off the mortgage on the new house.

She traveled to Rockfield with him some days because she was lonely out in Hamilton. But other than meeting Nick's supplier in the foyer of a burned-out apartment house on Hanson Street to relieve Nick of the chore, she didn't have anything to do in the city. She stayed away from the Royal Lion; Nick said now that she was married to him, her being seen there would jeopardize his firm. She passed by the Luccheses' deli sometimes and, avoiding Mrs. Lucchese and Sal, peeked in the window, but Pia was never there. She didn't dare venture near India. And so she began to watch Nick in court.

The first case she attended involved a university boy who had been charged with stabbing his roommate to death in a drunken brawl because the roommate had called him a faggot. It went on for several weeks, and for long periods of time in the courtroom nothing at all seemed to be happening. Fatma had imagined that all lawyers must be good actors to talk to jurors the way they did on TV. However, she learned that most of them, including Nick, didn't in the least talk the way actors did; most witnesses never broke down hysterically; and, without moving background music, the courtroom scene was quite dull.

In another case Nick defended a government employee who had kept his nephew and mother on his agency's payroll for years, although they had never actually worked, according to the prosecution. Fatma watched Nick carry heavy ledgers from his table over to the judge and then back to his table. He rattled off lots of numbers, and the monotonous sound of his chanting lulled her to sleep. One day a dead silence woke her up. Nick had stopped in midsentence. The judge and jury screwed up their faces, trying to understand what Nick was getting at, but he couldn't seem to get back on track. The judge called a recess.

Nick lost that case. He also lost the one with the boy, and Fatma started to believe that her presence might be bringing him bad luck.

"I hadn't expected to win," he said, taking a gulp of scotch at Edelweiss.

"How can you defend guilty people?"

"I didn't say he was guilty."

"I don't understand."

"It's my job, Fatma," he said. "Everyone deserves to be defended. I've told you that. Sometimes you just hope for a lighter sentence, maybe cut a deal." But he couldn't hide his disappointment.

She stopped going to court. The nice weather had arrived, and she didn't need to get out of the cold when she went into Rockfield. She started walking all over the city, to places she'd never been. It amazed her that she'd lived in the city as long as she had and yet there always seemed something new to see: a house painted an interesting color, a building being renovated, a new store opening. One afternoon she wandered into a park that Daniel had warned her to avoid. She didn't see anything worse going on than she'd seen in the alley and bathroom of the Royal Lion. The park wasn't very big, and there was little grass and a few trees inside its gates, but there was a large greenhouse with milky glass panes. She needed to go to the bathroom, and she needed a fix. Cocaine had taken her fast.

"How much?" she asked a lady sitting behind a desk in the foyer.

"Nothing, dear. It's free. The greenhouse is maintained by the Oliver Lyttle estate."

She didn't know who Oliver Lyttle was; all she knew was that she had walked into paradise. There were blue and purple crocuses, white, red, pink, yellow, and orange tulips, and air as sweet as Auntie's cologne. One little room was almost entirely taken up by a display of pots; more flowers attached to chicken wire cascaded down the walls. She could have stayed there the rest of the day, but she walked on, into a room that was hot and humid and familiar, with enormously tall palm trees, and wide-leafed rubber plants, ornamental banana plants, quinine trees. She recognized the tall thin bark and fernlike canopy of the tamarind from East Africa – from home. And there she sat until it was time to meet Nick.

"Why you never take me there?" she asked Nick on their ride back to Hamilton.

"To tell you the truth, I never knew about it. I only *work* in Rockfield, remember. I've always lived in Enfield."

Daniel had never mentioned it either.

"You have to come, Nick. It's beautiful. Like Mombasa."

"Why don't we build you your own greenhouse? That way I won't have to worry about you wandering alone all over the city."

"Build a greenhouse where?"

"Right outside the bedroom doors. I was going to have a patio put in there. We'll have a little conservatory attached to the house instead. I see them advertised all the time. I'll call about it tomorrow."

By early summer she had a greenhouse – not nearly as big as the one in the park, but a greenhouse all the same, and something to occupy her when she wasn't getting high. She potted and repotted, watered, trimmed dead blossoms and leaves, and fertilized plants. Nick and she bought from a local nursery where they taught her how to grow chrysanthemums from seeds, and in the fall her greenhouse was bursting with color. While she couldn't have all the tropical plants she'd have liked, because the conservatory was too small, and without temperature control, she did have a few rubber trees and one that grew miniature oranges.

She was in the conservatory the Saturday Nick went crazy. It was the following spring, but her tulips hadn't come up quite like the ones in Oliver Lyttle's greenhouse despite the fact that she *had* spent her winter days in the conservatory – mostly dreaming however – and smoking, and wondering from time to time why there had been no more mention of Mombasa or Hussein from Nick *or* her. No more mention of the baby that had never come. But then those thoughts evaporated as quickly as they had come. The car door slammed; there was some mumbling and a series of bangs. When she looked out, she saw Nick in the driveway, back from golfing, cursing and swinging one of his clubs every which way, whacking at the asphalt over and over again as though he were beating it to death. She ran out.

"What is wrong?" she asked, careful to keep her distance from the flailing club.

"Fucking bitch! Fuckingsonofabitch!" was all he kept saying.

Frightened, she crept back into the house and waited in the greenhouse until the sun set and the moon appeared. Until Nick's evil jinn retreated to its dark hiding place. Until, calm as a dhow docked in Mombasa harbor, he came looking for her, fixed her dinner, and took her to bed.

Nick stopped playing golf that day. He stopped going in to work regularly too. At first he said Tom was handling most things and that he was cutting back. Maybe he would sell him the practice. But Tom took off about a year after Fatma had met him, just about the time Emma left. They couldn't work for nothing. According to Madison, who had felt some kind of obligation to call Fatma, word was going around about Nick's growing unreliability. He was missing appointments and was incoherent in the courtroom. Nick said he had fired Tom.

"Time to get a new associate," he announced. "And a new secretary."

Tom and Emma, however, had been his last staff, because

things were changing for Nick. The tight band that had held his cool façade together finally snapped, and he began to spin out of control, whisking Fatma up in his whirlwind.

The house was laid out so their bedroom windows faced west. The early morning sun didn't disturb them; instead, they had a great view of it setting on summer evenings. Still, in the six years they lived in the house in Hamilton, they were too far gone to appreciate the red sunsets, the falling snow, the colorful palette of autumn leaves, or her precious greenhouse, where the plants dried up from neglect and died just like everything else in the house that Nick had bought for her. In time, they would light up right after breakfast. They'd drink to come down faster, shower, then light up over and over again until suppertime, always chasing that next hit, that next high.

She lost track of what was happening in Somalia: warlords hunted down by American military; civilians fired upon during the searches; the children's wing of a hospital bombed. She had no idea what was happening to her family, and they had no idea what was happening to her. Auntie must have worried herself sick about Fatma, thinking she had dropped off the face of the earth. But she hadn't. She'd just slipped into a subterranean part of it where other things and other people ruled. As Isaac once said: "No lions and tigers in this jungle, Fatma. Just people who act like them."

Frustration grew in Nick as his savings disappeared faster than a road in Katundu during the rainy season. His taste in drugs and liquor became less discriminating. There were no more trips to Vegas, the Bahamas, Puerto Rico, or even Boston. Edgy, he followed her around the house until there was no space she could be in without him being in it too. As their appetites waned, they stopped going to the supermarket and restaurants and had food delivered every now and then, cases of cheap alcohol more often. He got depressed. She lost so much weight that her chest looked almost as flat as Nick's. They began to bait each another, satisfied only after pushing their limits, and they invented a dance far more intimidating than any dance the Kornmeyers had engaged in. Arabs say you are not born a warrior, you become one. Nick and Fatma turned into their own private armies.

The night he told her to go out to the car for a carton of cigarettes because he was already undressed, he locked her out of the house. After banging on the windows and doors and screaming for an hour, she lay on the carseat until morning, grateful for unseasonably warm weather. When he opened the car door, she punched him in the arm.

"Why the hell you do that?" she shouted.

He looked at her as though she was a raving lunatic. "*Did you. Did you* do that. And it was a joke, Princess. Just a joke."

She got out of the car. He got in and took off, and didn't come back until the following morning.

His solo outings were becoming common. He would return with a dozen roses or fancily wrapped pieces of lingerie. When she accused him of fooling around, he sulked, and she felt a need to make up to him for her accusation.

One night she walked into the great room wearing a new teddy he had recently given her. She put on sexy music and stripped for him, trying to pretend she was enjoying it, still uncomfortable with no curtains on the windows and the moon – like a spotlight – shining down on her for all to see. Only, just as Nick had planned, there was never anyone to see or hear her in the house he had bought her. No one but Nick.

"Come here," he said when she was naked. He told her to kneel on the floor in front of him.

She waited for him to put his penis between her breasts the way he liked. Instead, he got off the couch and turned her over. He pinned her arms to the floor and forced himself into her from behind over and over again.

"Don't make me go out on you, Princess," he begged, as though it was she who controlled his behavior.

There were times on their trips to Rockfield when Nick started in on her before they even reached the car. A certain look came over his face – a slight smile, as though he had just remembered where he had stashed a thousand-dollar bill. The kind of look a lion has when it sniffs the air and senses fair game – a satisfied look, pleased with what it sees through its cold stare. Thus Nick looked at her on those nights with keen interest while she talked like a child without a thought in her carefree head, always thinking this was the night that would change everything. And he listened and nodded at her babbling like a lion with many thoughts in its head, smacking its tail on the ground as though drumming in the jungle, waiting to make his move.

"You know, you walk funny," he'd say. "Must be because your feet are so small." So she'd try to walk straight, one foot carefully placed in front of the other, because she figured that she must walk funny. Otherwise why would Nick say she did? She'd get into the car and sit there, waiting for him to quiet down. If he didn't, she began throwing punches, hitting him anywhere she could, knowing well what he'd do in retaliation, because no pain from his fists hurt as much as his words. One night he pulled her by the arm across the driver's seat, back out of the car, and into the house, her legs scraping along the gravel and then the brick walk and steps. She screamed, but soon she made no sound at all. He slapped her face. He punched her in the mouth. Her head hit the floor as she gagged on her own warm blood. He went into the bathroom; she could hear the water running. *He's going to drown me*, she thought. He came back, his hands smelling of soap. He had put on a clean shirt and pants.

He kissed her head and kept telling her how sorry he was. He took her to Hamilton County General and, as they wheeled her to the x-ray department, told them she had been mugged on the street, to spare no expense. In the waiting room he looked worried about her while he watched TV, drank coffee from a machine, and stepped outside to smoke cigarettes.

"Where were you mugged?" A young doctor asked her as he stitched up her lip.

"Rockfield."

"Then why didn't you go Commonwealth or Saint Joe's? What are you doing all the way out here?"

She shrugged her shoulders.

"Do you want to report the – mugging – to the police?"

She didn't answer.

"Look. You don't have to go back with him. We can find you a place to stay. We can call the police. We can help you."

On her way out, he handed her some brochures from the Everywoman's Center: *Warning signs for perpetrator* and *What you should know about your abusive partner.* In the years that followed the hospitals and doctors would change, but the scenes would remain the same. The pamphlets sometimes varied. *Cycle of violence* was a popular one; so was *Is he really going to change?* Whatever the pamphlet, a hotline number appeared in large bold letters at the bottom. She would become used to them, and to the small white cards with a list of emergency numbers they sometimes gave her. She threw them into the trash before she reached the waiting room. The doctors never understood why she wanted to go home with Nick. It wasn't because she was afraid of him. It was because she loved him, and she was sure that, if she could figure out how his mind worked, she would know how to act. She could make the relationship work again, too. She could make it be like before. It was up to her, because deep down, Nick was right: she had turned into a skinny, ugly junkie. She was everything Nick said she was. In a way, she was grateful that Nick *could* hurt her, could make her feel again, though it seemed that he could never beat that evil jinn out of her.

Only the jinn had five heads now: Walter Kornmeyer's, Daniel's, Uncle Oliver's, Isaac's – and Nick's. She kept looking at the five-headed monster as it led her into the bedroom and picked up the pipe and passed it from one head to the other. How could one hit last that long? she wondered. Then the monster passed the pipe to her.

"This'll make you feel better," he said. "I'll never hurt you again."

She climbed into bed; she took the peace offering from the monster, and she forgot that she was losing control over everything. She lay back down on the pillow; she closed her eyes. When she opened them again, it was morning and the monster was gone. Nick was carrying a tray of orange juice, toast, scrambled eggs, and cocaine to her. Breakfast in bed.

They ventured into Rockfield that day. Pure goods from his discreet former dealers had long ago become far too expensive, so Nick dropped her off on a corner of Gaylord Street where he would have stuck out like a white giraffe. She could scurry in and out of those alleys and deteriorating Victorian crack houses with boarded-up windows, caving-in porches, and trash piled high. She could prowl the tenements (their palatial stone-column entrances marred by ugly gray steel doors signifying what Gaylord Street had become) unnoticed, just another black junkie crawling up the anthill, looking for a dealer. Just like Nick had always known she could, from the moment he had seen her in Café Venezia, because he too had always had a plan.

That particular afternoon she turned onto Trumble Street instead and rang India's bell. It had been so many months – or years, she couldn't remember – since Fatma had seen her. She had no right to go there after she'd betrayed them, but India buzzed her in all the same. Nothing had ever ruffled India's calm demeanor. It was like the flat line on some hospital ICU machine and steady as the basket Lisha balanced on her head in the marketplace in Mombasa.

India recoiled on seeing her – more from pity than from anger, yet she let Fatma in.

"What you see?" Fatma asked India, who, her hair elegantly swept up into a tight knot, her nails clean and shiny and long, set two cups of coffee on a blue checkered tablecloth.

"You want to know what I see?"

"What he does when he come to Rockfield?"

India put both palms on the table and leaned her weight onto them.

"He's stinkin' like a dead dog. Pickin' up women. That's what I see. But it's not about what I see." She took Fatma's arm and pulled her out of the chair and over to a mirror. Fatma saw the drug-glazed eyes, the face bruised like a piece of tarnished silver in Auntie's china closet. "It's about what *you* see."

Nick had borrowed money anywhere he could. He sold his coin collection for eighty thousand dollars. When pieces of the jewelry he had bought Fatma disappeared, he tried to convince her that she had lost or misplaced or had never been given them. She was afraid her diamond ring would be next, and she wanted to protect it, not because it was so valuable but because it symbolized their marriage. If it disappeared, so might they. She phoned India, intending to arrange a time when she could give her the ring to hold. Fatma knew it was a stupid thing to do; Nick didn't like her to make phone calls.

She was using the kitchen phone and had barely said hello when Nick told her to come to the sofa and watch a show with him.

"In a minute," she said.

"Now, Princess," he called out. "I need you to come here *now*."

"One minute."

"Fatma, who are you talking to?"

"Nobody."

"Good, because I can't hear the TV with you talking."

Fatma hung up just as India answered. She buried the ring in a can of coffee; Nick never made coffee. She went over to him.

"Why you need me?"

"You know I don't like watching TV by myself."

"I talk low. It don't bother you, Nick."

"Now you're complaining because I want you to be with me?" His voice had climbed an octave without getting louder, as though he was trying to keep it in check. The little red veins on his temples popped out.

"I just say I can't even talk on phone."

"'*Talk on phone*?' You can't even talk!" he said, laughing.

"Stop!"

He kept laughing. She slapped him.

Her face was raw and wet and burning when he finished with her that night. He poured whiskey into her mouth to kill the pain, he said. It dribbled out and set her face on fire. Then he helped her to the bed.

"Jesus, I'm so sorry, Fatma. But you shouldn't have done that. You shouldn't have pushed me. I hope I didn't ruin your beautiful face. Here, Princess. Have some water."

She couldn't move her mouth to swallow anything. Every breath hit her torso like he was kicking her all over again.

She closed her eyes that night. She stopped thinking and feeling. She nearly stopped breathing. The next morning her lawyer phoned out of the blue and told Fatma she had a buyer for the house on Poplar Street – Daniel. Was she interested in selling? Fatma hadn't talked to Jeannine Fournier in years but she had taken her advice. She had held onto the house, never telling Nick. And lately – like so many other things – she'd even forgotten about it.

"Who called?" Nick asked.

"Wrong number."

Then she told him she was pregnant, more to test his response than as an excuse to go to Rockfield. He had never mentioned children again after that one time, never seemed upset that she hadn't conceived.

"What makes you think that?" he asked.

"Same way all women know. I miss periods."

"You've missed them before."

"Never this many."

"It seems like you just had it."

"You confused."

He furrowed his brow as if straining to remember, but she knew he'd never figure it out. He couldn't remember where the bathroom was these days.

Had he been happy about her news, she might have told him about the house – the house he never knew she owned. And she would have tried hard to get pregnant. Instead, she said she was going to Rockfield to arrange for an abortion. Nick said he would have taken her, but he was feeling sick.

She was afraid to see Daniel, who would instantly realize that she had turned into something far worse than the contrary child he had brought out of Katundu. She didn't want him to see her broken, with her cheeks bruised and her Mombasa eye swollen. But Daniel wasn't there.

"It's fallen apart," Jeannine Fournier told Fatma. "I tried to reach you. Daniel got cold feet about moving back into the house. Said he had personal reasons for changing his mind."

"You said who you was when you called me?"

"Almost. But I decided not to. Let's say your husband sounded a bit out of it. Don't worry – there'll be another buyer along soon. The neighborhood is changing for the better." Then she said icily on her way out: "And get yourself some help before it's too late."

A deep sadness began growing inside Fatma that day. It moved from between her ovaries into her uterus and stomach, and up into her heart. On the way home she carried that sadness until her body could no longer contain it, until she thought it might sink down to her vagina and, right there in the taxi, exit in painful convulsions, the way Hussein had.

When she returned she found the front door of the house slightly open. On her way into the bedroom to check on Nick, she heard rustling and groaning. Loan sharks must have finally worked him over, or worse, maybe they were still there. She first went into the kitchen and dug her hands into the coffee can, relieved to find the ring still there. She slipped it back on and grabbed her grandfather's pistol, which she kept in the breadbox they never used for bread, and walked into the bedroom. Nick was on his back, naked, oblivious to Fatma, a woman between his legs, her face in his groin. Then Fatma could see nothing. She could only feel – feel blood rising up, her heart pounding, her stomach muscles tightening, her body hot. The Kikuyu say that if a person is roasting two potatoes at one time, one potato is bound to get charred. She fired twice.

The first shot grazed the woman's butt. Fatma had always been better with a rifle than with a pistol. The woman jerked her head up and screamed. Fatma stared at the blurry image of her face in disbelief. The next shot – aimed at Elsa Martinez's head – missed its target. Fortunately, or Fatma would have gone to prison for life. She shot Nick's thigh instead.

IV

★

Daughters of Muhammad

★★★★★★★★★★ ☆ ★★★★★★★★★★

There were more drugs, of a greater variety and a higher quality, at Shelby County Jail and House of Correction than there were on the streets. Not long after her arrival, Fatma discovered the dealers' circle. It wasn't hard. Seated around a table in the common room, just like the women on Oprah's book club on the TV screen on the wall, and holding playing cards in their hands or setting tiles on a scrabble board, the dealers' circle also discussed things, but it wasn't books. Using code, they learned who had what. "My man came by yesterday. Said my baby girl put on at least five ounces" meant that an inmate had more than that amount of heroin hidden in the library. Shelby allowed inmates to greet their visitors face to face, to kiss hello or goodbye, as long as a correction officer was present in the reception room, a CO who didn't give a damn about an inmate's rehabilitation and saw her time at Shelby as something that would be repeated over and over again.

And so the little packet hidden under the visitor's tongue was easily transferred to the underside of the inmate's tongue. Some of the inmates had brought in their own plastic-wrapped heroin and coke. Held by tightly contracted muscles between the walls of their vaginas, the drugs had escaped detection during the welcoming strip search in which the women were ordered to bend over and cough. They later carried the booty to their cells. There it went under the mattress until they could get it to the library. There it was placed in a bookcase – for example, 150-199, the second shelf from the top at the beginning of the aisle, sixth book in: *Studies in Semantics of Generative Grammar* or another obviously donated book that no one had touched since the day it was shelved. Most inmates hadn't gotten past eighth grade.

At their meetings women who belonged to the dealers' circle set prices, elected leaders, and banished women for weakness or resistance. Transactions were carried out even more discreetly: a quick pass in the library, a pretense of making out with another inmate by kissing her or putting a hand up her shirt or down her pants. Women could have expense accounts at Shelby: they could do just about anything except drive a car and sleep with visitors. Money was transferred from inmate to inmate; a little went a long way in jail. Fatma quickly learned that it was no different on the inside than on the outside – those who had ruled. As always, she wanted to be among those who had, but thanks to Nick's isolating her, she hadn't established close enough friendships with suppliers for them to want to visit her in jail, so she was kept out of the dealers' circle. She could still be a customer, however, since Jeannine Fournier had been right about the house on Poplar Street: it had recently sold, and Fournier, who continued to manage the proceeds, made a monthly deposit into the Shelby account intended for sundries like cigarettes, magazines, and toiletries.

Drugs could also be got from COs in exchange for sex, or were administered by the medical staff to prevent the pain of withdrawal or to sedate difficult inmates. Without the drugs the doctors gave Fatma, she would succumb to uncontrollable fits of rage in an effort to rid herself of Iblis, who, like an alien, was painfully working his way through her insides and threatening at any moment to break through her flesh. She swung at nurses and doctors and COs. She flailed her arms and legs. She cursed and kicked and screamed. When they approached her with needles or pills, she knocked the trays out of their hands, until they strapped her down and injected her. After three months in Shelby waiting for her trial, she felt crazier than ever. She should have expected it, she thought. *Those who seek revenge should always remember to dig two graves.*

"We'll ask for a jury trial," her court-appointed attorney, Bernard Kosakowski, told Fatma as she sat across the table from him in the orange jumpsuit that signified she was a pretrial. "A jury will be sympathetic to you. More women than men serve on juries. A woman would certainly understand the overwhelming urge you had to shoot your husband, having found him and your friend in a tryst." *Tryst.* It was a word she had never heard before: probably an old-fashioned one, because Kosakowski's skin hung from his jawbone like hide from a dead goat's carcass. His blue eyes swam in pools of yellow and his hand trembled when he scribbled down things Fatma said.

Nick invoked what Kosakowski called marital privilege and refused to testify against her, much to the district attorney's disappointment.

"Don't think this is because he loves you," Kosakowski said. "He knows this business. He knows I'll make drugs a case and in turn make him look unreliable and guilty to boot. Of course, you won't look squeaky clean in any scenario."

Fatma had told Kosakowski how Nick must have made Elsa hide the coke and paraphernalia in a drainpipe and then stuff some socks and briefs up it to keep the junk from falling out. That had always been their plan should the police show up at their home for any reason.

"Unfortunately, you aren't married to Elsa. The DA will certainly call her, and she can't be too pleased with the burn on her behind. I'll get the jury to see her as an unreliable witness – slip that lousy record of hers in there by accident."

The jury selection and trial were over in two days. The eight women and four men seemed to regard everyone concerned, including Kosakowski, as unreliable, and were eager to have the whole thing done with. The judge sentenced Fatma to two years for shooting Nick, one for carrying a firearm without a license, and five years' probation for attempting to shoot Elsa. She was upgraded to a green jumpsuit, which meant she wouldn't be leaving Shelby anytime soon.

Shelby was a coed facility, with men and women housed in separate buildings that were right next to each other. There were more men than women, and the men had the run of the place. The women could hear the men marching on the grounds as though they were in boot camp – a drill instructor shouting, the men chanting back. When the women arrived or when they were being taken to and from court, the women could see them shooting hoops in their airy recreation deck. And the women knew that the men thought they were better than the women.

The women's recreation deck was a fifty-by-fifty-foot room between the first and third floors with only one screened wall to remind women that there was an outside. "Can't even see a bird fly overhead, sugars," Miss Sarah, the deputy superintendent, said with her southern twang, angry that the men had so many more privileges.

When Fatma stood in the corner of the deck, Lauinger never failed to show up. His stocky body was too big for his legs, which looked as though they must have been cut off at the knees. Fatma never played basketball or volleyball or kickball as the other women did. Women didn't do such things where she grew up. Instead, she'd lean against the wall and pretend she had better things to do than run around like a brainless hen in a coop.

"Cunt," Lauinger would whisper in her ear. "Stupid fucking African cunt. Can't even kick a little ball. Can't even speak English. Stupid African cunt."

The showers were ranged along the wall of the common room, and male COs like Lauinger, stationed up on the catwalks or on the floor, eyed the women as they walked to and fro and waited for a breast or pubic hair to peek out of their loosely drawn robes. That's why Fatma didn't like to take showers, even though they were allowed three a week. One day, though, she had gotten to the point where she couldn't stand the smell of her body, so she scooped up her soap and towel and marched through the common room. She was about to open the shower curtain when Lauinger stopped her and pushed her against the wall, acting as if he were checking out her assigned time. He moved his thigh between her legs for a second; he was famous for doing this, but the women would be sent to segregation if they made a fuss. Miss Sarah tried to keep her eye on COs like him, but she couldn't be everywhere at once, and she couldn't risk losing COs.

"I can get you whatever you want," he whispered. "Crack, heroin, privileges. See you in your cell at lights-out?"

"Fuck you." The thought of Lauinger's body on her was disgusting.

His nostrils flared, and little orange hairs stuck out like needles on a porcupine. "Stupid fucking African cunt."

She kicked him with the same force she had used to punch Nick, but she didn't stop there. While he was bent over cupping his balls and writhing in pain, she boxed his ears. Before she knew it she was off to the "hole," because they said she was out of control.

They wore blue in the disciplinary segregation unit. Fatma assumed blue was supposed to have a soothing effect. Here there were no privileges: no TV, no radio, no hardcover books. You got one hour of recreation a day, but only in shackles. A five-month-pregnant hooker was brought into the cell next to Fatma's, where she wailed morning and night because she could not be taken off methadone on account of her pregnancy. She imagined that the methadone was killing her baby. Perhaps that would be better, Fatma thought, since they were going to take the baby away from her anyway, just as Hussein had been taken away from Fatma in another world long ago. Still, the hooker kept wailing, and the memory that Fatma had tried so hard to bury worked its way up like rising dough until it perched on the tip of her brain and dove all the way down to her heart.

"Shut your fucking mouth!" Fatma screamed over and over again at the top of her lungs.

"Bitch!" Lauinger said, and took her up to Mental Health, where they wore purple. Valium was their first choice to calm her, but it took too long to kick in. So did Ativan. The injections kept coming until she became deaf to the world.

"This is a goddamn shame," Fatma heard Miss Sarah mutter under her breath. "You can't work with a person on benzos." Miss

Sarah thought no one could hear her, but Fatma did. Fatma wanted to tell Miss Sarah so, but she was so drugged up she couldn't even form a word. *I hear you, Miss Sarah*, she wanted to say. *I hear you, Auntie*.

When Fatma was let out of Mental Health, Miss Sarah tried to persuade her to take some of the courses offered at Shelby, such as Channeling Your Anger or Surviving Trauma. Fatma enrolled in art class and made postcards. She drew palm trees next to a toilet, or orange groves behind an electric chair, or a noose dangling from a tree. Her artwork was juvenile, like that of a first grader, but the messages she wrote on them for Nick were clear: "Miss(ed) you, but I won't next time." She sent her postcards to the house of the five-headed monster and waited for a response that never came. Then she quit the class.

Fatma finally agreed to sit in on a class called Breaking the Silence, but she wouldn't open her mouth. She listened to other women's stories – their fear, their feelings of helplessness and loss of control. She always found ways to differentiate herself from them and Nick from their brutal husbands and boyfriends. Her teacher suggested that she take an addiction education class instead. "You'll never win one until you deal with the other," Miss Sarah agreed. She sat through a few classes, missed most, and learned nothing. When the course was over, she went to graduation not because she was graduating but because Miss Sarah had asked her to go.

The ceremony was held in the chapel, which was decorated with two pots of white lilies on a table in front of the crucifix. Miss Sarah wore her tangerine colored suit. She usually wore bright colors to lift their spirits, Fatma supposed, but on occasions like graduation she favored lime green or raspberry pink or lemon yellow, because she said those days were as special as a bowl of sherbet on a sweltering summer day. The county sheriff spoke about his commitment to the women of Shelby. "There is a lot of good in me. I do have strengths," he told them to repeat to themselves every morning and every time they felt on the verge of relapsing. He was tall and trim, with thick white hair parted on the side, and he seemed anxious to get the graduation over with so that he could go back to more important things like his job, or maybe out to lunch so he could have a drink. The graduates nodded and clapped, a sea of green uniforms in the wooden pews.

The guest speaker was a former addict. They always were. Kendra had wiry orange hair and freckles that matched Miss Sarah's outfit, and she told the story of her life with drugs, which started at age six. By eight she was out of the house, stealing to support her habit and to get away from her alcoholic father. Twenty-five now, she looked forty, her thin white skin prematurely wrinkled from drugs and alcohol. She had found God, who had helped with her rehab and her three kids. "Recovery is so hard, especially for those of you with children. Only God loves your kids more than you do. Get down on your knees and rely on God to take care of them while you're in recovery." She had a good job now: people trusted her. Fatma thought no one would ever trust her again like that.

"None of you are just statistics," Miss Sarah said. "Like Kendra, you've all come from someplace. You all have stories. You all have reasons."

One of the graduates belted out a black gospel song that filled everyone's eyes with tears and brought the house down. Miss Sarah presented the awards: Inmate of the Month to the woman who had made significant improvement, Woman of Distinction to a tearful Manuela Aguilar, who had made the most. When the graduates had received their certificates, it was all over. The women went back to their cells.

"Still angry at the world? Still fighting yourself?" Miss Sarah sat down alongside Fatma in the common room afterward. "Life's hard, sugar. But we can learn how to make it easier."

Fatma trusted Miss Sarah, although she knew nothing about her except that she watched over her – over all of them.

"What does your name mean?" Fatma asked, to Miss Sarah's surprise.

"Sarah? I think it means princess," she said, giving a little laugh as though she was embarrassed to have such a regal name. "My daddy was a farmer down south. Where does you name come from?" she asked in turn.

"Fatimah, daughter of Muhammad."

It was a dreary late autumn day when they told Fatma she had a visitor. She had awoken to the sound of rain several times during the night, which was unusual because she was sleeping soundly these days. She was back on drugs, compliments of a new CO who asked for nothing but money in return. The rain that woke her was heavy and pounded against the narrow strip of windowpane in her cell. In the morning she could see that the trees on the edge of the prison grounds were bare. The rain had taken the leaves down and blanketed the sidewalk and parking lot with what looked like a soggy orange, red, and gold quilt.

She didn't know whom to expect as she walked into the reception room. No one ever came to see her. There was only one person she could think of who would always be able to find her, but she was too far gone to primp even for him. She had taken a look at her reflection in the metal mirror of her cell: her eyes were puffy from too much sleep and greasy strands of hair fell around her face while the rest was loosely tied back with an elastic band. She hadn't showered for days. Without makeup, her complexion seemed as green as her uniform, and her visitor's exquisite appearance only made Fatma feel uglier. The visitor wore a white trench coat with a belt cinched tightly around her almost nonexistent waist. Her long body bent in a graceful arc as she reached down toward her extended foot to remove some leaves stuck to the heel of her high black leather boot. She looked as if she were assuming one of the yoga postures Fatma had learned in exercise class. Slender fingers with red-painted tips peeled the dripping hood off her head. Her highlighted hair was pulled back into an elegant knot, making her black eyes seem even bigger, her small nose rounder, her lips fuller. Perfectly applied makeup gave her skin a flawless, airbrushed appearance. She had been well named, for *Jamila* meant "beautiful." She looked at Fatma and blinked: two black spiders gently swept over her eyes.

"Jamila?" Fatma didn't think she was real.

She stiffly put her arms around Fatma, as though this was what she should do in front of the CO. She pretended she didn't want to get Fatma wet, but Fatma knew Jamila didn't want to touch her. She might have been an actress, but she couldn't hide her repulsion at seeing Fatma in such shabby condition. She loosened her belt and unfastened the coat's buttons but she didn't take it off, making it clear that she wasn't staying long.

Fatma hadn't seen her half sister since Jamila was eight, long before Jamila had been discovered by the English photographer, but she recognized her immediately. She'd watched her mature on the covers of teen magazines and in films. The only child of Fatma's father's relationship with Jamila's mother, Jamila had inherited her mother's dusky copper-colored skin and long neck, and their father's height. A little younger than Fatma, she had never had much to do with the rest of Fatma's family. When she was eighteen she was cast in a James Bond film and became every man's fantasy. Despite her lack of talent, her beauty captivated audiences. It was her marriage to a famous British actor that really made her famous.

"What you're doing here?" Fatma asked.

"What are *you* doing here?" She spoke English perfectly, with a British accent.

"How did you find me?"

"Brother Hamal gave our sister Rihana your phone number and address – I used to see Rihana on occasion when I was on modeling assignments in Milan, and Hamal guessed she'd be able to get in touch with me. He knows I travel to America."

She paused. Her eyes darted around the room as though she was searching for a cue card or anything to stare at other than Fatma, but the entire place made her uncomfortable. Settling on a spot, she continued.

"There was no one with your name at that phone number, so I went to the address on Main Street, but the people in the store below said that you had remarried and moved. They gave me your husband's name to look up. When I called, he said I would find you here." Her voice trailed off.

"He said anything else?"

"No. Just to send you his best."

"How you get to Rockfield?" Fatma tried not to slur her words. She forced open her eyelids, but they were too heavy to stay that way for long.

"I'm on location in New York. I took a limo."

"That must shake up Luccheses, you coming for *me* in limo! How come you never look for me before?"

Jamila stared at the floor, somewhat embarrassed.

"I was young, trying to make a name for myself. I couldn't take the time. In the beginning you have to do what everyone else wants you to do. You can't imagine what that's like."

"I can."

"Besides, I didn't come to America *that* often. I was lucky to get small parts. I still don't come that often. Let's be honest, Fatma, we were never really close."

"You go back?"

"To Somalia?" She looked at Fatma as if she were insane. "Do you know what's going on there? They hate all of us."

"A lot of family – *my* family – is left there?"

"I guess."

"You help them?"

"It was just a fluke how I left. I couldn't even get my mother out in time. She only permitted me to go with the photographer because she knew it would be my last opportunity to leave." Her expression saddened. "Money can't buy everything, you know. They said my mother died of pneumonia soon after I left. I think she starved to death. I assume those who left early enough are scattered now all over Europe, Morocco, Kenya, Nigeria."

"I'm only one here? In America?"

"Yes, according to Rihana."

"You know how my auntie is?"

She took a breath, as though they had finally gotten to the meat of this reunion. "Hamal wrote to Rihana and told her that your auntie had a stroke. He and Rihana were hoping I could find you on one of my visits here and tell you. Your auntie asks for you. It's her one wish – to see you. You *are* her daughter, you know." Jamila's voice carried a tone of reprimand.

"They know about me?"

"No. And I won't tell them if you don't want me to. As I said, I don't really keep in touch. I can tell Rihana I didn't find you."

"I saw one time you get married to Michael Randall," Fatma said.

"We're divorced. I'm engaged to François Paquette, the French skier." She held out her left hand for Fatma to admire the large oval diamond held high on white gold prongs. Fatma was sorry she couldn't show Jamila *her* ring, but it was being held for her at the jail, along with the few belongings she had come in with. Fatma had never heard of François Paquette.

They talked some more, mostly about the time they had gone on safari with their father. Of all Fatma's father's children, Jamila was the closest in age to Fatma, and their father had once brought Jamila along on Fatma's annual birthday outing with him. Fatma had been jealous of her then: it was supposed to have been her time alone with her father. She also hated the way their father catered to Jamila, the way he lifted her delicate body and dreamily brought her extraordinary face close to his, as though he were taking in the scent of a fragrant flower. Jamila changed the subject and told Fatma what living in England was like.

She got up as though she had heard the whistle for a train she was about to board. She seemed glad to have this ordeal almost behind her.

"Can I help you?" she asked, knotting her belt. For a moment she appeared sincere.

"No, I don't think so. Thank you." *Maybe if you had found me sooner,* Fatma wanted to say.

She fished in her black alligator purse for a pen; she wrote her number on a folded tissue, and handed it to Fatma as though to say: *Whatever it's worth.*

"Your pictures are popular in here."

"Great," Jamila said, rolling her big eyes. She got up and hugged Fatma, this time more warmly. "I have to go now."

"Your limo waiting?"

"Yes."

"What color?"

"White."

"Like your raincoat."

"You still have them!" Jamila eyed the tattoos on Fatma's arms.

Fatma hadn't thought about them in years; they had faded so much she had forgotten they were there. Even Nick had mistaken them for black and blue marks.

"And you?" Fatma asked.

"I had them removed years ago."

"Goodbye." That was all Jamila said. What else could she say? *Gee, I'm sorry your life is in shambles. Thank God our father isn't alive to see you.* They hadn't promised to keep in touch – they knew better than to promise anything. For Jamila, the visit had probably alleviated some of the guilt for not having tried to find Fatma earlier and perhaps for not helping the rest of the family. But for Fatma, not since the visit with her father in Washington had Africa seemed so close: she could touch it; she could smell it; she could hear it. A longing for it gnawed at her stomach. She was starving.

She cried that night. She cried for the suffering her family endured. She cried for her auntie, who was sick and whom she had disgraced. She cried for the child she had abandoned, wondering if he even knew that across continents there existed another mother – his real mother. She cried out of humiliation for the pathetic condition that Jamila had found her in. She cried for war-torn Somalia. She cried for herself.

Her family had undergone the unthinkable, and still they had maintained their dignity, on that she would have bet her life. There was no dignity in selling mothers of innocent children poison. There was no pride in being beaten by her husband; her father had treated her mother like a goddess. She looked down at the tattoos on her arms and cried for the life that was slipping away. She cried into the night. She cried the next day. She cried for a week. She cried until the tears no longer came, and the water seemed to well up inside her, trapped. She cried until the wet sobbing became the dry moaning of a wounded animal in the desert, until her thoughts lost their clarity and she no longer knew why she cried at all.

In the days after Jamila's visit she longed to write to Auntie, to speak to her, but she couldn't until she got herself straight. If Jamila kept her promise of silence, the family might continue to consider her merely selfish and rude and ungrateful. She would return eventually, and when she got there, she would be whole and beautiful and loving, and they would love her back. She would make it up to all of them. Now she was getting ahead of herself, because there was much to do before her plans could take shape: an empty sack cannot stand, her mother always said. But her time at Shelby was almost up, and she had wasted most of it.

She was afraid to leave Shelby, to face the outside again. Then, just when the trees beyond the fence were the palest green and the air smelled like rain and a new beginning, she had another visitor.

Nick was tanned and healthy looking when he planted a kiss on her cheek. She turned away.

"I've missed you, babe."

"Well, I don't miss you."

"That's not what your postcards said."

"You get them?"

He nodded.

"Bastard," she said.

"I've been away – Florida. I needed to sort things out."

She didn't know how to behave. She was angry and excited at the same time.

"I don't blame you for being pissed off, but shouldn't I be the one to carry the grudge? After all, *you* shot *me*." His smile said he knew her better than she did herself, that despite anything she said or did, he knew what the outcome of his visit would be.

"And I would do it again," she told him.

"I didn't testify against you," he reminded her. "Doesn't that carry any weight?"

Her heart soared, but she kept her face expressionless. He asked her to sit down with him on the sofa.

"I've done a lot of thinking this past year and a half, Fatma. And I've done a lot of work. No more drugs. No more booze. I'm trying. I swear. And I'm going to help you stay clean too – after all, it was me who really got you into this mess." He looked down. "I fucked up big-time."

Fatma was silent. She wished there was a glass wall between them and they were talking through a telephone, so great was her urge to touch him. He was her worst addiction.

"Why somebody else?" she asked. "Why Elsa?"

"Men are weak, Fatma. And when you're not with me, I'm

even weaker. I made a big mistake. But I've changed. Living without you has taught me a lesson."

"What lesson?"

"I need you."

"Me and you like oil and water," she said, knowing full well they were more like a magnet and a piece of iron.

"I moved into a new condo on the waterfront in Rockfield. I've even got the practice back on its feet. It'll take some time to get it to where it was. It may never be exactly there, but it's going well. I put in some calls to a guy I went to law school with who works for the State Department. He thinks he can find a way for us to get your son here for good. Hussein Kornmeyer, right?"

"Al-Nassar. My mother's family name."

Remember me? Your flesh and blood? a sleeping voice within her said. *The one you let go of. The one who still clings to your insides like moss does to stone. The one who, like the sun and the moon, will never go away. The source of all your sadness.*

Nick took her hand in his. It was large and smooth and warm. She let him. "I'd like you to come home with me," he said. "I want to take care of you. I don't know if you've heard, but there's a nut out there. It's not safe, and I'm worried about you."

She knew all about what was going on in Rockfield: a serial killer on the loose whose targets were black female addicts. Women were breaking parole to be sent back to jail, just to get off the streets. One woman's frozen naked body had been found in an alley off Gaylord Street, pantyhose stuffed down her throat. Another was discovered in her home, her nude body sodomized with a vase. Yet another had been found under some bushes behind the post office, propped up in a grotesque sexual position. All had been raped and strangled. Every new inmate had come in with stories.

"I need go to Mombasa. My auntie's sick."

"I know."

"You come back, Nick?"

"Every visiting day. We can do it, Princess. We can start over. Trust me."

Nick did return – every Sunday for the next three months. She began to take her shower on Saturdays. She bought perfume and deodorant and mouthwash from the Shelby store. She took care to fix her hair the way he liked it. But when he showed up, she was nasty to him. He absorbed her abuse as if it were something he deserved and expected. After five or six visits, she began to soften and hungered for his hand on hers, his hello and goodbye kisses, first on her cheek, then on her lips.

The morning she was released she left with Nick, against the advice of Miss Sarah, who slipped her card into Fatma's pants pocket on her way out. Fatma got into his car just as she had on the day of the feast years before. He said they could be like Isaac and India, who had finally gone straight and bought a house and a dry cleaning business in Worcester. The last he'd heard, India was pregnant. They would travel, Nick said – back to Africa and Saudi Arabia. Back to Mombasa.

His condo was a remodeled paper factory set between Silva's Fish Market and Lambert's Restaurant Supply. From the balcony of the condo, you didn't see them or the decaying city; all you saw was the river and the beautiful bridge that arched from Rockfield to Carlington, where Daniel had first brought her. And so Nick took her to the balcony, where she made the mistake of looking straight ahead and never behind.

"A toast to a new beginning." Nick held out a glass of champagne. "Just a toast, that's all," he insisted.

*

She'd been out only a few weeks when Nick suggested they take a vacation in Key West, where he said he'd been living for a good part of the time she was in jail. He wanted to show her the place that had helped him get it all together.

"What about my probation officer?"

"I'll call him for you. He won't mind if you skip one or two visits."

"I don't know, Nick."

"*Come on*, Princess, I've already arranged time off." He was annoyed, and those little red veins popped out at his temples.

"Okay, Nick."

"You're happy about this, aren't you, Princess?"

"Yes, Nick. I'm happy."

They went shopping for beach clothes. He bought her bikinis and robes and hats and strapless long dresses for the evenings of dining and dancing on the pier. He bought her a pair of sunglasses with 14-karat gold designs on the frames. He didn't know what to do to make it all up to her. It was he who undressed her now and tried everything to bring her pleasure, and she remembered how much she had missed being loved.

They flew down to Miami and rented a red convertible, because Nick thought it would be fun to drive to the Keys instead of taking another flight. He sang all the way: "Runnin' down the road tryin' to loosen my load / I got seven women on my mind ..." And Fatma laughed as they crossed bridge after bridge connecting the islands. She pulled her hair into a ponytail, but the wind was strong and whipped it around her head. Strands of hair escaped and stung her cheeks. They drove so far, to the end of Key West, she thought they would go right into the water.

"This is where we'll watch the most magnificent sunset and eat fresh mahi mahi and Key lime pie. Hear that?" he said of the Spanish music on the radio. "It's from Cuba."

"How close we are?" she asked.

"Ninety miles or so."

"Let's go!"

"Why would you want to, even if we could?" he asked, laughing.

"I think it be nice there. Like heaven. Like Mombasa."

A Higher Power

********** ⭐ **********

Fatma should have known when they pulled into the Sunny Glow Motel that something was wrong: Nick never stayed in places like that. He liked valet parking and bellboys and room service. Her father had taught her never to drop the stick until the snake is dead, but she was hot and sticky and tired from the long day of travel. She went to take a shower; Nick brought in their luggage.

When she stepped out of the bathroom, with the thin scratchy towel barely covering her breasts and fanny, Nick's eyes had the expression of a rabid dog. He had never forgotten the shooting; he hadn't testified only because he had wanted her to get alone to seek his own form of justice. This time he didn't wait for her to take the first punch. His hands dug into her shoulders; the skin on her hip and leg burned as he dragged her along the carpet. His grip tightened; her head crashed into the wall. Fists met her eyes, then her mouth; her teeth cut her tongue and the insides of her lips. Next she was flying through the air like a rag doll. She lay curled up where she landed. He kicked her in the back and tried to pull the diamond ring off her finger, but he couldn't. "Fucking bitch!" she heard him say. "I'm gonna kill you. By the way, I had a vasectomy twenty years ago, and I have no friends in Washington."

It was dark when she came to. She didn't know how long she'd been lying there or whether Nick was on his way back to offer her a fix or finish her off. She crawled over to her suitcase and dressed. When she phoned the front desk and asked for a taxi, the clerk told her she owed him for two days. "Fuck it," he said when he saw her hobbling out of the room.

She had only enough money for taxis, so she called Jeannine Fournier and asked her to have a ticket waiting at the Key West airport. The attendants there were kind, trying to understand the words she uttered through clenched jaws. They called for a cart to drive her to the gate, and in Hartford they arranged for a taxi from Bradley Airport to Commonwealth Medical Center.

Her eyes were swollen shut as they wheeled her into X-ray, but she heard loud and clear a familiar voice, and she dropped her head so the woman speaking couldn't see her.

"Fatma?" Pia whispered, kneeling in front of her broken friend. "Is that you?"

The injection they gave her for the ruptured disk barely relieved the pain radiating from her lower back to her buttocks and down her leg like a steady bolt of lightning. So they admitted her and fed her more drugs that wrapped her in that blanket of numbness and sent her traveling so far in her dreams that she found herself in Mombasa, walking up Biashara Street. Only it didn't look like Biashara Street, at all but Main Street in Rockfield.

"Who are you? Where are you going?" Pia asked. She was wearing a black *buibui*.

"You speak very good English," Fatma said.

"I studied hard. Now tell me, where are you going?"

"*Nyumbani*," she said in Swahili. Home.

"Speak English. Everyone speaks English here now. No one understands Swahili anymore."

Fatma couldn't remember which way it was to Auntie's house, and so she walked and walked in the town she had known like the palm of her hand. The more she walked, the more lost she got. Then she saw the blue Indian Ocean behind the tall towers where the lawyers worked, and she knew that Auntie's house was near. She began to run, but she never reached the ocean. Another woman in a *buibui* appeared again out of an alley. It was her old maid Lisha, and Fatma was ecstatic with relief.

"Lisha, take me to Auntie."

"Where are your clothes?" she asked coldly.

Fatma looked down and saw she was naked.

"You are not Fatma," Lisha said. "You are American. American women are naked."

"I am not naked. I had a towel. I must have dropped it."

"Maybe Iblis took it from you. Do you remember Iblis?"

"Yes."

"You did not listen to me. You walked under the baobab when you should not have. You are not Fatma. You are not an American. You are Iblis now. Shame on you. Go now. Go away. Shame on you. Go. It's time for the parade."

A large statue of the Madonna was being paraded by a bunch of little children. She was dressed in the same clothes as the Madonna in Rockfield, only she was not the Madonna, she was Auntie – a giant Auntie. And she was headed toward Fatma.

"She does not know you anymore," Lisha said. "Go."

"Wait!" Fatma cried. "Please. I am Fatma. Take me home."

She tried to speak English, but the words came out in Swahili. The children kept marching; the statue came closer, until it was about to run her down.

"What's wrong, honey?"

"*Gina langu ni Fatma*," she sobbed. I am Fatma.

"Fatma," the nurse said. "That's right, honey. That's what your chart says. Just a bad dream. Here, this'll make you sleep better. No more bad dreams." The nurse injected her arm. "Just nice ones."

In the morning she asked for her clothes. An orderly brought her the brown paper bag containing her belongings, saying her doctor would have to discharge her before she could go. And if the doctor wouldn't? She would leave on her own; she was good at running away.

"Where do you think you're going?" Pia said when she found her dressing.

The swelling had subsided somewhat, and she could see Pia better now. She wore a white jacket and her hair was cut short.

"You look beautiful. Like grown-up lady."

"I *am* grown up."

"What you're doing here?"

"I'm a resident here. I was in Boston for a few years, but I've come back. My mother isn't well."

"Like mine."

"Is your auntie sick?"

"You my doctor?" Fatma managed. It was too hard to explain anything else.

"No. But the doctor who admitted you yesterday will be in to see you soon. Who did this to you, Fatma? And where's Nick?"

She put her head down.

"Oh my God, Fatma. It was him."

"I need to go."

"You can't even walk."

But she couldn't stay there with the drugs and the patient moaning in the bed next to her, the constant pricking of needles and drawing of blood, the strange hands all over her body. She needed to go. Pia was a doctor; she must have known all along about Fatma: Fatma's interior must always have been as open to Pia as those of the cadavers she worked on in medical school.

"What can I do for you?" she asked.

"Call Miss Sarah."

"Sarah who?"

Fatma had no idea what her last name was or what had happened to the card she had given her. "At Shelby. At jail," she whispered, hoping to soften the admission of where she'd been. "Just say Miss Sarah. They know."

She took the ring off her finger and offered it to Pia. "Keep this for me." It was too nasty out on the street, and she didn't want to lose a finger for it.

"If I were you I'd sell it, or better yet, I'd throw it away."

During her stay in the hospital, they treated her eyes with drops that were more effective than anything she'd used before. They also hooked her up to machines that diverted the messages her damaged vertebra sent to her brain. She was given massage and physical therapy, but only drugs alleviated the dull aches and burning spasms.

"I always want to be on my own," she told Miss Sarah when she arrived. "I make so many mistakes."

"We all make mistakes, sugar. Some just show more than others. Some have greater consequences."

"What I do now?"

"You violated your probation. Missed two visits. If you're brought up in front of a judge, he'll send you back to Shelby."

"But Nick called the probation officer. He said it's okay."

Miss Sarah looked at her as though to say, You still believe in him?

Fatma should have known that Nick would never kill her; he would never jeopardize his freedom with a murder charge. She should have known there was no breaking probation without consequences; Nick had planned to have her locked up again.

"Under the circumstances, I might be able to convince your probation officer and the judge of an alternative," Miss Sarah said.

Miss Wilma wasn't as sweet as Miss Sarah or as cold as Jeannine Fournier. Behind a slight stature and eyes like two pieces of coal set into smooth mahogany-colored skin lurked a mind as quick as a fox's. There was nothing phony about her, from her alligator shoes and tailored suits to her matching silk scarves, gold jewelry, and frank tongue. She didn't waste time telling Fatma and other new arrivals to Haven House that she was the product of alcoholic parents and a heroin-addict husband who had overdosed at thirty-five, because she made one thing very clear: you either kept up with Miss Wilma and life at Haven House, or they moved on without you.

Even though Fatma had come from the hospital, they deloused her at Haven House as if she'd come from prison or the street. They gave her a urine test and made her shower several times. Then, after Miss Sarah left, Miss Wilma took her down to the cellar, where there were racks and racks of clothing according to size.

"They're donated," she said. "The underwear is new, a gift from Sundry Undies here in Willowsville. Pick out something to sleep in, something to wear every day, and something you'll feel special in. When you graduate, you'll get a twenty-five-dollar gift certificate to the Salvation Army Store."

Fatma pulled off the rack the first three things she saw.

"Which one's for every day and which one makes you feel special?" Miss Wilma asked, eyeing the flannel work shirt, the sweatshirt, and a pair of jeans at least three sizes too large for Fatma. "Life's about making choices, good ones, and here's where you start. Try again."

Fatma found a pair of jeans in her size. She kept the sweatshirt, which was just like the one Pia used to wear. She then selected a yellow cotton nightshirt, a pair of black velvet pants, and a cream-colored lace blouse that was missing a few buttons. She was already wearing black heels.

"You'll need a comfortable pair of shoes to work in." Miss Wilma pointed to a shelf lined with everything from slippers to knee-high suede boots. Fatma grabbed a pair of worn sneakers. She took three pairs of panties out of a cardboard box that had "Medium" written on it, and fished for a size 34 bra out of another box marked A. All the underwear was ridiculously sexy for a bunch of women living together.

"I'll give you a needle and thread and some buttons. The most important thing you'll learn here is to care," she said. "About yourself."

"No maid service?" Fama said as she had to Daniel on her first day in Katundu.

Miss Wilma didn't think this was funny. She raised her eyebrows. Another privileged one, she thought. Just like the congressman's daughter who was there, because Fatma was also paying for her stay at Haven House, unlike many of the women sent by the courts. That had been part of the deal. The money came from the same place it had when she was in Shelby: the sale of the house on Poplar Street. "You come first," Miss Sarah had insisted. "Worry about your family later, because without Haven House, there won't be any visits back home."

Haven House was a two-story white clapboard tucked away in a wooded area a few miles from the center of Willowsville. There was no fancy trim or shutters on the building. It had a kitchen and a living room, two bathrooms, three bedrooms, and a year-round porch that Miss Wilma used for her office. Although the furniture was clearly secondhand (like the lavender leather couch with duct tape covering a few tears), every inch of Haven House was immaculate. Four other women were there during Fatma's stay. She shared a room with Justine – the youngest, the congressman's daughter. She was only nineteen, the victim of one bad mistake. She was shy, naïve, and malleable, which made her an excellent target for harassment.

Laurel had just finished doing ten years at the state prison in Framingham for killing the husband who had beat on her for twelve years. Haven House cut down on her prison time. Sweet spirituals flowed through the space left by her missing front teeth like a breeze through a window on a hot summer day as she cleaned or did other chores. Mary Ellen was a born liar who sweet-talked you this way and that, twisting the truth and making no sense at all. Teresa was the bully, no bigger than Fatma but with a mouth as wide as the Grand Canyon and a tongue to match.

"So much pink," Fatma said to Miss Wilma when she showed Fatma to her room.

"My, ain't we fussy. When your creative juices start flowing, you can redecorate."

Living in Haven House was different than being locked up in jail, where the outside was restricted to glimpses of trees and the parking lot through a six-inch-wide window or the sole open wall of the recreation deck. At Haven House Fatma felt the nip of frost on her neck when she rose at sunrise to perform her community service. She would sweep the downtown streets or rake newly fallen leaves from the lawn of the town common, where a local band played in the gazebo in the evenings. She sat next to a child who tried to trap tropical fish on the side of a glass tank in the dentist's waiting office. When she stepped out of AA meetings at the Unitarian church or sessions with her counselor, she met mothers guiding baby carriages, shoppers carrying bags of freshly baked bread, and young people with green hair sitting at tables on the sidewalk, laughing and sipping coffee through pierced lips. At Haven House, waking up at dawn really did mean seeing the light of day.

Yet even in little Willowsville – with its pizzeria, microbrewery, and café with exposed brick walls on the inside – scum floated. Pushers looked for the weak link, the chink in the armor. They showed up in the courthouse lobby and waited for the parole or probation officer to disappear into the restroom just long enough for the probationer to step outside for a fix. They hid in the shadows, waiting to give the vulnerable the swift kick that would smash the fragile shells they had constructed.

Miraa comes from the leaves and bark of a tree that grows in the muddy state of Meru, in Kenya. Somali travelers used to chew its woody stems to stay awake and feel confident while going long distances. It made them feel good. Fatma's old maid Lisha had a cousin in Lamu named Kalil, who chewed *miraa* much of the time. Kalil, however, had a good jinn who monitored his behavior. When Kalil chewed *miraa*, or drank alcohol, or neglected to pray five times a day, the jinn would possess him, and Kalil would cut himself with sharp objects, scratching the skin all over his body, or slam himself against walls. People in town would watch him and think he was going mad, Lisha said. And he was, but at the hands of his *good* jinn, who sought to have the craziness take a toll on Kalil, so that Kalil would come to understand that if he behaved he acted sanely, but if he sinned he was possessed.

While Fatma's evil jinn might have gotten her into trouble in America, it was her good jinn that now tortured her. There was nowhere to hide at Haven House. Not even sleep protected her. In her dreams Nick found her; they all found her. Some nights she ran up Gaylord Street naked, shackles weighing her down, but Nick always managed to run over her with his convertible filled with flowers, crushing her lungs beneath the tires. Other nights he shot at her with her grandfather's gun. Sometimes he got out of the car and strangled Fatma. If it wasn't Nick, it was Elsa. She'd pry open the door to Fatma's old apartment on Main Street with a knife and then chip away at Fatma as though she were a block of ice, taking shallow stabs all over, until Fatma was bleeding like a fountain with a hundred spouts. Miss Wilma would find Fatma in the morning, sitting on the edge of the pink bed, watching out for the sleep that always came to destroy her. She would find her with her skin all scratched, nails bloody, a sheet wrapped tightly around her neck, face and knuckles bruised, the wall stained.

"You're safe," Miss Wilma would say, wiping her sweaty body with a cool washcloth. "You're safe."

She *was* safe, and she hated it. Because the more she got herself straight, the more her jinns battled for attention and the worse her nights became, the more she wanted a drink and a fix, the more she needed to ease the pain.

"To stay sober and straight, you have to believe in a higher power," Miss Wilma said. "Because we can't do it alone; we can't do it our way. Our way is negative. But spirituality is positive. If you're doing something that's wrong, you know it can't be related to anything spiritual, because spirituality is a good thing. That and service to community."

But belief in a higher power had been the source of Fatma's trouble in the first place. Her mother's hatred of Christians and her sense of superiority even over Somalis had led her to manipulate Fatma with promises. And so while Fatma was sweeping Main Street and her overseer stepped into Dunkin' Donuts for a cup of coffee, Fatma walked off down an alley and several blocks over to the bus station, where she took out the hundred-dollar bill she had slipped in her vagina the day she left the Sunny Glow Motel and later tucked into the lacy black bra that Sundry Undies had donated. Like a love note she had kept the piece of green paper each day between the folds of her breasts, and on that warm late summer morning, she bought a ticket for the 6:20, all the while listening to the voice within that promised that if she rode the bus long enough, it would take her all the way to Saudi Arabia, it would take her to Hussein. But she never made it to Saudi Arabia; the last stop was Rockfield.

THE CLOSET

********** ⭐ **********

S he didn't notice the students boarding the bus to New York or
the old women holding shopping bags from Toys R Us to take to
their grandchildren. She smelled the piss of a man urinating on the
side of the building while a pimp cursed a teenage hooker wearing
hot pants so short the bottoms of her buttocks were exposed. A
young Hispanic junkie carrying her infant begged for bus fare at
the station entrance. These were the citizens of Rockfield with
whom she identified; these were the people in the stratum of the
city to which she'd belonged.

When a dealer Fatma recognized from Gaylord Street
approached her, she could feel that first hit, she could taste that
first drink. She conjured up an image of Nick at the Royal Lion,
sitting at the bar, using his finger to stir ice cubes around in a glass
of scotch, and she would surprise him, and they would return to
life the way it had been in the beginning, before they lost control,
before it all went wrong. As she took a wad of twenties out of her
bra, she felt two arms encircle her. She heard the familiar snap of
an illusory undercover cop's silver bracelets. And she saw Rockfield
in its finest state of decay for the first time. Panicking, she bought
a ticket for the next bus back to Willowsville.

That was the same morning Miss Sarah confided in Fatma and their true friendship began. She was leaving Shelby. She had been made a deputy sheriff, and she was going to work with women on the outside. She planned to follow them after prison, teaching them how to shop and save money and get a job, deal with people. She was tired of just helping them get out; she wanted to help them *stay* out.

"Now we're *both* onto something new," she told Fatma.

"I'm scared."

"Like standing at the edge of a cliff?"

"With devil pushing me."

"No, he's pulling you back. Jump, Fatma."

They were putting in a vegetable garden on the grounds of Haven House. The nursing students from the university brought over donated plants. On days they didn't lead classes on hygiene, sexually transmitted diseases, and nutrition, they taught the women to hoe and plant. Fatma liked the garden just as she had liked the greenhouse. With her hair tucked into a bandana she had found in the basement "department store," she spent hours in the sunshine, preparing herself for the luminosity of Mombasa, thinking how much better off she was here, working in the dirt, than back in the city living in it. She kept to herself, concentrating on taking that leap Miss Sarah had talked about. But her stamina was low. Thanks to the sessions with English tutors so she could begin to prepare for a GED diploma, the medical appointments for her back, the nurses' survival meetings, sessions with her social worker, and AA meetings, she barely had the energy left to deal with Miss Sarah, who came every Monday.

"You don't pull a knife on the clerk at the checkout counter because she says your lane is closed," she lectured at one of her skills session. "You don't cuss them out either, sugars." The women had learned a certain set of rules in the streets and in jail; now they had to find a way to stand up for themselves without taking another person down. After class, Miss Sarah took Fatma out for coffee or to a discount store to pick up nail polish or a hair clip – things that she thought would perk her up. Fatma could barely stay awake, so little had she slept.

During the day she longed for the old Nick she thought she knew, but at night she ran from the real one, trying to stay awake by concentrating on Justine's even breathing and observing how the night air dried out her lips. After a while Fatma's body would give in, and in the morning she would wake up on the floor, her face black and blue, her knuckles red and swollen, with Justine standing over her, frantically screaming for Miss Wilma. Now Justine became afraid to sleep.

"No use us both losing sleep," Fatma told Justine one night as they lay in their beds staring up at the ceiling. Fatma could see Justine's eyelids lowering every now and then, but the girl would catch herself and her eyelids would fly back up like a windowshade with a broken spring. Fatma was touched that Justine watched over her, even though she was far too petite to be able to restrain her. Or perhaps Justine was simply afraid that Fatma would attack *her.*

Linda Stern, Fatma's counselor at the Department of Social Services, thought that when the serial murderer was caught, her nightmares and violent behavior would stop. Fatma didn't say much to her, since she found therapy a waste of time. What made Fatma tick? The counselors and psychiatrists had no idea.

"You anorexic?" Fatma asked Stern, breaking her silence. She was tall and as thin as kindling. Fatma could snap her in half.

Listening to the annoying questions emerging from her long flat face, Fatma wanted to do just that.

"No, I've always been like this," she said, shocked and at the same time angry, as though she was tired of being taken for some kind of freak. That day Fatma saw a weakness in Stern: years of being made fun of, adults staring in disbelief, rejection by boyfriends who demanded breasts to suck on, children pointing at her. She saw a heart that beat and blood that flowed through that deformed body. She had found the chink in Linda Stern's armor.

"I'm not disrespecting. I just never see someone so skinny— except my sister who's actress." This wasn't really accurate. Jamila wasn't emaciated like Linda Stern.

"Does it bother you that I'm so thin?" Stern asked.

"You mean I'm jealous?" Fatma was glad to be putting on weight. She'd already gone up two sizes and bra cups since she arrived at Haven House. Miss Wilma said the additional pounds were a sign of her beginning to reach wellness. "All monkeys cannot hang on same branch."

"What?"

"Everybody's different."

The therapist smiled, amused.

"Was your body type a problem with your husband? A source of his anger and violence?" Stern asked, eager to reestablish their roles.

"Fat me or skinny me?"

"Either."

"Everything about me made him angry," Fatma said.

"What things?"

"Everything." She had said all she had to say for that session and for many more sessions to come, because she couldn't talk to this woman. There were things she couldn't say to anybody, not even Miss Sarah.

✶

Some Mondays, Fatma wasn't able to get out of bed, she was so exhausted from her battles of the night before. But Miss Sarah came nevertheless and, sitting opposite her on Justine's bed, talked and listened.

"It might help you to write your thoughts down on paper," she said one afternoon.

"Why?"

"It's a form of release, of ridding yourself of ghosts that haunt you."

"And then?"

"You can lock them away, or rip them up, or burn them."

"I can't write good." Fatma had done little writing since school, and now found it nearly impossible; her English lessons were primarily conversational. Thoughts often whizzed by like shooting stars that she grasped for with fists that came back empty. Too many drugs and too many beatings had dulled her, incapacitated her. At times her memory was lucid, as vivid as a Mombasa sunset; then it faded, and she had trouble recalling her brothers' and sisters' names. Of course, taking into account all her father's wives, there were thirty-one of them.

"I have a better idea." Miss Sarah reached into her bag and fished out a tape recorder smaller than her hand. She popped out a tiny cassette and put in a different one. "I use this all the time to dictate my notes at the end of the day while I'm driving home. Then I type it onto my computer. Keep it. I have another one." She showed Fatma how to use it. The recorder sat on her dresser for a month before she picked it up one night when she thought Justine was sleeping and began to whisper into the little black box.

"Are you talking to me?" Justine asked.

"No." Fatma got out of bed, opened the window, and threw the tape recorder as far out into the snow as she could.

Mary Ellen usually prepared dinner: corned beef and cabbage or chicken fingers or spaghetti were common fare. Meals were important at Haven House: most of the women had survived for too long on cigarettes and coffee. None of them had given up either of them. In fact, Fatma was smoking more now than ever before. But cigarettes were allowed at Haven House. Getting rid of one vice at a time was more than enough for anybody to handle. Mary Ellen was good about providing protein, vegetables, and salad when she cooked, and the regimen was obviously working for Fatma.

One evening when Mary Ellen had the flu, Justine volunteered to make supper. She topped frozen chicken wings with barbecue sauce, surrounded them with peeled sliced potatoes, and put them directly into the oven – which wouldn't have turned out too terribly, except that she had no concept of how much time it would need to cook. At six o'clock Justine called the women to the table. She had taken extra pains to make the occasion festive, bringing down from her room a potted ivy for a centerpiece and placing the white paper napkins in the shape of crowns in the center of the plates.

Teresa the bully took her place at the table, eager to find fault. She didn't have to look far. Justine nervously set the cookie sheet of pale chicken wings and semi-boiled potatoes swimming in steamy orange liquid before them. Indifferent to Miss Wilma's presence in the next room, Teresa blasted Justine's meal nonstop until a distraught Justine threw the pan into the garbage pail and, sobbing, ran up to her room. That's when Fatma lunged at Teresa, wrapping her hands so tightly around her neck that Miss Wilma and Laurel were unable to pry them off as Fatma elbowed them away. Miss Wilma picked up the Rubbermaid pitcher from the table and poured ice water over Fatma's head. Fatma released her grip, and Teresa's head dropped onto her plate as she sucked in air like a vacuum cleaner.

Justine thought the entire incident, including the restrictions placed on all the women, had been her fault. Fatma begrudgingly apologized to Teresa, who in turn apologized to Justine. But in her heart Fatma wasn't at all sorry, and in fact found the fracas had been worthwhile, because she and Justine grew closer once their caretaking had become mutual, and no one took advantage of Justine again.

"What do you think about this violent side of yours?" Linda Stern asked at the next session. "Why did you attack Teresa?"

"She make me mad."

"The way Nick did?"

"Nick. Nick. Everything Nick. Things make me mad before Nick."

"And did you react violently to them?"

Fatma shook her head. Uncle Oliver had never hit her, yet she feared him. Her brothers would have killed her had she raised a hand to them, even in defense.

"When did your anger become physical? When did you begin to put yourself in actual danger?"

The answer, she had to admit, was Nick.

"Do you identify with Justine when Teresa gets on her case?"

She didn't know. She had wanted to protect Justine, that was all. She had just wanted to take care of her. She cared about

Justine. Not the way she had been attracted to Elsa, though being attracted to certain women just seemed to make it easier to be friends. But Fatma felt no sexual attraction to any of the women at Haven House, nor for any of the men she encountered outside it, for that matter.

They were all gathered in front of the television when they saw a burly black welder who was handcuffed and shackled say to a judge, "What took you so long to find me?" His wallet had been found near the body of the latest female victim. DNA samples would later confirm him as the perpetrator.

"Bless the Lord!" Laurel hummed *Amazing Grace*.

"Ain't no more ladies gonna come here no more now dat it's safe on da streets," Teresa said. She was squatting (her big behind like two oversized throw pillows in navy stretch pants) as she tightened the screws of a doorknob. Teresa was handy; she could fix a leak in the kitchen faucet, adjust the circuit breakers when a fuse blew, repair the torn screen on the porch door, silence a whimpering dishwasher. "No ma'am, Miss Wilma. Ain't no more ladies gonna come here now dat it's safe in da streets." She stepped back and admired her work. Then she looked up at the crack in the ceiling, shook her head, and contemplated her next project. "Dis place goin' to pot. You ladies lucky I relapsed."

That night in her sleep, Fatma tried to strangle herself with a bedsheet.

"I heard you had another bad night," Linda Stern said.

"Who told you?"

"Miss Wilma."

"That's allowed?"

"I don't tell Miss Wilma what *you* tell me, if that's what you're concerned about. Of course, that's easy – you don't tell me much of anything."

Fatma smiled with satisfaction.

"I can't help you if you don't talk to me."

"You have cigarette?"

The therapist swept her tongue over her front teeth; she had a habit of doing this.

"It's not permitted in the building. Besides, smoke bothers me."

"You married?"

"Yes."

Stern was not pretty. No one at the Royal Lion would have thought she was. Yet somebody did. Somebody loved her with her long sad face and her drooping eyelids and her flat chest. Somebody wanted her, chinks and all.

"In fact this is my second marriage," she admitted.

"Your husband die?"

"We got divorced."

"He hit you?"

"No." She shifted in her seat and opened her mouth a little but nothing came out, as though she was having second thoughts about answering.

"He love you?"

"Yes. But sometimes love is not enough."

"You were how old?" Fatma asked.

She took in a deep breath. Fatma was getting too personal, and Fatma could tell that Stern was wondering how she had gotten herself into such a corner. She placed her elbow on the arm of her chair, rested her head in her hand, and closed her eyes, as though she had to think. "When I got married the first time? Twenty-two."

"I was twelve when I marry first time. When I marry Nick, I was twenty-four, but twenty-four for me in America was like being twelve in Mombasa. I only see what was on outside."

"You mean you couldn't see the red flags – the problems that would lie ahead."

"It's different here. People. The way they act. It's different."

"Tell me about your first husband."

Fatma still didn't want to talk about Daniel. Even though he had made her mad, he had been good to her. She *had* mentioned him once when she talked about the bad part, the part about Hussein. Stern suggested that maybe Fatma didn't like people being too nice to her. But that wasn't true. Fatma had liked it when her father was nice, and Auntie, and Ayasha, and even Hamal – and Sarah. Nick had been nice to her once. But she believed she liked it better when he beat her. She used to think the reason for that was the drugs he gave her afterward – the drugs that made her forget Hussein. But she didn't tell any of this to Stern. She just waited for her to say their time was up.

Fatma was in the bathroom at Haven House when the doorknob got stuck. She banged on the door. She kicked it. She called out. No one heard her; they were all outside talking about the location of the vegetable garden and the flowerbeds they would plant in spring. The bathroom had no window. Her heart began to beat fast and loud. She picked up the metal wastebasket and hit the frosted glass panel on the upper half of the door. The crashing sound brought Miss Wilma into the house, where she found Fatma on the floor in a fetal position, surrounded by shards of glass, hands cut and bleeding. Teresa unfastened the lock with a screwdriver. "Lord! It was only stuck, girl!" Miss Wilma reprimanded Fatma at first, irritated that she had damaged the door because of her bad temper. Then she bent down and cradled a trembling Fatma in her arms. "What's this about, child?" she asked as she rocked her.

Stern said the episode was a breakthrough. It only depressed Fatma. How could she have forgotten about the closet? The therapist said Fatma had had no choice but to forget.

There had been times when Auntie went to Saudi Arabia to visit Grandfather, leaving Fatma in the care of Uncle Oliver and the maids Lisha and Kiah. The first time it happened was when she found Uncle Oliver in Kiah's room. She must have been eight or nine and was looking for Kiah because Lisha had gone shopping. Uncle Oliver was naked, lying on top of Kiah. Fatma remembered standing in the doorway for what seemed liked a very long time, staring with fascination. She had never before seen a man's rump, let alone her uncle's smooth white behind twisting and bobbing up and down like a whale in a black sea. Kiah gasped when she caught sight of Fatma; her uncle looked over his shoulder toward the door and ordered her out.

He got dressed and locked Fatma in her dark stuffy closet to forget, to wipe what she thought she had seen from her mind, because, in reality, she hadn't seen anything, he told her. If she hadn't seen anything, why was he putting her in the closet? she asked him. So he didn't have to look at her, because he was sick of her, he said. Sick of the rude, naughty, outspoken child who was always in the way, the child he had taken into his home only to please his wife. If she told Auntie, he said, Auntie would send her away.

"It's because of your evil jinn that you must be punished, that's all," Lisha said when she returned home and tried to console a sobbing Fatma from the other side of the locked door. "The jinn has made you behave badly, made you offend your uncle" (though Fatma guessed Lisha never knew why Uncle Oliver was cross with her, or maybe Lisha had wiped it out of her own trusting mind). Then Uncle Oliver called Lisha away, and Fatma remained petrified that when he let her out, she would discover that soldiers had come to their door. There would be pools of blood higher than her ankles. And there would be Auntie, and Lisha, and even Kiah and Uncle Oliver lying in them, with their heads blown off and their brains stuck to the walls. And if she whimpered or made the slightest noise, they would come back for her too. So she kept quiet. And in time she did forget what she had seen in Kiah's bedroom just as she forgot what she had seen in Mogadishu the morning the soldiers woke her up and ordered the family outside in their nightclothes and into the center of town to witness the executions.

"You feared for your life. You feared for your auntie's life, but mostly for your mother's life – a mother who had already abandoned you. How could you ever capture her love if she died?" The therapist said more that day than she had in months.

"But she did die."

"And you never secured her love."

Stern asked whether taking drugs and drinking were the same as being in the closet. *How could drugs be like a closet?* Fatma asked herself. She had no idea what she was talking about; she had never done drugs. Fatma decided that Stern and the counselors and psychiatrists she had seen at Shelby, and she herself, were all crazy.

✷

They went back to the silence. *Fine with me*, Fatma thought. If Stern didn't have anything to say, neither did she. On one visit, they were sitting there, both of them quiet, when Fatma started to say something. The therapist picked up her pen.

"I hear voices at night."

"Are you sure you aren't dreaming?"

"I'm not always sure."

"What do the voices say?"

"They tell me I'm bad. I don't want repeat what they say."

"Things that your second husband told you?"

She nodded.

"It's common to relive terrifying events – imagine the words that Nick used to brutalize you, to make you feel worthless. It's called post-traumatic stress."

"But maybe it's not Nick."

"Who else might it be?"

"Maybe it's Iblis."

"Who?"

"Devil – my bad jinn."

She really stumped Stern with that one. If cocaine had been the devil and Fatma wasn't using anymore, or if Nick had been the devil and he was gone, who was beating her up at night? Stern wanted to know. Fatma tried to tell her that it was her bad jinn, that she'd been hearing him since she'd stopped using and drinking, that he was telling her to do bad things to herself.

"I'm born – I *was* born with evil jinn," she tried to explain.

"When I walked under baobab tree, I anger my good jinn."

"You have *two* jinns?" Her eyes opened wide.

Fatma nodded.

"Who is your good Jinn?"

"How can I know? But he punishes me when I do bad things."

"But you're not using or drinking right now, Fatma, so who is beating you up at night?"

"Maybe my *bad* jinn."

"Fatma, you're beating *yourself* up."

"Because my bad jinn tells me to."

"How can you get rid of an evil jinn?"

"No one in America can help me," she told Stern.

"Why not?"

"Only healers can chase away evil jinns."

"And where are the healers?"

"In Kenya."

"I see." And she really did look as though she understood.

"You think it's my jinns?"

"I think that you believe it is. That your culture says it is. So I guess the answer is yes."

Fatma felt good about Stern that day, and she stopped protecting Nick and Daniel and began to talk about them in a way she had never done before. Fatma wondered if the therapist had been right, if her opening up had had something to do with the murderer having been caught. She began to wonder about a lot of things having to do with other things, thinking differently about things than she had before. In the months that followed, she talked about her childhood, her mother and father, Auntie and Uncle Oliver. She unlocked the box she had been carrying around with her for thirty years. The secrets flew around the room like bits of confetti. Some mounted through the skylight and were carried off by the wind, never to return. Some, however, like the memory of the closet, came back and hit her on the head harder than a punch from Nick ever had.

Her therapist kept saying that Fatma had been "traumatized" by what she'd seen in Mogadishu. Over and over again she used the word. She said that it had all gotten jumbled: the executions, the abandonment by her mother, Daniel's deception and weakness, Nick's beatings. "I choose Nick. He wasn't weak," Fatma insisted. Stern nodded and raised her eyebrows, as though that had been the response she was looking for. Hadn't she been searching for a hero? Someone to save her? The only thing Fatma still saw was that she was stupid – had always been stupid. That was really why Nick had turned on her, why so many people hadn't wanted her. "And by the way," Stern added, "abusers are the weakest."

"Why did you start doing drugs?" Stern asked.

"Nick. I already tell you."

"Why did you get involved with Isaac?"

"For money."

"That you needed?"

"That I wanted."

"Why did you drink so heavily?"

"Elsa."

"Really?"

"I liked how it make me feel."

"How did they all make you feel?"

"They make me forget."

"Same as cocaine."

Fatma nodded.

"Kind of like being in the closet. And the executions. They were your fault too."

"No. How can they?"

"They couldn't be, but you believed they were your fault, didn't you? Because you were bad. You were *so* bad that your own mother gave you away. Wasn't that the reason your uncle put you in the closet? Not because you were stupid, but to forget what you had seen, because, like Lisha said, it was *all* your fault?"

"That's why they send me away to America."

"And is that why Nick beat you? Not just to give you drugs afterward."

"I wanted to get high because I wanted to forget Hussein."

"Do you think Nick ever really loved you?"

"Yes."

"Then why did he beat you?"

"People who love me turn on me."

"People like your mother? Like your uncle? But why do they turn on you?" Her eyes were fixed on Fatma's; Fatma couldn't look at her.

"I don't know." She was crying now.

"Why wouldn't they turn on bad Fatma? Daniel must have been weak. Why else would he love you? Everyone turns on Fatma. Bad Fatma. That's what you think, isn't it? You're a bad little girl."

Tears streamed down Fatma's face. They dropped onto her hands that lay folded on her lap. She didn't wipe them away. She wanted Stern to see them. She waited for her to say she was sorry and apologize the way Nick used to, after he hurt her. But Stern never apologized.

Sarah said that, when Fatma didn't release her thoughts, they fermented like soured wine that she angrily spit out. "You may act tough," she said, "but you're feeling worthless." She told her to picture the places that made her happy and secure: the beach in Mombasa, the corner in Lisha's room above the kitchen where she used to hide. She taught her to repeat: *I am valuable and so I protect myself; I have courage to make good choices; I face the unknown with confidence.* When Fatma was lonely, she asked Laurel or Justine to take walks with her. And, remembering that her father's blood flowed through her as freely as her mother's, she found her own higher help. Muhammad Hakeem, the mighty warrior, had been humble enough to acknowledge his weaknesses and wise enough to ask for help in desperation. Now she too reached out, reminding herself over and over again what her father's good brother had told so many years before. *You are strong, little Fatma — you are brave; you are the good general Muhammad's daughter.*

Iblis quieted down somewhat, which made her nights more tolerable. Sometimes he never surfaced at all. But she knew he was there watching and waiting. She could feel him roaming her mind, searching for that crack through which he could emerge, ready at any moment to lay a hand on her, a force always to be reckoned with.

*

It was common for the women who had shown some progress at Haven House to get a job, small occupation in town to help them become accustomed to being on their own, to assume responsibility. Fatma began to work four hours a week at Sundry

Undies. From cartons she removed bras and panties, bathrobes and nightgowns, slips and teddies, and hung them on racks or placed them on shelves, being careful not to mix up the sizes. Sometimes she had to iron garments that had become wrinkled in shipping. Other times she took inventory and counted how many of each style, color, and size were left on display. They were quality garments, ones Nick would have loved.

It was work similar to what she'd done at the African Artifacts shop, and a chance to get away from Haven House and do what she had always loved to do – make money. But most importantly, it helped her self-esteem because the women at Sundry Undies trusted her. They weren't afraid to be with her in the store without a supervisor, nor were they reluctant to leave her alone by the cash register while they were in the storeroom or dressing room with a customer. They trusted her with the money they gave her for coffee and sandwiches. It was only four hours a week, two hours on Tuesdays and two on Thursdays. Four hours of working with legitimate businesswomen like her mother had been. And on the mornings she couldn't bear to drag herself out of bed because even the simplest routine was too much, her father's strong hand pulled her from the covers. *You have not yet slid away!* he whispered.

She'd been at Haven House a little over a year when green buds were forming on the trees and Miss Wilma took her aside. "I think it's time we begin planning your trip," she said, her eyes wide with excitement, her smile vast. Defiant gray hairs had begun to spring from her straightened black hair like corkscrews. It appeared to Fatma that Miss Wilma was eagerly anticipating the departure of all five of the women at Haven House and that she was throwing Fatma out first. Reading Fatma's thoughts, Miss Wilma placed her palms squarely on Fatma's shoulders and stared into her eyes. "Sarah and Linda Stern and I believe you're ready, and that it's necessary at this point for your recovery to go back to Africa. To find your son. To revisit the life you closed the book on long ago."

A New Identity

********** ⭐ **********

"When's the last time you renewed your passport?" Sarah asked.

While Fatma had more than enough money left to finance her eight-week stay in Mombasa, she couldn't remember the last time she'd seen her passport.

"We'll go to the post office and put in an application today. Passports can take months to process. You'll need some identification of citizenship. How about your marriage certificate?"

Fatma showed the piece of white typing paper handwritten in Arabic and signed at the shiek's home where she and Nick had been married, and that had lived in her purse forever, and had followed her in and out of jail.

"There's got to be something from the state, something with a seal. The imam must have registered your marriage. City Hall will have a record."

"We never go to City Hall."

"You never applied for a marriage license? Never took a blood test?"

"No."

"Is that why you still use Kornmeyer for your name?"

"With Nick I used Benson. Then I go back to Kornmeyer."

"Just like that. Why?"

"Maybe inside I always know I'm not Nick's wife."

Sarah took in a deep breath. "How about your marriage certificate to Daniel?"

"Don't know."

"Think hard, Fatma. You must have kept your papers somewhere."

There was a limit even to Sarah's patience. Fatma felt like a child who couldn't recall where she had put her mother's best piece of jewelry she had secretly played with. Then she remembered. The passport had been somewhere in the dresser drawer in her apartment on Main Street.

"It's gone," she told Sarah.

"What is?"

"Everything. Mrs. Lucchese, my landlady, burned it."

Sarah made a call to Pia, who said that although nothing had been burned, her mother *had* thrown everything out.

"You'd better locate Daniel and your marriage certificate, because right now, sugar, you're a woman without an identity."

Just as Fatma was feeling she had become too American for her own good, America was telling her she wasn't American enough. She wasn't Kenyan or Somali either. She was nothing.

"We got married in Mombasa."

"It will show that you were legally married to an American and that your name is Kornmeyer. Maybe that will be enough. You have to call Daniel."

"I have been in American jail. They know who I am."

Sarah tried to regain her composure. It was as though all her years of dealing with drug addicts, thieves, and filthy-mouthed liars had reached its culmination, and this little matter of lost identification was the last straw. These irresponsible people couldn't keep their lives straight from second to second. She spoke slowly and with determination.

"Listen carefully. There are rules in America, very strict ones about proving who you are. A passport can prove citizenship and identity, because you've already submitted proof to get it. Without it, you need certain documents. And you, sugar, have none of them!"

Daniel answered the phone with his friendly "Hi." He always sounded as if he anticipated that caller, whoever it was, would be someone he knew intimately. It threw people off sometimes, particularly strangers, and made them remind themselves that yes, they had called Daniel and not simply bumped into him across the wires.

"It's me. Fatma. How are you?"

"Fatma?" He was surprised, but his voice was upbeat. "Where are you?"

"Haven House in Willowsville." She might as well make it known right off. "You know it?"

"I do." Of course he did. He was a social worker.

There was an awkward silence. She knew he was taking her feelings into consideration and needed time to figure out his response. He wouldn't want to appear stunned.

"How long have you been there, Fatma? The last I heard from that lawyer of yours was that you and your husband were living somewhere in Hamilton."

"A lot happened." It would have taken another ten years to tell him where she'd been. "Daniel, you have our marriage license from Mombasa?"

"Our marriage license! I have no idea what happened to that. Did we ever take it with us to Katundu?"

"I don't know. I think so. I think it get thrown out with my passport."

"Why would you want that?"

"I'm taking trip – to Mombasa. I need my passport."

"What's wrong with your marriage license?"

"I'm not married any more."

"I'm sorry. Look, why don't we get together?" His voice assumed a tone of concern.

"I don't think it's good idea."

"Just for a cup of coffee. I can meet you anywhere on a Saturday or Sunday, and any other day after five."

Her legs weakened; she sat down at the kitchen table.

"Look, if you'd rather not, that's fine. I only thought – "

"You can come to Willowsville?"

"Sure. I'll come to Haven House."

"No."

"Okay. Where then?"

"Red River Café. You know it?"

"I'll find it. Six o'clock okay?"

"Yes."

The moment she hung up, she knew she had made a mistake. How could she bring herself to tell him about the life she'd lived after she asked him to leave? The last thing she wanted was his pity or his advice, and yet she was excited to see him again. She thought about the first time they had seen one another face to face at their wedding; the first time they held hands; the first time she let him touch her in Katundu.

"Who is he?" Miss Wilma asked as she drove Fatma into town.

"Why you think I'm meeting man? Maybe I'm meeting nobody."

"Who are you kidding, going out all dolled up like that?" She worried about her women getting involved with pushers and other addicts.

"It's Daniel, my old husband – about marriage certificate," Fatma lied.

"I thought he didn't have your marriage certificate," Miss Wilma said, casting a doubtful eye.

Fatma arrived before Daniel. It was the first really hot night of the season, and she wore a black spandex tank top that sat off the shoulders and a short print skirt. Her hair was still long and partially pulled back at the crown with a barrette, and large gold hoops dangled from her earlobes. Jewelry, she hoped, would distract his eyes from her face.

There is a certain handsomeness about men after forty that comes from being settled, from having direction. Fatma had always found it very attractive. Her father had it; so did Nick when she first met him. And now Daniel wore it. A little thicker around the waist, fuller in the face. Some gray in his sideburns, ponytail gone. Short hair combed straight back from his face. A few lines around the pale blue eyes. That gentle smile.

She remained seated with her hands around a glass of iced tea when Daniel walked in. He bent down and kissed her on the forehead, which surprised her. The earrings were of little use. He steadfastly averted his eyes from her to avoid seeing the unevenness of her cheekbones, the scars above and below her lips, the missing tooth, and the discoloration that had never gone away.

"You look good," she said.

"And you."

Daniel was always a gentleman.

"What are you doing now?" she asked.

She had asked that before she even inquired about his parents, whom she later learned were both still living in Carlington. His mother had Alzheimer's and breast cancer. Fatma felt sorry for her, the way you do when you hear that type of news about someone you've never met, a friend of a friend. Someone you see on the cover of a women's magazine.

"I'm still a social worker. I left the Department of Human Services a while back for a college counseling center."

"So you know Haven House?"

"It's a program for women in recovery." Then he smiled the way Daniel smiled when he wanted to tell you that he knew whatever it was you were trying to hide.

"You married?" she asked.

"Seven years."

"Children?" she forced out.

"Two girls. Four and six."

"That's nice." She was relieved that there was no boy.

"I never have more children." She needed to tell him that.

"I'm sorry." He apologized for the second time since she'd phoned him, looking down at the table as though he were looking for some script that would tell him what to say next. "I didn't handle that right."

"Maybe we both didn't."

"We were young. At least you were. And me, I was so taken up with doing the right thing in your culture, so trying to please your family – everybody, including myself. I thought I could be Muslim and Christian and agnostic all at once. A cockeyed optimist, an idiot. I shouldn't have brought you to America." Here it came: he was feeling guilty now, responsible for her state. "We should have stayed in Kenya."

"*You* stay in Africa?"

"I could have tried."

"What I do – did – is my fault. What happened in my life after you is my fault. I learned that from some smart people. There's bad people everywhere, just waiting. Waiting to take advantage, to hurt other people, so they can be king lion, you know? But Hussein – *he* was *our* fault," she said, unable to conceal her bitterness.

"How are your auntie and uncle?"

"Auntie is not well. *Walisema alliugua kiharusi.*

"I can't really speak Swahili anymore."

"They say she had a stroke."

"So you're going to see her." He stared into his cup as though in it he could see the past.

"And Hussein."

He looked up at the mention of Hussein.

"Can I help?"

"I don't need money. The house on Poplar Street was good investment. I sold it not long ago."

"You were right about that one."

"Why didn't you buy it?"

"My wife changed her mind at the last minute. I don't think she liked its history."

"What's her name?"

"Alison."

"She pretty?" Fatma asked, and then regretted it because she felt a little mixed up about Daniel at the moment.

"Yes," he said and changed the subject. "Your English has really improved."

"It didn't for long time. But I study hard here in Willowsville. Tutors come to Haven House. Sometimes college students, sometimes old people. It seems easier for me than before, but I still make lots of mistakes, too many mistakes."

"Maybe you've finally given yourself permission to speak it."

They talked a little more about small things – things that had nothing to do with them. Then he said he hadn't eaten and suggested they go across the street to a pizza place. She told him she wasn't hungry and that she had to get back. Neither was true, but she was growing anxious, and anxiety always led her in the wrong direction. She took the last sip of tea, which was really a mouthful of sugar that had settled on the bottom. Daniel paid the check and offered to drive her back. She wasn't ashamed; it seemed fitting. Before she got out of the car, he put his hand on her shoulder.

"Fatma, please know that despite the way we got married—*nilikupenda*."

She had never doubted that he had loved her. It just hadn't mattered.

"I thought you forget Swahili," she said.

"Seeing you has brought a little back."

"A lot," she said, smiling, and walked away and up the steps to the screen door, where Miss Wilma was waiting for her on the other side.

"Fatma," he called, "if you find Hussein, will you let me know?"

"Maybe," she said, with a sense of satisfaction.

The demons lay still that night, and she slept well.

"The picture is ugly," Fatma told Pia, as they sat having cappuccino at Café Venezia. She was referring to the two-by-two photo inside her crisp navy blue American passport. KORNMEYER, FATMA it read alongside it. It was Justine who had come to her rescue and spoken to her father the congressman. He contacted Citizenship and Immigration Services and had new certified copies of Fatma's papers issued. Miss Wilma believed that, because she was the only black woman who sat on nearly every nonprofit board in town, the congressman had helped out, because no politician wanted to jeopardize his tenure by crossing her. Fatma liked to think that it was on account of her friendship with Justine. Sarah had asked Fatma what name she wanted to go by. She said she had two choices. Benson was out of the question.

"It's not ugly, but you do look angry," Pia said.

Fatma had refused to smile for the same reason she always did – the tooth Nick had knocked out.

She had called Pia because it was time to get her ring back. She wanted to arrive in Mombasa like an elegant, well-heeled American lady, worthy of the lineage she hoped to reclaim. It was strange sitting in the café again, almost as if she had never been there before. She saw it all with new clarity: the refrigerated cases filled with colorful pastries and cookies, the shiny elegant espresso maker, the polished pink granite table and countertops, the reflections in the clear mirrors that she had once thought were smoky. At the same time an old feeling crept up from the terra-cotta floor and threatened to envelop her like a blanket in a snowstorm. I'll protect you, it said. I'll make you forget. I'll make it all easy. I'll smother you.

She struggled to stay clearheaded and to resist the hazy comfort of the familiar. They talked about her upcoming trip, and about Haven House. Pia was pleased that Fatma was getting her life together.

"You don't know, do you?" Pia said.

"Know what?"

"Nick. He's dead."

It was as if she had said that everything Fatma ever thought was real had just been a dream.

"He died last week."

"How?" She envisioned him lying on the floor beside their old bed in Hamilton, white like paste, lifeless from an overdose or bleeding from the stab wounds of an abused lover.

"Cancer," Pia said.

"That's impossible. He's never sick a day in his life."

"It might have been an aggressive cancer. One that gets bad really fast."

"I can't believe it."

"It was in the paper."

"I want to see."

"Fatma."

"I need to see."

"Fine. Suit yourself."

They walked over to the library on State Street. Pia picked up a pile of *Boston Globe* newspapers from the shelf. "It was in last week," she said. She carried the papers to one of the long wooden tables with a green shaded lamp in the center. "Here," she said, opening to the obituary page and placing the paper before Fatma.

> **BENSON** – of Enfield, CT. May 21. Nicholas A., age 59. Father of Carl Benson of Cambridge, Nicholas Benson, Jr., and Amanda O'Brien, and grandfather of Jessica O'Brien, all of Enfield. Companion of Carol Mason of Rockfield. Funeral services will be held Thursday at 9 a.m. from the D'Andrea & Sons Funeral Home, 100 Madison St., Cambridge, followed by a Mass of Christian Burial at Saint Bartholomew Basilica. Burial will follow at Mount Auburn Cemetery. Calling hours are Wednesday 5-9 p.m. Relatives and friends invited. Those desiring

may make donations to the Visiting Nurse Hospice
of Greater Boston.

Fatma had to read it several times to understand it. A Mass?
She had never seen Nick set foot in a church. And why Boston,
and not Enfield, where he was from, or Rockfield, where his
"companion" was from and where they most likely spent their
time? He had had a son living in Boston – in Cambridge, a son
from whom he must not have been estranged at all, but with
whom he must have maintained a substantial relationship,
because this son was clearly handling all funeral arrangements.
She realized that Nick and his son had been in touch all along.
That was where Nick went while they were vacationing in
Boston – not to take care of the business. She had been kept in
the dark about this son, and he about Fatma. But Carol Mason
had obviously known him. She was credited with being Nick's
"companion," not Fatma, who was his wife no matter what
legal documents were missing. Nick was dead. The pounding
in her head intensified. Nick was dead. "Relatives and friends
welcome." Had he mended fences with them all in the end? Had
they flocked to his bedside? Presented him with a sweet-faced
grandchild? Or had they sheepishly and guiltily only shown their
faces at his wake or burial? "Relatives and friends welcome." Not
his wife.

"I can't believe it." She choked on the words.

"Let's get out of here." Pia took her by the arm and led her to
the stone steps of the library, where they sat like schoolgirls.

"It's the best thing that could have happened to you, Fatma.
If you couldn't free yourself from him, then maybe God did it
for you. Don't you think? Keeping him in your life would only
jeopardize the progress you've made."

"I'm mad! I want to tell him things, things like: Look, I made it without you. Six years with him and he's never sick. And now he's dead. I'm mad. It didn't even mention me."

"Why are you really *so* angry?" Pia searched for a tissue in the woven sac she carried over her shoulder and handed it to Fatma.

"I guess I was always thinking we would get back together one day. One day he was going to get straight and there was going to be hope. He was going to find me again. I can't believe he's dead."

"How could someone who hurt you like that ever love you?"

"I can't explain. I just always hoped that one day he would change and we be happy. It's just like that. The hardest thing to accept for me is that I can only change *me*."

Pia sighed.

"His companion! *I'm* his wife. He always called me his wife in front of everyone."

"Because he never wanted any other man to come near you. He possessed you."

"I never wanted other men. He was only one I ever loved. He took my heart and he played with it. Because of him, I can never trust another man. Now he can rot in hell."

"Maybe you don't want to see that ring now. If you won't sell it, at least wear it on your right hand. And think of your trip now. Your future."

"I have my son. They're going to bring him to me in Mombasa. There's going to be a lot of questions. I hope he understands. But I won't be able to take him back with me. He's too young to leave on his own. I can't take him out of country until he's twenty-one. And I want to come back to this country. I love this country." She was rambling now, still trying to process the news that Nick was dead.

Pia glanced at her watch. "I've got to get back to the hospital."

"Thank you for coming," Fatma said when they approached the Café Venezia where Sarah, who had driven Fatma to Rockfield, was already waiting for her.

"Tell your mother hello," Fatma said.

"I will."

"Pia, you're what kind of doctor?"

"I'm a plastic surgeon," she said. "Didn't I ever tell you that?"

"I probably forget." Fatma could see as Pia stared at the scars on her face – the split lip – that she was waiting for Fatma to request one more favor, but she only kissed Pia on the cheek and headed over to Sarah's car.

Sarah drove Fatma to Logan Airport on the second of June. Fatma was wearing high heels and a rust silk suit and a cream-colored top with gold threads running through it. It was hot, and she held the jacket over her arm.

"It gets cold in the plane," Sarah said. "You always need something."

She wore the ring and some new jewelry she had bought. She was all gold and sparkly, like a bottle of champagne whose cork has just been popped. It would be a long trip, with a layover in London. "That's trouble," Miss Wilma said. "Drugs and pickpockets everywhere. Watch yourself. And call us," Miss Wilma said.

"Anytime," Sarah added.

She hadn't informed her family of her visit to Mombasa. She would surprise them and return from America like a girl in a movie she had once seen who came home from Paris: sophisticated, mature, and – most important – whole, or almost so.

At 6:10 in the evening she was airborne somewhere over Connecticut when Mary Ellen answered the telephone at Haven House. Because Mary Ellen liked to lie, it took a while before Miss Wilma believed her when she said that a man claiming to be Fatma Kornmeyer's son had called from Somalia.

V

SHANGAZI

********** ⭐ **********

S he landed in Nairobi at eleven in the morning, twenty-three hours after departure. Afraid to set foot in the London streets after Miss Wilma warned her of pushers and pickpockets, she spent her six-hour layover at Heathrow seated at the gate, her arms embracing the handbag and carry-on on her lap.

The Nairobi airport was more drab than she remembered, with its flat, tan concrete buildings, and about as busy – which is to say not very. Security officers with machine guns outnumbered passengers. The main building had never been enlarged; rather, new smaller ones had been constructed. Since there was no need to provide shelter from the cold in Africa, unlike the large terminals at Logan and Heathrow where she had just come from, little distinction was made between inside and out. With no moving walkways or shuttle buses or trains, she walked a good distance in high heels from the international to the domestic terminal. She arrived with blisters popping on the balls and heels of her feet.

The tiny white-tiled airport in Mombasa did not disappoint her, however. *I'm home*, she thought as she descended the escalator, exited the building, and got into a taxi. It was hot – she had forgotten just how hot – and it was humid. Shifting her body on the torn leather seat inside the stuffy, gasoline-fume-filled cab sounded as if she was ripping adhesive bandages from her thighs. Her undergarments soon became soaked with perspiration.

"Where you goin', mama?" the driver asked.

"The first hotel you come to."

As they drove into the city, her eyes adjusted to the sprawling, run-down, strip-mall architecture, the abundance of *matatu* buses and bicycles in the crowded streets, and the scarcity of cars. There appeared to be a greater presence of Somalis and other outsiders than she remembered. A sleek United Arab Emirate Bank skyscraper looked boldly out of place. Trash was everywhere. She found the heat unbearable. Her mind juggled images, trying to reconcile the disjunction between America and Africa, between the past and present. Had her memories been real? Had her mind simply painted comforting yet distorted visions from childhood? Or had drugs and alcohol completely warped her memory? She felt as though she had slipped into a soft and familiar sweat suit that had shrunk and now subtly nagged at her: too tight in the crotch, too short at the ankles.

"Where you been?" the cabby asked.

"On vacation." She wasn't in the mood for talk.

"It was good vacation?" he persisted.

"Very long one." She tried to trap the rising nausea in her throat.

"This okay, mama?" he said after fifteen minutes of silence.

"Fine." She hadn't even taken a good look at the hotel. Grateful for the end of a bumpy ride, she rushed to get out of the stifling car, only to find the air outside wasn't much better.

She paid him the thousand shillings he requested. The equivalent of ten U.S. dollars may have been an outrageous amount, but she was no longer used to bargaining over cabfare.

The hotel was a cheap one. There was no real mattress, just a foam pad. Nor was there a private bath, or even a fan. She collapsed on the bed and slept until the sound of squabbling between a man and woman in the next room wakened her. She took the towel at the foot of the bed along with her bag of toiletries and headed for the bathroom in the hallway. She washed with the mushy piece of used soap in the shower stall, put on fresh clothing and makeup and, already glistening with new perspiration, set out for the streets of Mombasa.

On Biashara Street she bought a big bar of scented soap and some cheap underwear. At the rate she was sweating, she would run out of what lingerie she'd brought faster than she could wash and dry it. She continued to walk, expecting to see someone she knew or someone who knew her. Years ago, everyone knew everyone in Mombasa. A young boy purchased some *miraa* from a kiosk for three dollars a kilo. He pulled the leaves off and chewed on the sticks, then spit them out into the street. She wondered what the margin of profit was for the kiosk owner, assuming she could do better. She edged her way past shoppers bargaining for clothing and household merchandise and occasionally examined a silver teapot or feigned interest in a rug or a *kanga* – the housedress Kenyan women wore at home – so that she could pause in the shade of a shop's awning for relief from the sun.

On Digo Road, men seated at tables on the balconies of an endless string of tearooms read newspapers in front of open windows framed with faded brown shutters. Grease-stained curtains escaped from the windows and waved like flags in the Mombasa dust, beckoning other men upstairs into rooms that were dark and dingy and so unlike the sparkling Little Venezia Café in Rockfield. As she made her way through the crowds toward Hanawi Street, she was struck not so much by the number of Somali women she encountered as by their appearance. What had always distinguished a Somali Muslim woman from a Kenyan, who wore the solid black cover-up called a *buibui,* were their colorful outfits. But that was no longer the case. Many Somali women were now also covering their faces with veils, just as her Saudi mother used to do.

She entered the pastel section of the city, where a few homes were still graced by massive carved wooden portals. Star-shaped spikes protruded from the doors, protection in former days from invaders' elephants.

"Where you goin'? What you doin'?" A toothless old man took her by surprise. The neighborhood watch had long existed in Mombasa.

"*Nyumbani,*" she said. Home.

Hearing Swahili, he smiled.

"*Sawa,*" he said. Okay.

"*Sawa,*" she echoed, happy to have the familiar words bounce back and forth from tongue to tongue again.

She wandered on through the dirt passageways of Fort Jesus. A tourist asked her to take a picture of him and his wife at the entrance to one of the caves. At first she thought they were Americans: he with his jeans, white T-shirt, sneakers, and backpack; she with her long linen travel skirt and sandals. But they informed her they were South African, which surprised her. The South African tourists of her childhood had been white, not black like this couple.

She walked beneath the remains of a mud-brick arch that opened onto a quadrangle of green lawn similar to the town common in Willowsville and sat on one of the blue painted chairs at a long table beneath a tree. The sun was beginning to go down, but not the temperature. Fort Jesus had been taken for granted when she lived in Mombasa, a relic of the past that tourists made sure not to miss, a marker of the Old Town. For the first time she wondered what it might have been like to retreat into the fort for protection from evil forces. She wondered what evil had been at work within its thick mud walls. What women had been violated? What children compromised? What men humiliated? Man against woman. Tribesman against tribesman.

✳

In the morning she prepared herself to meet her family. She put on a white shirred stretch-lace top. Her silk suit jacket had perspiration stains under the armpits, but if she folded it a certain way and carried it over her arm, the stains were hidden and it added elegance to her outfit. The night had been filled with the anxiety and fear that her tortured sleep might leave her bruised, but it hadn't. She took her coffee and rolls at daybreak and checked out of the wretched hotel as quickly as she had checked in.

"Five hundred shillings, mama," the taxi driver said when she directed him towards Auntie's.

"Two hundred," she countered.

"Four."

"Three."

They settled on three-fifty. Soon they were riding along the beach, which seemed narrower than she remembered.

"What are they doing?" she asked, watching two men empty large plastic bags into the ocean.

"Dumping trash," he said, matter of factly. "The water's full of seaweed anyway."

She told him to stop at a fairly decent-looking hotel.

"This new?" she asked.

"The Giriami? No, mama."

It wasn't familiar. She didn't ask how old it was, because the driver was only a boy. What did he know about time? It might have been erected after her departure or had been there and changed hands in her absence. Maybe it had simply fallen into one of those black holes of her damaged memory.

He took her bags out of the trunk; she paid him.

"The Giriami is very nice hotel," he said in anticipation of a bigger tip. She gave him an additional fifteen shillings and told him to wait.

At sixty dollars a night the Giriami was indeed quite posh, with private bathrooms, air conditioning, in-room phones, two pools, and real mattresses. She told the clerk she'd be staying only a night or two, until she got settled with relatives. Taking no chances, she insisted on accompanying the porter who took her bags up to the room before she continued on to Auntie's. It was June, and she imagined her family would be preparing for the annual reunion. After all, Auntie's health was failing; everyone would surely come.

When the driver pulled up in front of the house, Fatma almost told him he was mistaken. The once-proud villa, as orderly as the bricks that sat one on top of one another, appeared as tired-looking as a hooker who'd been out on the street too long, its neglected gardens like a woman in wrinkled clothing.

Her brother Hamal answered the door. Middle age had not treated him as well as it had Daniel. Political, financial, and social ruin had produced a forty-five-year-old who looked more like sixty-five or seventy. They hardly recognized each other.

"*Hujambo*," he said, surprised. "*Umekuja*." You came.

Nearly two years had passed since Jamila had brought Hamal's message to her at Shelby, yet he didn't question her tardiness, and she offered no excuses.

The rooms were as cluttered and filled with old and new as the streets of Mombasa: a television on top of an old refrigerator, a high chair alongside the sofa, T-shirts and several pairs of jeans draped over Auntie's carved Arabian sideboard, toys scattered here and there. Hamal, who had always preferred to communicate in Somali, spoke only in Swahili.

"Excuse this, but there are a lot of people living here. You should have called. Jumaa!" He summoned the houseboy, who came running. "Bring my sister a Fanta orange."

This was hardly the welcome she had anticipated. But should she have expected to reappear after years of silence, and so long after Jamila had delivered his message, and receive a warm embrace from the brother who had beaten her for running away on her wedding night? That he had tried to get in touch with her had been for Auntie's sake, and probably also had had something to do with ensuring his own comforts. This was, after all, *her* house, for she, not he, was Auntie's child. But there was a Somali tradition, one she had forgotten about but that Auntie had not: when a mother dies, a sister assumes her role as parent of her children. So it is too with fathers and their brothers. Auntie, who had been unable to conceive, now had fifteen children. She was Hamal's mother too; when he spoke of her, he no longer referred to her as *Shangazi*, or Auntie, rather as mother, as only Fatma had done in the past.

"Mama has taken a turn for the worse," Hamal said. "You did not get here a moment too soon. She suffered another stroke two weeks ago."

"Fatma is here, Mama," he called out, leading Fatma into her room.

She was lying in bed; several pillows propped up her gray head. Her face was crooked, as though it had been made of clay by a creator who, unable to decide how to arrange it, had left it unfinished and drooping on its right side. Fatma sat on the bed and took her mother's hand.

"*Binti*." With great effort, her lips tried to form the word for daughter. "*Binti*," she repeated, her speech slurred.

"*Sawa*, Mama."

Fatma hoped that her vision was blurred too, that she could see none of her imperfections, that she appeared as unblemished as the girl who had left so many years ago.

"I am sorry," Fatma cried. "I am sorry for having stayed away so long."

Auntie nodded, as if to say she knew why Fatma disappeared, the way only a mother knows things. The way a mother senses danger or feels a child's pain.

"There are reasons," Fatma persisted.

"You are here," she whispered.

Fatma rested her tear-streaked face on Auntie's breast; Auntie rested a hand on Fatma's head.

Later, Hamal told her how Uncle Oliver had left Auntie and gone back to Liverpool a few years after his venture in America failed, salvaged his declining business. Hamal and his wife had taken care of Auntie. "I've tried to help any family members I could," he said. Hamal's wife's cousins were living on the second floor, along with Hamal's own children and grandchildren. Auntie's house had become a boardinghouse, in which every room was a bedroom. The houseboy Jumaa slept on a cot in the kitchen. In Kenya there was always someone worse off and willing to work for next to nothing; Jumaa came from the lowliest tribe of the oldest slave port, Takaungu.

At first Fatma resented them all for descending on what had once been her home, but she soon felt grateful to Hamal. He and his wife had cared well for Auntie after her stroke, attending to her day and night with feeding tubes and bedpans. "This is still your home," Hamal said, but they both knew that culture and circumstances had undermined that legal claim. Fatma owed her family the same generosity Auntie had offered them. They, in turn, owed her nothing. Besides, she had never planned to stay in Mombasa, and she couldn't take anything away from her family, which was no longer rich and or united even in spirit. There would be no feast this summer, no party to mark her homecoming. She had been deluded in thinking there might be; there hadn't been a celebration in years. Fatma was not the only one who had suffered. She was not the only one whose situation had changed.

Fatma returned to Auntie's house the next morning and, against Auntie's advice, called her sister Kamilah in Saudi Arabia. Fatma would confess everything, and Kamilah would understand and send or bring Hussein to Fatma, at least for a visit. She might even ask Fatma to come to Saudi Arabia. Disagreeable Kamilah had not changed, however, one bit and was outraged at Fatma's phone call; she hung up the moment she heard her voice. Fatma called again.

"You've been gone too long. He's not your son anymore." Her tone was as flat and dry as the desert. *Not your son anymore. Not your son.* The dust of her Arabic choked Fatma's ears and throat, and it took her a while to respond.

"Only because of Grandfather – and Mother."

"No. You could have come for him. You could have tried to see him. But you never did."

"How could I come? Grandfather would never have permitted it."

"He forbade you to *raise* Hussein. He never said you could not visit him."

"That's a lie!" But in reality, Fatma could no longer remember the exact details of her departure. There were many things she could not remember.

"You do not know what life has been like in this part of the world. It is no longer your world. As far as Hussein is concerned, he's no longer yours either. It's too late. He's only fourteen. He doesn't need to take on your mistakes. He doesn't need to try and understand. He's had to understand enough. He knows that his real mother was my sister. He knows that his father was American. That is all he needs to know. That is enough. Believe me. He goes to school. He has friends. He's happy. He's all I have."

"Just let me speak to him, Kamilah, *rajaan*." Please, Fatma begged.

Kamilah slammed the receiver down.

Fatma phoned again – ten, twenty times. Kamilah didn't answer. She had taken a knife to the rope Fatma had knotted inch by inch and struggled to climb.

Fatma planned to fly to Saudi Arabia. She wanted only to talk to him, she told Auntie.

"Is this the only reason you have come?" Auntie asked. Her twisted face could not conceal her disappointment.

"No."

Auntie told Fatma that Kamilah had been good to the family, that she had spent most of Grandfather's money supporting their brothers and sisters in Somalia. Because of her, one had managed to get to Switzerland and another to France. But there had been only so much she could do.

It took Auntie a long time to say these things. Such hard work. Slowly, she spoke the wisdom of selflessness and true love possessed by one who has given it yet lived without receiving it.

"All I ever wanted was for you to be my daughter – only mine," she whispered, her crooked mouth struggling with every syllable, her eyes glistening. "To me, you were and are my daughter. But my sister could never relinquish her role as mother. She was a holy woman, an intelligent woman, much smarter than me. She was a stubborn woman, and a selfish woman. I say this to you now, and I ask Allah's forgiveness for speaking of the dead so. But it is true." She paused and took several long breaths, then began again. "It pained me when you returned from your visits to her so sad. I knew why, and still I sent you all the same. I felt obligated to her. Without her, there would not have been you for me." Her eyes filled up with tears that rolled down her cheek. Fatma gently swept them away with her fingertips. "Because of her selfishness I was never free to raise you truly as my own. But it was because of her selflessness that I had you at all. We are all capable of the two. You had two mothers: one strong, one weak. Forgive me for being the weak one, for letting her interfere and control what she should not have. At the time I thought that to go against her would have brought you more misery. Just as I thought to go against your uncle many times would have brought the same."

"Oh, Mama." Fatma sobbed to see her trying to say all this.

"Do not repeat the sins of the past. Learn from the mistakes of others."

She had to stop now. She was exhausted. Fatma gave her some water through a straw. She coughed, closed her eyes and slipped into a sleep from which she seldom woke. Two days later she suffered another massive stroke that sent her, hemorrhaging, to her death. Fatma closed Auntie's eyes. Hamal brought a clean sheet and covered Auntie's body.

Hamal's wife took charge of caring for Auntie even after death. She immediately washed her body in rosewater and wrapped it in a new white cloth. Auntie was then taken to her favorite square in Mombasa, where an imam stood in front of her, his back to the family and townspeople who had gathered, and prayed in silence. As was Muslim custom, Hamal and his father-in-law and the other male mourners accompanied Auntie's body to the cemetery, where she was laid in her grave on her right side, facing Mecca. Fatma removed her own earrings and diamond ring, as tradition forbade the wearing of decorative clothing or jewelry. Along with Hamal and his family, she sat quietly in the house for three days as neighbors brought sweets and fruit, and offered their condolences.

All the time Fatma was mourning, she told herself that, if she truly loved Hussein, she would stay away from him. After all, what did she have to offer him? In time he would grow into manhood, and perhaps then he would learn about her and she would learn what it meant to be a mother like her *shangazi*. She would learn the meaning of sacrifice. She must not fall victim again to the false pride and greed of Iblis. This she tried to tell herself, but she could not accept it.

Fatma had paid for Auntie's funeral. It was the best they could get under the circumstances. After her nieces and nephews had all come over to the Giriami and seen what the money of their American auntie could buy, Fatma left the hotel on the beach and went back to the busy center of town, where rooms at the Sapphire Hotel were only thirty dollars a night. One more person was too many in Auntie's cramped house. Besides, she needed time alone to sort out what she had found and what she had left behind, and to gain a clearer image of where she was going. She also needed to use her money more wisely. She spent much of it on her nieces and nephews and their children, taking them shopping and enjoying being the rich American *shangazi*. She bought them what they believed were stylish products, but even Fatma noticed the misspelled labels that read NIKI or ADDIDAS. She didn't tell them; they were so proud of what they thought were authentic American fashions.

Hamal, who had once been a high-ranking member of the military in Somalia, now delivered soft drinks to hotels and grocery stores. And, while his family wasn't starving, the tourism industry had suffered a blow from the terrorist bombing of the U.S. embassy two years before. There was an end to Fatma's riches too, however, and she still longed to help those who had not escaped Somalia. It was in doing for others that we find a reason for living, Miss Wilma had told her on her first day at Haven House.

While the Sapphire was comfortable enough, it was smaller than the Giriami and more run-down. There was a bar next door, not much more upscale than the Royal Lion, and it tempted Fatma. She phoned Miss Wilma once but could barely hear her for all the noise in Fatma's room which had become a destination for her nieces and nephews. Going to see *shangazi* broke up the boredom of their day.

"Who's there? Who's with you?" Miss Wilma asked suspiciously, imagining the worst, when Fatma phoned.

"My family." Fatma never phoned again. Miss Wilma and Sarah were in Willowsville, a world away, in a very big country that could never fit into Kenya.

Some days she left them all in her room, sprawled on her bed watching TV, and took a matutu to the most beautiful beach in Mombasa, more beautiful than the beaches of Hawaii and Jamaica that Nick had taken her to. It was one of the few whose white sand and blue waters were devoid of garbage. It was also not frequented by the German tourists who, beneath umbrellas at their luxury hotels, lay with child prostitutes who had been included in their package deals, boys and girls who gave themselves to tourists with the hope that a European would take them away from the poverty of Mombasa. She scooped up a handful of the smooth white sand and for a few moments held in the palm of her hand the weight and texture of her childhood. As hard as she tried to hold on to it, it always slipped through her fingers.

While having tea with Hamal and his wife one afternoon, she told them she intended to go to Somalia. They nearly choked on their biscuits.

"My dear sister," Hamal said. "There is no going to Somalia."

"But they're there. So many of our sisters and brothers, their children and grandchildren. And Ayasha. I want to see her again."

"The borders are closed," Hamal's wife said. "And there are pirates on the seas." She was a small trim woman with graying hair that she covered begrudgingly when she went outside. She had been a real beauty in her youth and, while the years had taken their toll on her too, the independent spirit that had impressed Fatma as a child was in no way diminished.

"Your family got through," Fatma said.

"That was years ago," she retorted. "And do you know how? Yes, there are many places where you can sneak across illegally with a man who takes you to another man who takes you from there. You pay them a high sum of money, but it is still dangerous. There are shiftas on the Kenyan side – mercenaries who make money killing elephants and rhinos for their tusks. They are all Somali born, and they will rob you, even kill you. Plus, there are lions and other wild animals at the border. Sickness – malaria. No, Fatma. There is no going to Somalia."

"Then how can we reach them?"

"We'll go to the Barakaat office," Hamal said. "That is the only way we can make contact from time to time. There are no addresses left in Somalia. The country is in shambles. That is the best we can do."

They gave the name of their family tribe and the neighborhood they lived in, and the agents at Barakaat told them to return three hours later. When they did, the man said he had located one of the sisters and she was taken to the Barakaat office in Somalia. At five-fifteen the call came through. They could not talk long; the connection was bad and might be cut off at any moment. Their sister told Fatma that most of the family was living in the part of their mother's house that had not been bombed. There was no plumbing or electricity, no postal system, no airlines. She named the nephews and brothers who had been killed by guerrillas, her husband and son included. And Ayasha? She and her husband were dead. He had been killed instantly; she had been wounded and later died from lack of medical treatment and antibiotics. Her son? He was alive – a good boy, a bright boy, who had been working as a photographer for passports. But there was no longer any use for passports, since no one left Somalia. "Father is blind and not well. Send money if you can. We have nothing." The line went dead.

"Father! What was she talking about?" Fatma asked Hamal.

"Father has been dead for years."

"Uncle Abdullah," Hamal said, smiling. "Father's eldest brother. He is ninety-five now." He was the frail kind man of Fatma's childhood who had gone on safari with her and who had always seemed one hundred years old. "He assumed guardianship of all of us after Father's death. He is the head of this family now. He is our father, and he will see that what you send is distributed fairly."

Fatma wired money right then through Barakaat; there were no banks left in Somalia. *We once were the richest and most respected family in Somalia*, she thought.

"What's happened to our family?" Fatma cried.

"There is a conference going on now in Djibouti. It is an attempt to restore order in Somalia. The tribes are arranging for an election of a new president, someone who will be good for the country, someone who can put an end to the anarchy. Ever since the ousting of that bastard uncle of ours, Siad Adan, the tribes that overthrew him remain splintered and continue to fight among themselves for power. Not like America, is it, my sister?"

"People fight for power in America. People always fight for power."

Later that evening after dinner, Fatma asked Hamal why so many Somali women were wearing veils like their mother did, when they never used to.

"There was a man – a Saudi, Osama bin Laden," Hamal said. "He went to Somalia for a while to fight against the Americans who were there in what they thought was an attempt to restore stability. He brought strict notions of Islam. He preached men's control of women, made slaves of them. You know the old Arab saying: The mule and the woman are equal."

Hamal's wife took her napkin from the lap of her *kanga*, the brightly colored apron with a matching top she wore, and threw it onto the table in disgust.

"It is not *my* saying," Hamal assured her.

Yes, Hamal had changed. Hardship had turned him into a better man, a compassionate one who valued life and family. His stern manner with outsiders masked it, but the gentleness with which he treated his wife and grandchildren made it very clear. Nick, Pia said, would never have changed.

"You too have come through hard times," Hamal said.

"What did Jamila tell Rihana about me?" Fatma asked.

"Jamila said nothing. That is how I know."

That night, Iblis surfaced. She dreamt Nick was driving his big car filled with roses down Biashara Street with that frantic look in his eyes and shouting: "I'll get you Fatma! I'll get you, whore!" She was wearing a black *buibui* with a veil, and he could not pick her out of the crowd of Muslim women like her who seemed to be multiplying and filling the streets. But then, as a bloodhound smells a scent, he zeroed in on her using his car to mow down the ranks of black-draped figures, drawing closer. He was on her heels when she became aware that she was dreaming and woke herself up. Shaken, she dressed and walked downstairs and into the tiny bar to drink away thoughts of Nick and Hussein and her family.

At the door, the odor of whiskey and urine and cigarette smoke pulled her in like groping hands. A young Kenyan woman in western clothes was flirting with several men at the bar when a man brushed by Fatma so roughly he nearly knocked her down. He walked straight up to the woman, yanked her off the stool by the hair and dragged her across the floor and out into the street. Fatma's stomach muscles contracted; her insides burned. *You are strong. You are the daughter of Muhammad*, she repeated to herself as she turned around and crept back upstairs.

LAMU

********** ⭐ **********

Auntie's maids, Lisha and Kiah, had been gone for quite some time. Kiah had married and moved to Nairobi not long after Daniel and Fatma left for America. But Lisha had stayed on in Mombasa, giving up her room to Hamal's in-laws and moving into what was no more than a large pantry. She had died of an intestinal infection five years earlier, and the news of her death saddened Fatma. Lisha had been loyal to Auntie, who had taken her in and given her work when she was only twelve. She had loved Auntie; she had loved Fatma.

Hamal couldn't understand why Fatma cared to go to Lamu now with Lisha gone. Had she ever met members of her family?

"Do you believe in jinns, Hamal?"

He laughed.

"Perhaps that was what killed Lisha," she said.

"What? Some evil jinn roaming around in her bowels?"

"Maybe."

"And you have been in America all these years? Fatma, she died of colitis. All those other stories Lisha may have told you are old wives' tales." He looked around to make sure his wife wasn't listening; the expression would have insulted her. "Ignorant people believe in jinns. Or people who can't take responsibility for their own actions."

"I've made many mistakes, and I do take responsibility for them. But – "

"Look, if you want to go to Lamu, go. No one will stop you. They say it's beautiful, if nothing else. But fly. There are bandits who are notorious for robbing *matatus* on the road to Lamu, and the trip is six or seven hours long."

She did want to go, she needed to sweep out every corner.

She rode in a *matatu* an hour and a half north to Malindi, where she took a small plane over to the island of Lamu. There are no roads in Lamu: the town isn't big enough for vehicles, with the exception of the deputy commissioner's car and the coastal services tractor, which collects trash and dumps it into the ocean. One either rides a donkey or walks, which at least makes for clean air. She hadn't brought much – several changes of clothing and a bathing suit. She didn't intend to stay longer than a day or two.

She wandered past stone buildings huddled close together along with labyrinthine passageways, admiring the intricately carved doors (much more beautiful and ornate than those in Old Town Mombasa) that graced even ramshackle dwellings. A small shop resembling an ill-equipped American convenience store was, she would learn, the only establishment of its kind on Lamu, where most shopping was done at the open-air market. As she purchased a can of Coke and cleaned the top with the underside of her skirt, a young couple in scanty beach attire strolled into the store. Tourists like them were everywhere, like ants crawling among the citizens of Lamu, who went about their daily routines. The contrast between the exhibition of flesh and the hiding of it in religious Lamu was more striking than in Mombasa.

The shopkeeper, an elderly man in western dress, seemed to appreciate Fatma's long batik skirt and long-sleeved white top. His wife appeared in a bright green, blue, and yellow *kanga* over her clothes, with *I like your behavior* written in Swahili on the skirt as part of the decoration. This perhaps meant that she had chosen to wear the particular *kanga* because she was pleased with her husband's current conduct. She smiled at Fatma and disappeared as quietly and as quickly as she had presented herself, obviously returning to their home, which must not have been far – maybe even upstairs. Fatma took an immediate liking to the clerk because of this dress. She asked him if he knew of Lisha and her family, and he did – everyone knew everyone in Lamu. Though Lisha had lived for so many years in Mombasa, she had traveled back home often. Did Fatma want to visit her family? No, she told him. What she was really looking for was a healer. He raised his eyebrows in curiosity but not surprise; her connection with Lisha had taken their relationship to a more intimate level. Fatma was sure it never crossed his mind to ask why she sought the healer; the people of Lamu are considerate.

There was an assortment available. Assuring her that the one he recommended was a good choice – a traditional healer – he directed her to a hotel.

"*Asante!*" She thanked him.

"*Bila asante!*" He said. Don't mention it.

Abd-al-Rahman's white stucco house was hidden behind ferny foliage, red blossoms, and tall palms. A thatched awning amid the branches indicated where the doorway was. She knocked, and a man in his forties or fifties who resembled Denzel Washington, with a short black beard in a long prayer gown, appeared. A round white embroidered pillbox covered his crown. Her attraction to him alarmed her.

"Abd-al-Rahman?"

"Yes."

"You're a healer?" she asked in Swahili.

"Yes," he said, and waited to hear her purpose for being there. She stood silent, intimidated by him.

"You're not what I expected," she said, then quickly regretted the remark.

"*Hujambo*. I hope I have not disappointed you."

"*Hujambo*. I have come to make an appointment with you."

"For when?"

"For whenever you're free."

"I'm free at present, and it seems that so are you."

He led her through a small courtyard with two cement benches built into the low wall surrounding it. Vines with wide leaves twisted up the whitewashed walls. As they climbed a flight of stairs to another courtyard, she could see a small primitive kitchen in an alcove. They continued up one more flight to a salon, from where she could see another room with a finely carved bed. They seemed to be alone in the sparsely furnished house. He motioned for her to sit on one of two wooden chairs that were as elaborately carved as the bed frame. He left and returned soon afterward, carrying a large silver tray with a teapot and two cups that he placed on a small table. He sat across from her as he poured the tea. He watched her drink. She was worn out from her trip, and the tea was soothing. Leaving his cup untouched, he continued to observe her, which made her feel awkward. He put the tips of his fingers together as if in prayer and bowed his head, giving her permission to speak first.

"Can you cure me of an evil jinn?" she asked.

"You are possessed?"

"Yes."

"What makes you believe so?"

"It comes to me – especially at night. It calls me ugly names. It gets me angry. It makes me do bad things." She told him her story, leaving out significant parts, like jail, and playing down her addictions. She told him her mother had been a priestess and that she had neglected to take her to a healer at birth. That she had perhaps picked up another jinn while walking under a *baobab* tree. She told him of her ghastly nights and of the jinns' attempts to have her kill herself. He listened impassively even when she admitted that she had come from America and that all her difficulties had begun there. She began to relax and speak as she might in the ER, listing flu symptoms.

"Not every malady is caused by a jinn, you know."

"You don't think I have one?"

"I'm not sure."

He remained so aloof that she wondered about his authenticity, and looked around for diplomas like those one sees in a doctor's office.

"Where did you learn to heal?" she asked.

"The ability to heal is not learned. One is born with it."

"Have you cured many people?"

He nodded. "There are a lot of jinns in Lamu, because the people here believe in them. But," he said sadly, "their numbers are decreasing. Electricity, you know – too much light. They have no place to hide."

"Isn't that good?"

"Good for evil jinns. Bad because good ones who protect are also leaving."

"But the cure – it's certain?"

"Generally. Sometimes, however, the jinn is simply too strong."

"What happens?"

"The victim dies." She gasped. "Not right away. A fatal evil jinn will make a person sick for a very long time before death comes." Probably concerned that he might have frightened her into leaving, he spoke in a lighter tone. "But *your* evil jinn, if you do indeed have one – and I sense that it is only one – does not seem to be of that nature; a fatal jinn is usually the result of witchcraft. In any case, you must remember that even the most evil jinn enters a person with God's blessing. Before a person can cast a jinn on another, God must agree or it cannot happen. God has reasons."

"Can you help me?"

"I will try."

He went over to the side table and picked up a gold pendant the size of a silver dollar. Dangling it by its chain in front of her face, he instructed her to concentrate very hard on it. He began chanting in Arabic, and that is all she remembered, because he hypnotized her so that he could talk to her jinn and see what it wanted and what she had done to deserve it. She awoke to the sweet smell of burning incense. Abd-al-Rahman was still sitting across from her. He told her that he had read some verses of the Koran and burned the coriander because its scent was pleasing to inns.

"Did it work?" she asked.

"I think so. But only time will tell if your jinn has kept his word."

"What do I owe you?"

"Five thousand shillings will do."

A bargain, she thought. She paid him and stood up. He stood too, but kept on staring at her.

"What?" she asked.

"Strange," he said, "that you still believe in jinns."

She knew that he meant after having lived in America for so long. She did not know how to respond. She wasn't sure she did believe in jinns. She was learning to take responsibility for her actions. Yet she was sure the devil existed: she had seen him, felt him, tasted him, made love with him. *I am desperate*, she wanted to say. *And when one is desperate, one will try anything.* That much she had proven in her life. But she only nodded, expecting him to lead her out. He stood there as though waiting for her to say or do something more. She became aware of the bedroom again. He was drawing her in, or so she thought. She felt a tightening in her chest as she had on the night Nick proposed marriage: her hands grew cold; it was difficult to breathe and swallow. She wanted to run for the door, but her legs threatened to give way.

"You need to sit a while longer?" he asked and, with his hand on her shoulder, he attempted to lead her back to the chair. She recoiled from him the way a dog cowers before a brutal master.

"*Nakwenda*," she uttered sharply. I am going. Immediately he turned and began walking down the stairs. He had been polite, that was all. He had been waiting for her to leave first, instead of appearing rude by showing her the door.

"*Asante*," she whispered, drawing in the cool evening air.

He accepted her thanks with a nod and a look of concern. "Perhaps it has not worked," he said.

"*Asante*," she repeated, and hurried away.

She stayed in Lamu for a week. That was almost as long as it took for the black Pico dye to wear off her hands and feet. The henna proved a bit more stubborn. She hadn't had this done to her since she was a child, when Lisha painted her hands and feet before their summer feast. Auntie had been furious. In her eyes it was like putting heavy makeup on a little girl. Fatma loved it. Throughout the days of the feast she ran around and played, glancing down at her extremities every now and then to admire the artwork that made her feel as though she had leapt into the mysterious realm of adulthood overnight.

The woman who sold dyes at the marketplace had handed her a piece of paper with her address written on it and offered to decorate Fatma. It would be like having a manicure, Fatma thought. Not wanting to appear too eager, she arrived at the woman's home an hour later than she had said she would. Time was rather elastic in Kenya, and in Lamu, she was learning, it almost seemed to stand still. The woman's home was similar to Abd-al-Rahman's, only not nearly as elegantly decorated. The furnishings in the healer's house had been few but fine; whereas, the house of "Auntie," as she preferred to be called, was a hodgepodge of pieces. They sat on a couch with swirling turquoise, yellow, and tan upholstery, its carved wood frame scraped and worn. Beside it, a sink with ugly piping was attached to the whitewashed wall. After she had removed Fatma's sandals, the woman produced a splintering wooden stepstool on which to rest Fatma's feet.

She sat beside Fatma; the folds of her colorful and busy *kanga* fell over Fatma's batik skirt. Yellow, mauve, and blue swatches of clothing contrasted with the heavily patterned couch and worn oriental carpet beneath them. Dipping her thick brush into the bottles of Pico, she painted the tips of Fatma's toes and fingers black, and then, with a finer brush, painted designs on the tops and sides of her feet, all the way to her ankles. She filled in the outlines with orange-red henna, as if they were drawings in a coloring book. Fatma felt the same comforting tickling of the cool wet brush that had decorated her so long ago. And she became one with the woman from the marketplace and with the couch and the carpet. She became one with the colors and shapes and life forces of Lamu.

Fatma looked for Abd-al-Rahman everywhere in Lamu, but she never found him. Such a small place, so few people. Where was he? Once she thought she saw him at the marketplace. Her heart skipped, and she wrestled with how to approach him. First, she would apologize for her behavior. She would explain the attraction, then the fear of being cornered and attacked. When she finally decided that she would simply thank him again, he surprised her by heading her way. But a closer view proved that she had been mistaken; it was not Abd-al-Rahman. Her interest in him as a person frightened her, because she was not ready to trust her judgment about men. One has to be completely sure of oneself, and the desire from time to time for a glass of vodka told her she had not yet achieved this. After several days she wasn't even sure she could identify the healer. His image – no longer clear in her mind – became distorted, and she believed she saw him in almost any handsome male citizen of Lamu between the ages of thirty-five and sixty. She began to doubt whether she had actually visited him at all. Had he been an alcoholic's hallucination? A jinn himself?

She walked along the beach at sunset. The sky and water had turned shades of orange and brown as the foliage on the shore that cradled the water grew black. She stepped onto the wooden dock lined with dhows – exactly the kind she knew as a little girl. A fisherman was lying on the deck of one, staring up at the sky. In a few hours he would set out on a search for red snapper and yellowfin tuna.

"*Mshangao*," she called to him, but he didn't respond. He must have been half deaf like most fishermen, and she was glad, because she could not contain her laughter. She was remembering the first night she had run away from Daniel, when Halima's father, also deaf, hid her in his boat. She saw Auntie's face as she sat beside Fatma on the airplane that took them from Tanzania back to Mombasa, the smile that told her Auntie thought she had been nervy, maybe even clever, in running away. The look that said she was not such a bad girl after all. Her life began to roll before her like a film at her own private showing. Faster and faster the reel spun, and the more images she saw, the more she laughed. She was hunting in Serengeti with her father, riding the lion at the ranch in Mogadishu. Even the painful scenes with Nick forced a smile, because their reality was over. Her healing had begun long before she'd met Abd-al-Rahman. It had started with Sarah and Miss Wilma and Linda Stern. With the Luccheses. It had started with Auntie, and with her mother and the determination she had bequeathed her. Only her mother couldn't do what Fatma was doing: she could never look in the mirror and laugh at herself. She could never be humble. That's what had isolated her and made her brittle. Nick also lacked humility and used his physical strength to hide his weaknesses. The leader who survived her Uncle Ahmad was also a very powerful man, perhaps more powerful in the eyes of his subjects than her uncle had been. When the opposing clan killed him, his soldiers stuffed his body and for several days and pretended that he was still alive to prevent the enemy from storming the palace and to keep his supporters feeling secure and calm. That's what power is: the illusion of greatness, larger than life and bolstered by fear. A man full of hot air.

She, too, had never been able to back up, to admit to her mistakes and start again. And so she had stayed on the road, running faster and faster until she strayed too far and got lost.

It was peaceful in Lamu, but it could never be home. Mombasa was, to some extent, comforting, but it wasn't home any longer either. Despite her years of protest she was American now. While she no longer fit perfectly in either place, she had to choose. And so she chose to keep to her plan and return to Mombasa and eventually to her anchors in Willowsville. Because she had taken that step back, and she was afraid of what she saw. It was only a matter of time before she'd begin to run blindly again, then trip and tumble down into that dark abyss. Still she needed to take one more side trip before she began her journey home.

She wore a green and orange and red *kanga* she had purchased at the marketplace. But she was scandalously naked beneath the cloth she had wrapped around her and fashioned into a skirt. Abandoning the upper piece of the *kanga* set, she paced the hot hotel room barebreasted and waited for the electricity to be turned on again. *Your patience is becoming*, the printing on the *kanga* read. She didn't know why she had bought a *kanga* that said that. She hadn't really paid much attention to what had been written on it; she had been drawn to the colors. There were rolling blackouts in Lamu to conserve energy – power on one day, off another. Sometimes, they told her, it was three days on and three off. Electricity had become a big problem in Kenya, because it came from Uganda, and political disagreements caused the Ugandans to pull the plug, so to speak. Americans, her brother had told her, were planning to build massive generators for Kenya, but until then, power was at a premium, particularly on an island like Lamu. Even in Nairobi, anything electrical – for instance, the telephone system – had become undependable. The first two days of her visit she stayed at Petley's, where generators kept the luxury hotel's power going all the time. Her money was running out, however – the income from the sale of the house on Poplar Street dwindling away. She still planned to leave every cent she could to her family. Moreover, she planned to go to Saudi Arabia, despite her auntie's pleas and her sister's rejection. Just to catch a glimpse of her son and, if she should be so fortunate, to speak with him. She moved to the Millimani her last night, hand-washed some garments in cold water, there being no hot, and woke up with bedbugs all over her. Time to return to Mombasa – as soon as her underwear dried.

IMANI

Hamal shook his head as he eyed Fatma's stained hands and feet. "Did you find what you were looking for?"

"I think so."

"You should have. You stayed away long enough. You could have phoned, told us where you were. I was beginning to think you were kidnapped by bandits, or tried to cross the border, or stowed away in some dhow that got taken by pirates."

"There was a power outage."

"The entire time?" She smiled. "You find this funny? Is that what they do in America? Laugh at crime and danger? At respect for family?"

"I'm sorry. Thank you for worrying about me."

It had been selfish of her not to phone, but she hadn't even thought about calling. She had needed to separate herself from everyone she knew, to test her own strength. She had been made whole with the help of others, but not wholly with their help.

"Has anything new happened in Somalia?" she asked.

"The representatives at the conference in Djibouti have elected a transitional government. The city, however, is still carved up among clan-based faction leaders who were ignored at the conference. There's little hope for long-term stability."

There was still annoyance in Hamal's voice, as though he found her responsible for the atrocities. For the rest of her stay in Mombasa, all their attempts to phone the family in Somalia were futile.

"Hamal, I'm going to Saudi Arabia."

He looked at her with pity as he shook his head.

"But you promised Mama," he said.

"No! I promised nothing. I only listened. But I need to try, Hamal. I'm so close."

"And how will you do this? Your visit is almost over."

"I need to see him."

"Like Lamu."

"Yes. Like Lamu."

"Will you call Kamilah?"

"No!"

"I forgot. You like to make surprise appearances."

She handed the travel agent her plane tickets to America. She couldn't afford to extend her stay, and needed to coordinate her itinerary with her existing connections. The young man told her if she left that evening, after long layovers in Nairobi and Jeddah, she would arrive in Riyadh in late afternoon of the following day. That would leave her twenty-four hours to meet Hussein, or at least catch a glimpse of him, before she had to be back in Nairobi in time for her return flights to London and Boston.

"Can I see your visa?" the agent asked. She produced her passport and the visa to Kenya.

"To Saudi Arabia," he said.

She had never thought about getting that one.

"How do I get it?"

"First things first. You are an American citizen. All visas require a sponsor. And, by the way, all women must be met at the airport by their sponsors."

"I have family in Riyadh," she said, knowing full well that Kamilah would never agree to sponsor her.

"Even with a sponsor, securing a visa can take months."

"But I must go there today."

"Well, you'll just have to wait until your affairs are in order."

"I can't wait."

"There is nothing I can do for you," he said, looking over her shoulder at the next person in line.

"It was not meant to be," Hamal would say when she returned to their mother's home. "Not wise to play with destiny."

On her last day in Mombasa, she stopped at a marketplace for souvenirs, some small gifts to take back to Sarah and Miss Wilma. A man approached her as if to greet her. Suddenly, someone behind her pinned back her arms while the smiling man sliced the strap of her purse. "*Kumamayo!*" she screamed, waving her hands wildly like. "Fuck you!" There was so much noise and foot traffic around her that the incident went unnoticed – or ignored. The man who had grabbed her purse caught sight of her diamond gleaming in the midday sun and almost dislocated her finger as he yanked the ring off. The whole affair lasted only seconds. No one did anything. The police were nowhere to be found. When the officials at the station understood that she had only been robbed, they wanted no part of her. This was not how the Swahili people of her childhood behaved. She had to get to the travel agency in

Nairobi as soon as possible to arrange for a new ticket to be issued, knowing that nothing was easy these days in Kenya. At least she had put her passport back in the hotel safe, but her plane tickets were still in the purse. On her way back to the hotel she fought the urge to punch someone – anyone. She wanted to claw at herself for having let down her guard – at her vulnerability, her stupidity. But rage boiled over into tears. Kenya had stripped her of the bold façade she had arrived with and left her exposed for all to see. Despite her efforts to appear healthy and whole, she would leave Mombasa as herself – weakened and struggling, dependent on the help of others.

Everyone in the house contributed money for Fatma to take a bus to Nairobi; flying was out of the question. "You have enough for a modest hotel and food for your trip," Hamal said. She thought of the bug bites from the Millimani.

The goodbyes were difficult. More than ever, her family walked that thin line between life and death, but the robbery had left her too anxious to secure another ticket home for her to become overly sentimental. Hamal and his wife were grateful for her having left them Auntie's house. What was she going to do, take it to America? They said they would keep in touch. She knew they would keep in touch with their hearts. That was all. Life was too complicated to do more. Maybe there would be a letter or a call every now and then.

"Goodbye," Hamal said in English, as if to prepare her for her reentry in America. He kissed her lightly on her sunken cheek.

Change is inevitable, and it had come to Kenya, but Kenya had held the door open a little too long and allowed much of the good to slip out while the bad had muscled in. Although Mombasa had undergone negative transformations, Nairobi had become insufferable: crowded with immigrants, crawling with idlers, beggars, and thieves. It was impossible to walk down the street without men rubbing their bodies against her (most of them young, with nothing to do) or being tugged at by dirty, pleading street children whose hands had just rummaged through garbage. Hamal had advised her to stay in after dark. "They rape women in broad daylight," he warned. She had taken an overnight bus whose countless stops interrupted her sleep and made the trip interminable. She had survived the back streets of Rockfield, and then prison.

She went directly to a travel agency, and after waiting two hours in an empty office, an agent named Tarana Wachira, who hit the keys of her computer with the tips of her inch-long, gold-glitter nails and who displayed little sympathy for Fatma's plight, told Fatma she would take care of everything. It would take time, she warned, because they were shorthanded. Fatma was to fax from her hotel – if the power was working – and Miss Wachira would return the fax with a new ticket. Fatma doubted there would be a fax machine where she could afford to spend the night. However, she decided to worry about that later.

At a kiosk she bought a Coke. After all the explaining she had done to Miss Wachira (who had displayed greater concern for the chip on her fingernail) and the dry heat, her throat was parched. She was paying for the drink when she caught sight of a small hand reaching up to the counter to snatch the soda. Fatma grabbed the sticklike wrist it was attached to and nearly broke it.

"*Kumamayo!*" a little voice said, but Fatma held on and stared him in the eye. He was filthy – dressed in shorts and a tight-fitting undershirt – with a torso not much wider than the pathetic wrist. His eyes, an all too familiar sight, were dull, bloodshot, and glazed over. She knew that if she let go, he would run away. "*Don't!* Don't do this! *Don't!*" she shouted down at him in Swahili, like a mother outraged over her child's behavior, while he tried to wriggle free of her grasp and screamed obscenities.

"Get lost!" the vendor told both of them. "Go away. You ruin my business."

"*Fuck you!*" Fatma yelled at him.

"What's going on?" a man in a gray sweatshirt asked in English. He was tall and white and old. Fatma released the boy's wrist.

"She tried to kidnap me," the boy yelled in Swahili. "She tried to kill me."

"Sure she did," the man said. He swept a lock of thinning snowy white hair from his forehead. "Come along," he told the boy. "I'm sorry," he said in English to Fatma.

"He's little drug addict," Fatma blurted out.

"Yes. Most of them are."

"Where you taking him?" Fatma asked, but they had already started up the street, the little hand now wrestling with the older man's as the crowd swallowed them up.

She didn't know why she did what she did next. Perhaps she simply had nothing to do for the next two days in Nairobi, or maybe she felt responsible for getting the boy in trouble. More likely, she had seen too much of her conniving self in those eyes. But she caught up with them, and keeping two or three people as a screen between them, she followed them to a narrow rectangular building with a tin roof and blue plank walls. They were about to enter when the old man turned around and, as if he'd known she'd been there all along, asked her if she wanted to come in.

He motioned for the boy to sit down on one of the benches in front of several long wooden tables.

An African woman in a suit met them. "Who have we here?"

"This is Kwesi," the old man said.

"Come with me, Kwesi," she said, smiling and taking his hand, which no longer offered resistance.

"I'm Brother Frisone," the man said, extending his hand to Fatma. "Welcome to Imani Home."

"I'm Fatma. Fatma Kornmeyer."

He looked a bit confused.

"My husband," she said. "He was American. *I'm* American. And Somali. And Kenyan."

"I'm also American. From Buffalo."

"Cold," she said.

"Yes, very."

There was a silence, which appeared to bother only Fatma.

"What *is* this place?" she asked.

"It's a drop-in-center for some, a home for others. It's a stop for the weary. Can I offer you some lunch?"

She was hungry; it was almost noon. And she was still thirsty, since she had left her Coke on the counter. Still, she declined.

"Please," Brother Frisone said. "Be our guest."

The woman, whose name was Alicia and who Fatma later learned was a social worker, returned with Kwesi. He was washed up and there were Band-Aids over the cuts on his bare feet. They had given him a worn but clean T-shirt that read GO CUBS.

"A donation from America," Brother Frisone said. "The rest of the boys are in school now. There are eighteen of them living here with us at the moment."

Over a lunch of vegetable soup, Brother Frisone told Fatma how he had come to Nairobi ten years before to work with a Catholic priest, who had since passed away, and with Alicia in their efforts with street children. "Father helped with food and education. Alicia offered her services at the police stations and courts. With the aid of American sponsors, we have gone from a dilapidated mud house in the slums – with no electricity and running water, no toilets – to this three-room palace," he said with pride.

"I'm waiting for ticket back to Massachusetts," she said, disassociating herself from Brother Frisone's world. "Mine get stolen."

"Stay as long as you like."

"What happened to Nairobi?" she asked. "What happened to Kenya?"

"A sad but familiar story. A leader who encouraged dissension and tribal bloodshed rather than concede defeat."

She didn't understand.

"The violence the dissension caused drove those who opposed his government away from their homes. In turn, they didn't vote. The president won a disputed election and proceeded to run Kenya's economy into the ground. Who would vacation here with the crime? The bombing of the U.S. embassy sealed its fate. There are other places for rich people to go on safari. Imagine a man willing to see his country nearly destroyed rather than give up power."

That night she stayed at Imani Home. The boys, who returned around three, first took her for another social worker and buzzed among themselves, darting glances at her. But her lack of interaction with anyone gave her away. It takes one to know one, they say in America, and it wasn't long before she knew that they too had sized her up. She might have been older and neater and cleaner than most who came through the door, but she had more in common with them than appeared on the surface. Soon they ignored her and went about their chores much the same way the women at Haven House did. They did their homework, Brother Frisone and Alicia helping some with their English and Swahili lessons; they played soccer and card games; they cleaned up after dinner and then went to bed. Fatma slept on a cot in the dining room, the fingers of her right hand consoling the empty ring finger of her left. The diamond had been her last remaining tie to Nick, and the smoothness of her skin carved out a hollow in her gut. She had never been his wife, really. The thought still landed on her heart like one of his punches. *A piece of shit like you? Never. You were never my wife*, she heard him say.

It cools down considerably at night in Nairobi. She wrapped the thin blanket around her, holding fast onto the edges to keep her fists occupied. Not tonight, she whispered. Not here. Not tonight. The daughter of Muhammad in a drop-in center for street rats in Nairobi. Well, she had been in worse places. She sensed a familiar comfort in the shelter for these juvenile delinquents. This was a part of her that could never be exorcised by magic chants. There was one Fatma – one fragile Fatma with a tendency to stray. And she would remain fragile. The demons would always be with her.

Kwesi was eleven, a glue-sniffing orphan. Brother Frisone wasn't sure if the boy would stay. "*Imani*, as you know, means 'trust'," he said. "We hope they come to trust us here and let us help them make a future. But one never knows. One only hopes."

"And if he leaves?" Fatma asked.

"We'll hope he returns."

She had called Tarana Wachira earlier that evening and left the number for Imani Home on her answering machine. She waited all the next day. When the boys returned home, she helped them wash and hang laundry. Wachira never called. On Friday morning, the scheduled day of her departure, Fatma rose at 5:30

with the boys and ate breakfast. She slipped five hundred shillings underneath her plate before she said farewell to the good Brother Frisone, and set off planning to sit on the travel agency doorstep and wait for Miss Wachira to open up. Surprised and irritated to encounter Fatma when she arrived, Wachira let her in, took a newly issued ticket from her desk drawer, and without an apology or a kind word, handed it to Fatma with those glistening claws. Kenya had gone mad, Fatma thought.

Willowsville 2001

40 KILLED AS SOMALIA RENEWS FIGHTING

Mogadishu, Somalia, May 12 — The worst fighting in several years in Somalia's battered capital left 40 people dead today, including 21 civilians, and 100 people wounded after a fierce 15-hour gun battle between rival militias.

The intense fighting underscored the tenuous hold on power of the year-old transitional government in a city still fragmented among clan-based faction leaders. The government was elected a year ago in neighboring Djibouti in an effort to end the state of anarchy Somalia has endured since the overthrow of Siad Adan.

Doctors at Al Hayat hospital, where many of the dead and wounded were taken, said most of the civilian victims had been killed by random mortar and anti-aircraft shells that fell on their homes ...

A newspaper lay on the mat in the hallway, covering the bold black letters that spelled WELCOME, when Fatma opened the door of her efficiency apartment. According to the paper it was Monday morning; she had slept through an entire day. She didn't know why they kept delivering the paper anyway. She never asked for it, she never paid for it, and she never read it. Lately it was too hard to focus – unless, of course, she saw something that had to do with Somalia on the front page like this morning. The nighttime attacks on herself returned after her visit to Lamu. If a jinn had possessed her, the cure performed by Abd-al-Rahman had failed or, more likely, as Hamal would have said, there had never been a jinn. The loss of her wedding ring had also failed to sever her connection to Nick's ghost. As had her visit to the house in Hamilton.

Sarah had taken her to Hamilton four months after her return from Africa, right around Christmastime. She had just moved out of Haven House and into a one-room place in a newly renovated welfare-housing unit in downtown Willowsville: a fifteen-by-fifteen-foot room with a sink, dishwasher, and kitchen cabinets on one side and a bed, bathroom, and wardrobe on the other. Sarah had helped her fix it up with new lace curtains for its lone window, bedding, a red metal café-style table and two chairs, a small TV, a coffeemaker, and a microwave. Most important was that she was on her own.

The landmarks they passed on their way out to the house brought back that familiar queasiness. Linda Stern had suggested the trip as a way to provide closure to a part of her life and to put an end to the nightmares.

"Are you all right?" Sarah asked as she drove.

Fatma nodded, forcing Sarah to take her eyes off the road to read her face.

"You're sure this is your day off?"

Fatma nodded again. At least she thought it was her day off. She was working at Sundry Undies three full days a week now.

Some days she was late for work or didn't show up at all because she had overslept or lost track of the date. The problem was the drugs. There were pills that her doctor prescribed to take away the back pain that flared up from time to time. Pills to help her sleep deeper, to quiet the voices. Pills that left her groggy and headache-y and unable to speak coherently, that made her lose track of time. Sarah had given her a wall calendar on which she noted everything in order to become better organized. Yet sometimes, like this past weekend, she just couldn't wake up enough to get out of bed. The pills were necessary, the doctor said, or she might end up killing herself. He verified that she was at risk when he arranged for her to receive Social Security payments. The first of every month she sat at the kitchen table with Sarah and they paid bills, allotting so much for food and not much for anything else, except the tiny portion of her salary from Sundry Undies, that she set aside each week for her family in Africa.

They had started out early for Hamilton that Friday morning in December. Snow had begun to fall in Willowsville, cleansing it as one would a dingy kitchen with a fresh coat of paint. It was a wash of purification that forgave the town all its sins, the final touch to Main Street's holiday decorations.

"Are you sure you're up to this?" Sarah asked again. "We can do it another time." She was growing concerned about Fatma's silence.

"It's okay," Fatma forced out.

They pulled into the driveway and Fatma began to tremble.

"Shall we go back?" Sara asked.

"I'm just cold," Fatma lied, knowing she wasn't fooling Sarah.

The snowfall was heavier out there than in Willowsville and accumulating quickly. They stepped out. Soundlessly, their boots sank into the softness. Abandoned in the white woods, the house seemed to have been frozen in time. Fatma supposed that Nick's children and his "companion" were still fighting over ownership.

"So quiet here," Sarah said.

But not to Fatma. Despite the insulating snow that muffled sound, she could hear them: heels being dragged on gravel, floorboards vibrating, thrashing and crashing, yells and screams.

Slowly she circled it, drawing closer and closer until she could see inside the palladian windows and atrium doors, the panes of the conversatory. He was still there, larger than life, and as usual bellowing through the halls, his feet heavy on the marble floors. At least she feared she would see him – feel him – if they went any closer. Sarah was surprised to find the door unlocked.

"We never locked door here," Fatma said. "Even loan sharks rang bell before they came in."

The ache in her lower back made her uncomfortable; she leaned against the doorjamb. When she tried to walk again, the pain intensified and shot down her leg.

Sarah offered to help her to the car, but she refused. There was something she needed to get from the house, something she wanted badly.

She went directly to the black lacquered credenza in the great room. Like a safety net, Sarah followed ready to catch her if she fell. She couldn't remember exactly which drawer it was in, but she knew it was there somewhere. And it was, at the bottom of the third drawer she rummaged through: the tablecloth Pia had given her for a wedding present. They had never used it. Nick hadn't liked it.

Fatma didn't speak on the ride home; she tried not to wince or moan. She could tell that Sarah was thinking the whole idea had been a huge mistake. They drove directly to the hospital, where a young ER doctor gave her an epidural for the pain radiating from the bulging disk that compressed a nerve. After a week in bed at home without any other medication, which the ER doctor suggested she stop for a while, her body became fair game once again, the site of a free-for-all between her ego and Nick's spirit. Nick had early on found the chink in her armor, the defect in her personality that she had been born with that allowed him to speak to her when he wasn't really speaking, to berate and destroy her. And he had put a chink in her body that would never let her forget him. Even after death his spirit, like a bat in the dark, zoomed in through those cracks and made itself known. Now her days turned as monstrous as the nights. She found herself afraid to leave the apartment even to go to work, for fear that the house in Hamilton would be there on every corner in Willowsville. However, almost miraculously, after a week or two the images faded, along with any illusions she might have had about Nick. She no longer loved him and probably hadn't for some time, but she'd had to convince herself that she did, to justify having stayed with him for so long. Iblis too, in time, seemed to grow weary within her – but not weary enough, and so some evenings she resorted to the pills that dulled her pain, and stole her time, and put the demon to rest.

That Monday morning she drank a cup of strong black coffee. Sitting at the table she and Sarah had bought at Big Lots and covered with the tablecloth that had waited for her in the Hamilton house like a faithful dog, she smoked a cigarette and tried to read the newspaper article about Somalia through blurry eyes. She pictured her mother's house leveled to the ground, her sisters and brothers, nieces and nephews, and her father – her eldest uncle – roaming the devastated city without shelter. Perhaps they were all dead. She telephoned Sarah and explained in a slow, determined voice that she had to find out something about them.

Mondays were their time together, so together they went to the Red Cross in Rockfield. Fatma filled out lots of papers, one for each member of her family. Two months later a Red Cross official phoned: no success. There was something, however. During their search, the office in Washington, D.C., had sent them a copy of a letter they had received nine years ago from Fatma's sister Ayasha. She had been looking for Fatma all that time, but the Red Cross hadn't been able to find Fatma. The letter in Somali was short and merely Ayasha's attempt to reconnect with Fatma. "I am thinking of you, sister. We all do. Times are getting very bad here, and I must speak to you. Please write to me and tell me where and how you are. Perhaps you can help us."

How ironic! Fatma had been in need of Ayasha just when Ayasha had been in need of Fatma. Would the letter from her have made a difference in Fatma's life had it fallen into her hands on time? She would never know. A month after getting it, another unanticipated letter came into her possession.

"They tried to trick you," Miss Wilma had said when Fatma first returned from Africa.

"Who?" Fatma had asked.

"Your father's enemies in Somalia. They tried to get you to go there so they could kill you."

Miss Wilma proceeded to tell Fatma about the phone call Mary Ellen had taken from the young man in Somalia, the one who claimed to be Fatma's son.

"At first we thought your son was in Somalia, but when you told me over the phone that he was still with your sister in Saudi Arabia, we figured it out," she said proudly.

"You figure what out?"

"Who had called you. It was a trick. Your family's enemies. They tried to get you to go to Somalia."

"Why didn't you tell me about call?"

"Because we thought it best for your safety. We didn't want you to get caught up in the trap. Besides, Fatma, we didn't know how to get in touch with you anyway. You only called us once." There was chastisement in her tone.

Mary Ellen must have lied about the phone call, made the whole thing up for a little evening entertainment. That was the only thing Fatma could think of. It was not only highly improbable that Somali enemies would have bothered to track her down in America, it was absurd that they would have been so intent on killing her that they would lure her back to Somalia. It would have been even more unlikely that they had known she was heading for Kenya. Maybe the call had been some sort of prank from an American Fatma might have confided in while she was at Shelby or over a bottle of vodka at the Royal Lion. Maybe Elsa Martinez was up to some new trick. However, one year after the call had been made to Haven House, on a humid day in July, Fatma removed a brown letter-sized envelope from her mailbox in the foyer of her building.

The return address read: <u>Friend</u>: Ibrahim, 197 Middle St., London. The postmark was also from London. She carried the envelope up to her place and opened it with a kitchen knife, trying not to damage it. She read carefully and slowly, her hands shaking with every word. *Dear Mommy*, it began. Hussein had found her! she thought, nearly delirious with joy. But as she read on she realized the letter had been written neither in England nor Saudi Arabia; it had originated in Somalia with Ayasha's son Kareem. Ayasha had known her life was at stake and tried to make plans for her son. That's why she had looked for Fatma so many years before.

> *I write you because my mommy your sister Ayasha tell me you are my mother if she die. My American mother. I work for photographer. There is no much work now, only making false passports. Somali passports are no worth nothing. I learn English in the underground school since to study English is forbade. I hope you like my English although I know I make many errors.*
>
> *It is very terrible here. There is no more house. We live in tents and cardboard boxes. My father and mother die. Cousin Abdul die too. They kill them. They hurt many more. Many uncles shot dead or paralyzed.*
>
> *Mommy, I want come to America and live with you. I want study computers at university. America has much opportunities.*
>
> *Please to send me money when you can. I will save until there is enough for me come to America. I will give also to Father chief of family for everyone. Please, Mommy. Help me.*
>
> *I hope you like photos. I hope my friend Ibrahim reach England and send letter.*
>
> *Your son,*
> *Kareem Muhammad*

There was a small passport-size picture of Kareem (he had written his name on the back). He was a good-looking young man who resembled his Bantu father more than Ayasha. The rest were four-by-sixes: one of Father, one of Ayasha, one of four of Fatma's other sisters, and three of their children artfully posed under a canopy of sticks and blankets, some seated, others reclining on their sides, propped up on their elbows, heads resting in hands. They were smiling, trying hard to look happy, but their faces told another story. Suffering had aged them – like all the other members of her family – far beyond the natural passage of time, and they appeared much older than they should have.

Sarah and Fatma went to a Barakaat office in downtown Boston. Mr. Abdul Kiran was pleasant enough, a middle-aged man with a graying beard and moustache who wore a black suit, a gold striped tie, and a large gold ring. He would, he assured Fatma, find her family, and whatever money she gave him would be in the hands of her family's father, Uncle Abdullah, within hours. Mr. Kiran kept his word. A week later she received a call from Kareem, to whom she had passed her phone number through the Barakaat officer. Though they spoke less than a minute, Kareem was delirious with gratitude. Fatma began to send money regularly to Father – one hundred dollars a month – her entire salary from Sundry Undies. It would have been nice to buy some new clothes for herself instead of depending on hand-me-downs and the Salvation Army. Nevertheless, she was thrilled to be able to do something for her family. She heard a wise man say on the radio that injustice was not what people do to other people, but what people were not doing about it themselves.

Her life was confined within narrow parameters. Anything social revolved around Haven House, or an outing with Sarah, or an occasional cup of coffee with a neighbor in her building. There wasn't much she desired anymore; she was content with little, and afraid to allow herself too much freedom. No, she was better off with little money at this point. And a hundred dollars was more like thousands to her people. Besides, she was too busy to go out spending money. She had things to do: a future to plan for, preparations to make for the arrival of her new son.

Sarah helped her sign up for an apartment in a low-income building in town. There was no way two people could survive in her efficiency. The waiting list was long, she was told – maybe a year. She could wait. There would be an investigation into her character as a tenant in her present building. Fine. She had nothing to hide. In fact, she got along quite well with the manager, who liked to chat with her as she came and went. She was one of the "good" tenants, he said. One of the respectable and quiet ones who didn't give him trouble, like others who dealt drugs and pimped. Everything was going smoothly until September eleventh of that fall, when Arab terrorists flew two planes into the World Trade Center and one into the Pentagon.

"It's here," Fatma told Sarah, horrified.

"What?"

"Greed."

"What greed?"

"For power."

Fatma was staring, seemingly at nothing, but she was seeing so much – the end of her life in America, the end of this country.

"Does the manager of your building know you're part Saudi?" Sarah asked.

"Yes."

She frowned.

The next time Sarah and Fatma went to Boston, they found the Barakaat office closed.

"They're gone," a jeweler next door said. "Closed up by the government. The lousy Arabs were funneling money to that terrorist in Afghanistan. Stinking Arabs."

"But they get my money in Somalia," Fatma told Sarah.

"But maybe they didn't receive it all," Sarah said warily, seeming distant for the first time, as though for a moment she shared the jeweler's sentiments. Fatma almost felt she couldn't blame her.

"We'll find another way," Sarah said when she dropped Fatma off at home. "Fatma, be careful. Willowsville is a good community, an open-minded community. But in times like this … Just be careful."

She went by the name Kornmeyer. She wore western clothes. She did not attend a mosque. She spoke to few people, and even when she did, most had no idea of where she had come from. There were, however, aside from her landlord, others who knew of her Arab ancestry. There were the restaurateurs who swept the sidewalks in front of their Middle Eastern cafés that day with long shameful faces, the fearful faces worn when one of your own is found out to be a criminal. Faces that told how even fellow Arabs had begun to regard one another with a certain suspicion. Fatma began to wire funds through a Moneygram office in Rockfield. Kareem called her every second Tuesday of the month, and she gave him the code they had told her he needed in order to pick up the money. There was little time for conversation, except for a few words on the state of Father's health, which was declining daily. By the end of December the United States military had all but exhausted bin Laden's potential hiding places in Afghanistan. They assumed he had slipped into a bordering nation or possibly back to Somalia, where he had fought against the Americans nearly ten years before.

When her red phone on the wobbly wrought-iron stand rang, she could sense the urgency in the ring, and she knew that something very bad had happened.

"He's gone!" Kamilah cried hysterically. "He's gone! Hussein has run away! He left a note saying he wants to be an American like his father. You must do something. You must help me."

Oh, sister, this is what happens when you squeeze the sand too tightly.

"Please, Fatma, he is only fifteen – " The connection was breaking up.

"I'll try. I will call you tomorrow, Kamilah," Fatma shouted into the receiver. "We will find him."

There was only one other person who shared this responsibility. One person whose duty it was to right a terrible wrong. He had offered to help her find their son not so long ago. Now she prayed that Daniel had the courage to keep his word.

Daniel set aside everything and worked day and night. It took several days of telephoning, one call leading to another within the State Department and various senators' offices, until he received word from a senior staff person in the Department of Defense. His son had been found hiding in the storage room of a hangar at the U.S. air command center in Prince Sultan Air Base, and was being hand delivered to his home three hundred and eighty miles away.

"He hitched the whole damn way," Daniel told a relieved

Fatma. "Takes after his mother. Call Kamilah after tomorrow. He'll be home by then."

"Thank you, Daniel."

"Thank *you,* for not letting me forget."

Kamilah was so grateful to Fatma and Daniel that she agreed that when Hussein turned twenty-one, she would let him come to the States for a visit. If he chose to stay longer, she would not stand in his way. After all, he would be a man then.

"Do you know who I am?" Fatma asked him.

"Yes."

"And do you understand?" She wanted to know if he forgave her, but it was too much of a burden to place on a boy who had never even laid eyes on her, or at least not that he remembered. And if he said no? After all, she had never forgiven her own mother for giving her up. But he seemed wise, this stranger whose voice she found higher-pitched than she would have imagined, cracking at times, still making its way from childhood to manhood.

"My mother told me that it was not your fault. Can I call you Mother also?"

"Of course." She stilled the quivering in her throat. She would be strong for her son. But she could not slow the beating of her heart. She had waited what seemed like a lifetime for this moment, and now she wanted to end the conversation. It was too much too fast for both of them. They must go slowly, like children learning how to walk, step by step, conversation by conversation.

"Mother," he asked before they hung up, "does it snow where you live in America?"

"Yes, Hussein. Sometimes it snows."

✳

She hasn't sent money to Kareem in months: the United States has stopped all funds destined for Somalia for fear that they might be supporting the terrorist movement. She's been told by message services that there is no contacting Somalia at the moment. There is no more phone system. There is nothing. Even if she could find a way to send help, in all honesty, she is afraid to contact her family for fear that she will appear to be suspicious. She has come a long way from prison, and has no intention of returning. Even Sarah is afraid to contact Fatma's family for her; no one is above suspicion now. Fatma wrote to Kareem's friend Ibrahim but received no response – nor was her letter returned. What happened to Ibrahim? Was he questioned and was he now in prison in Cuba? Was he in fact connected with the terrorist movement? Is Father alive? She swallowed her pride and wrote to the famous Jamila, asking if she could somehow, through England, get money to Somalia. But Jamila had never been really interested in their father's other children. She sent Fatma a check for a thousand dollars. Fatma was going to send it back, but reminded herself that pride was what had got her into so much trouble in the first place. Jamila had come to see her; she had tried, and it was more than Fatma, ever jealous of Jamila, had ever done. Fatma sent Jamila a note of thanks and had Sarah deposit the thousand dollars in the savings account Fatma opened for when her sons come.

Fatma fears for Somalia and her family more than ever. Would a country that cannot bear any more self-destruction harbor a terrorist leader? To what end? For what gain? But she has seen madness before. She herself has been mad. And she has learned that prejudice and lust for power drives people to lose their minds and do the unthinkable. They are the same, she and Somalia: dried-up battlefields of self-destruction, starving territories raped by power-hungry beasts, bodies unable to rest in peace.

Some people who knew Fatma in Rockfield still expect her to be bad. Those who have never known her think she's a drug addict because she lives in the welfare house. At least she assumes that's what they're guessing when they meet in the elevator. Fatma doesn't return their looks; she might give herself away. It's the hardest thing to be honest. People like her never told the truth. It's not that she lied much – she wasn't raised to lie. She was, however, raised to keep silent.

Fatma imagined that, when she left Haven House, all her problems would disappear. But she gets frustrated. After all these years of having people tell her what to do, now she is by herself, and it gets lonely. Some days she's afraid to go out. She doesn't know who her friends really are; she doesn't know whom she'll run into. She is an addict. She is an alcoholic. She closes her eyes when she passes a bar. At times she gets this urge, and everything she sees and hears and smells seems to trigger it. Some days she really doesn't care. She tries not to think too much. She reads. She walks. She continues to study English. Every now and then she calls Miss Wilma and says, "Tell me what to do." "You're on your own now, you have to make your own decisions," Miss Wilma says. But she's afraid she'll make the wrong decisions. She's been sober for three years and eight months, but she can still taste the liquor and feel the high – and the beatings. She's become as delicate as life, which, she has always known, can shatter at any moment. She treads lightly through that life, like glass walking on glass.

She's made a new friend, a Somali woman. Her name is Halima, the same name as her old friend in Mombasa. The manager of her building introduced them. He's like Nick only inside out: a man with a rough and unkempt exterior and a kind and gentle heart. Halima is a visiting nurse who comes to see one of Fatma's neighbors. The manager recognized her accent and asked where she was from. When she told him Somalia, he asked for her phone number and gave it to Fatma. Fatma called her on her own, taking the chance that Halima would not want to meet. But they meet often now, and they have coffee. They speak Somali. Fatma thinks that meeting a person like Halima when she first arrived in America – someone who knew where she had come from, someone who had come from the same place – would have made all the difference. You can live without a brother but not without a friend, Somalis say. Halima recommended a tea that soothes Fatma as effectively as the pills. She's not so groggy and is rarely bruised in the morning; she even finds her pillow in the same place she put it the night before. The cigarettes are fewer. Sarah says she looks better too, and Fatma believes her: people don't stare at her when she's alert and smiling. And if she has a bad night, she knows that in the morning life will start all over again. Every morning – every second – is Monday morning.

More Somalis are coming to the area too – the Bantus. They were the first to suffer when civil war broke out in Somalia, robbed and murdered by warring clan members. Although many fled to Kenya, they are still not safe, living in filthy refugee camps, young girls being raped by Kenyan guards or other refugees. An American relief group wants to bring them to Rockfield because it has many vacant apartments and cheap rent. They want to establish a Newcomer Center, an apartment complex where they can settle and be helped to adjust and find work. They'll need a lot of volunteers, and Fatma intends to help. So does Halima. They'll teach them to manage the day-to-day business that they themselves had to learn – the messy parts of living here. Fatma knows how the Bantu have existed, in mud huts, cooking over wood fires. It will be truly shocking for them to come to the United States, even worse than it was for Fatma. She'll teach them to use a stove and to cook foods they have never seen, to go shopping, to adjust to the weather. They'll be happy to have someone they can speak Somali to, happy to have a friend.

The September 11 attacks slowed down the process of bringing the Bantu to Rockfield, but it's moving more quickly now. As soon as the city council votes on it, they'll come. They say that people in Rockfield don't want them, that there aren't enough jobs and too many people on welfare already, that the Bantu will only bring more Somalis and that there is enough racial violence in the city. Kenya doesn't want them either, nor do Mozambique and Tanzania, their countries of origin. The Bantu only want what everyone else wants: for their children to be safe, and a better life.

Fatma thinks that maybe she'll be able to give a little money too to the Bantu people. She's thought about calling Pia and using some of the money she earns to fix her face, but the funny thing is, it doesn't bother her much anymore. Besides, it's not bad to have reminders – like the chronic pain in her back, like the eye that sometimes tears – of how far she's come.

They trust her to open and close Sundry Undies. Sarah trusts her to be alone in her home. Miss Wilma trusts her to watch over the women at Haven House when she's gone. And their trust has given Fatma the confidence to trust in herself and in her choices. She is better able to decide who in America is a friend and who is not. She's learning to peek through a body's window, to put her nose to the pane and zoom in beyond all the looks – all the talk – and discover bits of truth, plain as day, lying on the mantle of the soul, hanging on its walls.

She doesn't know when she'll face the world again with the boldness that convinced Daniel to buy the penny house. Or trust a man once more in that special way. She can't imagine. She doesn't ever want to be owned by a man or country or devil again. She grows lighter by the day. One autumn morning she'll feel so airy that the breeze will come from behind and lift her up and carry her, like a bright red leaf, above the golden treetops, and she'll look down on Willowsville, and her Mombasa eye will weep with joy.

They're refinishing the floors and painting the walls of her new apartment. She can move in after the New Year, they say. She's bought drapes, leopard throw pillows, a zebra patterned area rug, and a carved wooden elephant – all made in China and purchased from a local discount store. The saleswoman there says that African-looking pieces have become big sellers and she can't keep them in stock. Fatma wonders if Uncle Oliver is behind any of this.

Miss Wilma gave her a set of clear glass dishes. She likes being able to see the food on her plate and only that. She wants a nice place – not fancy but nice, with good things that *she's* chosen. And she wants a bed – a real bed, not just the mattress and box spring that came with the efficiency. A big bed like the one the healer in Lamu had. A bed with a canopy that will protect her, a bed that will give her good dreams, because the nighttime is becoming less frightening, and because this time, unlike the day she left Mrs. Lucchese's apartment to live with Nick, she is really starting out new and leaving the nightmares behind her.

There's a balcony in her new apartment where she'll be able to eat breakfast on summer mornings and watch the stars at night. She's buying a sleeper sofa for when her sons come to live with her. She'll teach them that it is not in dominating others that one becomes a man, that pride is an overcoat for insecurity, that it is self-control and consideration for others that makes people strong. She'll show them how to love without holding on too tightly, how to keep it all from slipping through their fingers.

Telephone lines have been restored in Somalia for the time being, and Kareem phones when he can. They speak in Somali; the minutes are too precious for misunderstood conversations.

"Stay away from terrorists. Stay away from pirates, Kareem."

"There are days, Mama, I wake up believing it is the only way for my country to exist."

"Somewhere the violence must stop. Please," she begs him, but she does not ask him to promise.

There is still no way to send money. *Stay safe,* she wants to tell him. *Stay alive. Study English and master the language of your future homeland. Do not be like your mother; prepare for your trip to America.* There is so much she needs to tell him. But the time between each call grows longer and longer, and the fear for his life and the actions he may take becomes greater. She knows the consequences of desperation.

And when Hussein is old enough to travel away from his place of birth and face the lions on his own, she prays that he too will also come to know, and learn, and understand. On that day, they will all three sit beneath the shade of some great leafy American tree or, on a cool summer evening in the moonlight, on Fatma's balcony, and they will talk and laugh and cry about what has gone before and what is yet to pass. And they will remember that once upon a time, in a land far away, there was a nation and a family. There was a princess.

ACKNOWLEDGEMENTS

I am deeply thankful to the following: My agent, Laura Gross, who believed in this book from the beginning and wouldn't give up on it. Everyone at Guernica Editions, especially Michael Mirolla, Connie McParland, and Antonio D'Alfonso. My editors, Chris Jerome and Lindsay Brown. Hazel Robinson and Kate Decou, for taking me into the world of women's incarceration and recovery. Sarah Craig for sharing her research on jinns, as well as details about Mombasa and Lamu. Julie Rose, Joann Kobin, Betsy Hartmann, Mordicai Gerstein, Roger King, Anthony Giardina, Zane Kotker, and Tracy Kidder for listening, reading, and offering excellent feedback. Many thanks to Marilyn Levinson, friend and research companion; to Eileen Giardina, David Hoose, Charlotte Watts, Rich McCarthy, Shivohn Garcia, Barbara McCarthy, Marci Yoss and Peter Bigwood, whose specifics were most helpful; and to my wonderful parents, Michael and Viola Labozzetta, who gave me my first appreciation for literature and the importance of family. I'm especially grateful to my husband, Martin Wohl, who put up with my having this book on my mind for a very long time. And most of all, to A., without whom this book could not exist.

ABOUT THE AUTHOR

********** ⭐ **********

Marisa Labozzetta is the author of the novel, *Stay With Me, Lella* (Guernica 1999), and a collection of linked stories, *Thieves Never Steal in the Rain*. She was a finalist for the 2009 Binghamton University John Gardner Fiction Award and a Pushcart Prize nominee for her collection of short stories, *At the Copa* (Guernica 2006). Her work has appeared in *The American Voice, Beliefnet.com, The Florida Review, The Penguin Book of Italian American Writing, Show Me a Hero: Great Contemporary Stories About Sports*, and the bestselling *When I Am an Old Woman I Shall Wear Purple*, among other publications. She lives in Northampton, Massachusetts.

Printed in August 2012
by Gauvin Press,
Gatineau, Québec